Manouch

Anne Welters

Order this book online at www.trafford.com
or email orders@trafford.com

Most Trafford titles are also available at major online book retailers.

Printed in the United States of America.

ISBN: 978-1-4669-5565-3 (sc)
ISBN: 978-1-4669-5567-7 (hc)
ISBN: 978-1-4669-5566-0 (e)

Library of Congress Control Number: 2012916098

Trafford rev. 08/28/2012

Trafford PUBLISHING www.trafford.com

North America & international
toll-free: 1 888 232 4444 (USA & Canada)
phone: 250 383 6864 • fax: 812 355 4082

Prologue

She could hear the noise coming from the corridor outside her ward.

Her children and their spouses were all there as well as some of the grandchildren. Earlier they were all with her until a nursing sister asked them to leave the ward. Now she could hear them protesting to the doctor.

I know they are nearby, although I feel somehow detached. It almost feels as if I am floating on a cloud. I think it could be the injection they gave me earlier, but I am not sure of anything today.

And then everything is quiet in the corridor and I know they must have left. I am now alone, and yet I feel as if someone is with me. I call out but there is no answer. That is strange, my senses are very acute, after all, I have relied on them for a long time. I raise my head a little from the pillow and turn it slightly. Darkness is all around me but I am used to that. No, it feels more like a light mist surrounding me and I feel a shiver pass through my body. My voice is hoarse when I speak again. 'Who is here with me? Is it you Yvette?'

Still no answer comes, and I put my head back on the pillow. It must be my imagination, and I sigh. No, there I feel it again, and I lift my head up once more.

Gently I am pushed back against the pillow. The touch is light like the wings of a butterfly, and the voice is no more than a whisper.

'Ah! Manouch, I have waited so long.'

* * *

It is not a common name. I have encountered it only three times in my lifetime and it is of the first one I knew about, that this story is told.

As far as possible it is true and correct although there are times when feelings and emotions are expressed by visualizing such events.

Her name is Manouch, and she is ten years old.

I dedicate this book to Yvette . . . .

It was written because Norman asked me to

Part One

Chapter One

Two brothers, Eblen and Salem, sat on the wharf, waiting for the boats to dock. They were dressed in peasant clothes. One was a bit taller than the other and both had slim frames. They were both good looking, with black hair and dark brown eyes, with long eyelashes. Neatly trimmed black moustaches drooped down from their upper lips. Whenever they could get away from their daily tasks, they waited for the sailors to embark, and then questioned them.

"Where do you come from? How far away is it? Tell us about the country you come from.'

They listened and stored all the information away to later discuss it again with each other.

Four destinations were locked in their minds. Australia was the most preferred but offered more hardship and mostly agriculture work. England sounded more attractive but the weather made them reluctant to commit themselves. After much deliberation they chose America as their goal, and if that failed, then a young country at the foot of Africa would be next best. South Africa, the sailors reported, was booming. Gold and diamonds offered many opportunities and they spoke of riches beyond anyone's dreams.

Although the brothers loved their families their minds were made up.

Adventure was beckoning and they were eager to leave their village where a career was either going to a seminary or working the land. As children living on the mountains where majestic Cedar trees grew in clusters, overlooking the harbour miles away, they lived carefree and happy with their parents and siblings. These two brothers were often found standing on the crest with their hands, shading their eyes, looking out to sea. Religion was Maronite Catholic, and their family lived for the church. The brothers shared this deep-rooted religion but wanted more out of life and were determined to get it.

So it was that with their minds finally made up, they approached the captain of a ship in the harbour en route to South Africa, who agreed for them to work their passage to their destination, and gave them a list of documents that would be needed. The boat loaded with cargo, was due to leave in four days, which gave them enough time to obtain the necessary papers as well as to go and tell their family and take what little possessions they had.

Money was not something they had, but they were strong and willing to work, so with the appropriate documents, they boarded the boat.

When the boat left the harbour the two brothers were too busy with their duties on board to see their beloved Cedars, disappear from sight.

The journey was arduous. Many sailors got sick and succumbed and were later buried at sea. Fortune smiled on the two brothers, keeping them from getting sick, and after many months they arrived in Durban, South Africa where they were first put into a quarantine camp before papers were issued to allow them to stay in the country.

In the camp they heard about opportunities on the goldfields of the Transvaal and the two brothers boarded a train once they were cleared. The journey took two days and a night sitting on hard benches, but neither of the two complained. Crowds of people met them at the station in Johannesburg and it looked daunting for the two men with one small suitcase shared between them. Many foreigners could be heard talking and shouting with bundles of clothing or suitcases clutched in their hands. Women and children were everywhere. The two brothers stood bewildered, looking at all the people milling around, and then, out of all the commotion, they picked up a familiar language, and saw a man approaching, who was surrounded by other men, young and old.

'Excuse me.' Eblen lifted his hand and said to the man 'my brother and I could not help hearing you speak Lebanese.' Nodding his head, the man replied 'Yes and who are you?'

The two brothers, together with the other men, left with the man who said his name was Yusaf. He took the men to a boarding house on the outskirts of the city where he arranged for cheap lodgings. 'Here' he said 'you will meet people who can help you find work.' They thanked him and settled into a tiny room where two single divans with very thin mattresses, stood next to each other.

Threadbare candlewick spreads barely covered the beds with one flat pillow on each, but it looked clean.

They put their small suitcase on the floor and sat next to each other where they made the sign of the cross on their body and said a prayer of thanks.

They did not linger in the confined room and carefully locked the door behind them to explore their surroundings.

Further on in the same street, was a small diner, where they met other people who also spoke their language. They were warned by Yusaf to be careful as many people presented themselves as friends and then later stole what they could. Careful to heed his warning, they listened and made no commitments, staying close together. After a satisfying meal of lamb stew and rice they returned to their room.

On the second day, they realised that there were too many people around which made it difficult to get work, and decided to leave the city to travel inland to the East Rand where many of the goldmines were.

When the train pulled into the Germiston station, they took their small suitcase and waited for the train to stop. There were not as many people around as was in Johannesburg, and for this, they were relieved.

The station was in the upper part of town and they walked slowly to see what was around them. In a house near to the main road they saw a board in the window offering rooms to let. When they enquired the rental was reasonable and the room was clean so they decided to stay for a few days. They packed their meagre belongings into the small upright cupboard in the corner of the room. After many days of travelling they were tired, but finally felt as if they had arrived to where they wanted to be, wherever it was, and of this they were not quite sure either.

The bathroom was further along in the passage and although shared by all the residents, was clean and they each had a warm bath to wash away not only the grime of their journey, but also that of their past life. Refreshed and full of enthusiasm they could not help the feeling of excitement that made them laugh when they looked at each other. Together they kneeled at their beds and after making the sign of the cross by first touching their forehead and then their chest then their left and right shoulders and then their lips, they said a prayer of thanksgiving and asked for guidance and protection in their new surroundings. Their hearts were light when they rose from their knees and they kissed each other on both cheeks.

Chapter Two

Finding work was a priority and language was a liability. No language other than Lebanese was ever spoken in the village they grew up in, and now except for a few words, picked up while on the boat, they found it difficult to communicate with people.

The only work they managed to find was at the market, which fortunately, was not far from where they were staying. The pay was meagre and between them was hardly enough to pay for their room and a meal at night, but they persevered, eager to learn the ways of the local people.

Willing to work hard, and a friendly manner, made them popular among their peers, and before long the two brothers became part of the locals.

The languages spoken in the general workplace was also mastered within a short while and although the main language was English it was the Afrikaans language that was preferred among the workers. The brothers were well liked and even though everyone working there was poor by all standards there reigned amongst them, a feeling of friendship.

They were happy, even though the work was strenuous moving crates of vegetables and fruit endlessly from one place, to another. At night they made plans for their future. A wagon would be needed, so they could transport fresh vegetables and fruit to the mines, and they saved every bit of money they could.

There were many families living in the area from different parts of The Lebanon, and they were sometimes invited to family dinners, and the occasional social gathering. Daughters were usually presented, and although they showed friendliness and respect, they were careful not to show any interest for fear of being linked up with anyone. Their future lay before them and they had big plans, which did not include wives and children.

The wagon on offer did not look good. In fact it needed a lot of attention. They inspected it carefully and left. The next day they went back to the owner and looked some more at the broken wagon, and the following day they did the same. On the fourth day they made a small offer to the owner, pointing out the total disrepair, and the amount of work needed, if it could in fact, be used at all. A short haggling followed and the next evening they hired a strong horse from a local stable and some ropes. It took most of the night to drag the wagon to a nearby shed that they had hired. Later, after locking the shed carefully behind them, they led the horse back to the stable. Bone weary the two men fell onto their beds and fell asleep without even eating.

After work, and Saturday afternoons, they worked on the wagon. If the wagon was to carry the anticipated load, the axels had to be re-enforced and wood panels were built on the sides to give more height to the loading space. They worked till late at night, and morning saw them up early for work again. Enthusiasm kept them going, and when the time came that they felt the wagon was ready for use, they kneeled on the ground next to the wagon and gave thanks for having been able to complete the task they had set for themselves. That night they sat in their room each on their own bed, facing each other, and planned their next step.

The horse they bought was the same one they had hired to pull the wagon to the shed. The mare was not young but she was strong and they kept her at the stable, paying a monthly fee where she would be fed and groomed after each task. Now, on this first day of their new future, they carefully hitched the mare to the wagon, checking that the braces were all firmly in place, making sure she was comfortable. They named her 'Starlight' although they knew she probably had another name, but it felt right. Taking out a small bottle from his pocket, Eblen opened the cork and sprinkled the water over the horse and the wagon, while walking around to the other side, blessing everything as he went. This was the moment where they became the masters of their own future. The looks on their faces were of guarded excitement as they briefly hugged each other, and then Eblen opened the door of the shed.

Salem climbed on to the wooden seat, now repaired and varnished, and picked up the reins.

At the market, supplies were carefully chosen and loaded, and then covered with a tarpaulin. What lay before them they did not know but they were ready and eager to find out.

Chapter Three

The sky was already turning dark on the third day when they returned.

Most of the supplies were sold, and what remained, was left on the wagon.

Stiff from their long journey, they carefully took the harnesses off Starlight and locked the shed before they both walked her to her stable, where a young stable hand took her.

Although their bodies were tired and stiff after the long journey, they felt content as they entered the diner for a much needed warm meal.

The diner was very basic but the meals were tasty and satisfied them.

They did not linger once they had eaten and it was already dark when they arrived at their lodging.

Once they were in their room they made sure that the door was securely locked before they took off the leather money bags hidden under their shirts and emptied it onto the beds.

Their beds felt soft when they sat down opposite each other after the hard bench of the wagon. The money was counted carefully, and Eblen then wrote down the date and the amount, with a pencil, into a small book bound in a black cover, which he had taken from his cupboard.

After a warm bath, the men were ready for sleep, which came instantly.

The next day, being Sunday, they attended mass at the Catholic church, a few blocks away, from their lodgings. Later they went to the shed to take inventory of the goods not sold, which was also written into the small black book.

* * *

Early Monday morning found them at the market while everyone was still asleep to replenish their stock. They planned a longer journey this time, and expected to be away for at least four days.

Supplies of other items were now also on the wagon. Mine workers where they were, wanted blankets and clothing, as well as sugar, rice, tea, coffee, mealie meal, cigarettes and tobacco.

When they were satisfied that the load was firmly secured and that the tarpaulin covered everything, the reins were lightly pulled, and Starlight moved forward. The two brothers felt an inner excitement and it was as if they were going on a holiday.

Chapter Four

When the horse drawn cart stopped in the clearing in front of the veranda, the women sitting in the cool shade, greeted the men getting off, in a friendly, manner.

'Eblen, Salem, come and join us.'

|Three young girls playing further away at the end of the veranda, stopped their play momentarily, and then carried on taking no notice of the visitors.

The men greeted the two women with a kiss on their cheeks and pulled chairs out to sit at the table.

Well being of each was first asked, as per ritual, before any conversation could take place.

'How are you Auntie?'

'Fine, thank God, and yourself?'

'How are you Auntie?' They turned to the other woman.

'Well, thank God, and yourself?'

'Very good, thank God, and how is your family?'

'Fine thank God, and how is yours?'

This ritual took a little while but could not be rushed. That would be bad manners and everyone knew that, and they did not want to offend each other or their families, after all, everyone was connected to a family of a family, and they all knew the same people.

Refreshments were offered by the women, which the two brothers declined. Everyone knew that one never accepted on the first offering, and waited until the third offering before accepting. This was also customary.

The two men still had the same look about them as when they first began their journey to establish a new life, which was now more than a year ago. Their black hair was a little thinner on the sides but their brown eyes, which looked like melted chocolate, was warm and friendly. They each still had a moustache drooping down the sides of their cheeks that lifted at the ends as they smiled. One brother was slightly taller than the other and the tallest was barely five feet nine inches, with the other being an inch shorter. There was no doubt that they were both good looking and a charming presence surrounded them like a halo. Their teeth shone white as they laughed and little crinkles appeared at the sides of their eyes. Clearly they were well liked as the women plied them with olives and goats' cheese, which they ate with strips of soft thin bread. Black Turkish coffee was poured from a small slim coffee pot perched on a stand with a small flame flickering below it, into small cups. The coffee was strong and black and sweet and a ring of foam floated on the top as they sipped it slowly, savouring the richness and the aroma.

The fact, that the taller man, kept looking at the young girls playing further away, did not escape the attention of the women and after intercepting one of these glances again, she called the girls.

'Veronica, Bernadette, and you to Manouch, come here.'

Shyly the girls came to the woman who introduced them to the young men. The girls kept their eyes lowered and blushed, and said nothing. What could they say anyway? They were children and these people were grown ups. Old actually, they thought, and waited for the woman to send them back.

'This is Veronica' she said pushing the one girl forward. The men extended their right hand and solemnly shook her hand 'and this is Bernadette' as she pushed the next girl forward 'and this is Manouch.' The small hand placed in his hand was lost in the roughness but Manouch felt a warm feeling come over her as the man took her hand. When Salem held her hand, he wanted to hold it longer, but knew it would not be appropriate. He looked at the woman who was watching him intently, and nodded his head. The girls turned and left, but his eyes followed Manouch.

The two men kissed the women on both their cheeks and then climbed on to the cart and left. Salem had chosen his wife, although it would be more than two years before he would claim her as his bride.

Regular visits followed, with small gifts for the child, who would not be out of her mothers' sight at any time. A contract was a contract even though it was not written or signed, and the bride, when the time came, would be as pure as the day she was born.

Manouch felt special from that day on, although she had no idea why, and she enjoyed it when the two brothers came to visit and usually brought her a small gift. She played with her doll and her cousins, and sat with them on the floor when her mother told them all stories, of her own childhood in Australia. Manouch loved to hear these stories and sang with when her mother sang 'Waltzing Matilda, waltzing Matilda,' while clutching her doll on her lap.

Veronica was already twelve years old, and Bernadette was eleven, although she looked older, and Manouch wished she were more like them. She felt such a child watching them, as they dressed, marvelling at their fuller figures. True she was treated as a cousin, but she somehow felt as if they were jealous of her.

She knew it had something to do with the two young men that came to visit more and more often, but she did not understand it at all. When they came, they were always together, the two brothers, and her mom was always with her. Not that she spoke to them much as she sat next to her mother who seemed to ask them many questions. She knew that she was promised to Salem but did not quite understand what it meant. She knew every angle of his face from every side as she watched him. His eyes were to her like warm coffee and she sometimes imagined smoke was coming from them. His hairline was receding on the sides and there were flecks of grey in his moustache. What she loved most of all, was when he smiled.

His lips would curl up on one side and then a twinkle would come to his eyes, which made it look, as if his eyes were dancing. Sometimes he looked at her when he smiled and winked, turning her blood into jelly, and a warm flush to wash over her. Yes! She knew she was spoken for but still did not know exactly what it meant.

Chapter Five

When the day came that Manouch was no longer a child, but a woman, she was well prepared. Her mother, and her aunt, made sure that she knew what to expect. Excitement filled the air as the two women laughed and joked. The euphoria was infectious and Manouch felt so important. Her two older cousins had already passed this phase of growing up, and now finally, she was equal to them. Her cheeks were flushed, as the feeling of excitement emanating from the women, took hold of her as well. Her mother made her stay in bed for two days and brought hot soup on a tray. Oh yes! She felt special.

A whole new atmosphere filled the house. Laughingly the two women flitted from room to room. Visitors came and went while Manouch stayed in her room.

Even when Salem and his brother Eblen came to visit, she was not allowed to see them. On the fourth day, a dressmaker came to take measurements for her wedding gown.

She was so excited she thought she would burst.

* * *

The day before the wedding finally arrived. Many women, and young girls, were there to help prepare the bride, for her wedding the next day.

A big zinc bath was placed in the bedroom and filled with warm water, from big pots warmed on the coal stove. Fragrant salts and oils were added which gave off a sweet smell pervading the air. Manouch was stripped and helped into the bath of warm scented water. She sat down and her mom and aunt washed her hair and then her body, all the while the other women watched, and made ululating sounds. After she was washed she was dried with a towel and more fragrant scents and oils were rubbed on her body making her feel like a queen.

She went to bed early that night, and lay in the bed, which she shared with her cousins, thinking about the next day. Sleep came almost immediately, and she awoke early with the shouting and noise from the kitchen, where everyone was rushing around with the preparations for the wedding feast. Her mother brought her a tray with tea and a slice of toasted bread with a boiled egg. She ate hungrily and lay down again. There was nothing for her to do until they came to dress her for her wedding. She was twelve years old, and was being prepared for a wife, and hopefully soon, a mother.

The women towered over her small frame as they dressed her. The dress was beautiful with embroidered lace all along the high upstanding collar. A row of tiny buttons covered in the same fabric as the dress ran down her back and along the long organza sleeves. The top of the dress fitted snugly around her small body showing off her blossoming breasts, while the skirt flared towards the bottom beyond her height. The extra length was allowed to hide the box she was going to stand on, for the photographer to take their picture. Earlier her black hair was expertly coifed, and fell in bangs around her face. Her skin, the colour of crushed olives, showed off her glowing brown eyes surrounded by long eyelashes. She looked beautiful to herself as she looked into the mirror, and hardly noticed the ululating sounds all around her. When she left the room, the women called blessings on her.

'May you be happy.'

'May you be blessed with many children.'

'May you have a long life together.'

Manouch felt as if she was walking on a cloud. The skirt of her dress was draped around her one arm to allow her to walk while a bouquet of lilies rested in her other arm.

Salem saw her beauty as she came to him and his heart filled with pride and love.

She saw how handsome he looked in his black suit and bow tie, and her heart, leapt with joy.

Not much of the wedding mass, said for the couple, was remembered by the bridal pair, who only had eyes for each other. And who for the first time, since their first encounter, felt the nearness of the other. The feeling between them was like an electric current waiting to be connected.

The whole community, it seemed, was at the house where the wedding feast was to be held. Tables on the cool veranda were laden with traditional dishes of stuffed grape leaves, baby marrows, cabbage rolls, sheep intestines and whole sheep's stomachs filled with finely chopped mutton and rice. Big platters filled with raw mutton stamped to a fine consistency with crushed corn and greens, were in the centre of the tables, with chopped chillies, and olive oil, next to it. Fresh, flat round bread was on wooden tablets placed at the corners of the tables.

Jugs of water and glasses were also placed at intervals. There was no wedding cake and no liquor, but no one expected it. Instead strong Turkish coffee or tea would be served later with sweetmeats of cornflower biscuits topped with almonds.

* * *

We were not only brothers, but also good friends and companions. Salem and I were always together wherever we went. We worked together in total harmony, each knowing what the other needed or felt.

Salem made his choice in choosing a wife and I must say she is not only beautiful, but gentle as well. Her youth is of little concern. I know my brother will look after her as he has done for the past few years, and I know he loves her. Growing up, she did not disappoint him, and treated him, and myself, with the utmost respect. I know our parents would be proud if they could see him and how happy he is. I will write, knowing that someone there in Lebanon will read the letter to them. Perhaps I can include a photograph? I myself am as proud of him, as anyone can be. Our relationship will not change in any way, in fact, it will become richer, and his family, when he has one, will be my family.

Together, Salem and I, have built up a small business in transporting and selling goods, managing to save a little money. Salem had bought a narrow stretch of land on the outskirts of town. With the help of unemployed men, who lived in a camp nearby, we built a row of small houses attached to each other. Hundreds of men and women were camped in makeshift tents, living in poverty, on the outskirts of the town. Men, and sometimes even women, stood in rows each morning along the roads leading into town, hoping for work for that day.

There were three houses in total. Salem had prepared the first for himself and his wife, and children to come. An open covered space where the cart could be pulled in at night separated it from the two smaller houses alongside. These he rented out for some extra income. Salem wanted me to stay there but I was comfortable and decided to stay where I was.

Next to the house he occupied, he cultivated a large garden with vegetables and fruit trees. This piece of land, although he cultivated it, was not actually part of his property, but he used it anyway. Behind the row of houses was an open field stretching out to the railway track on the crest. The area in front of the houses, were also of open field leaving the row of houses quite isolated and made it an ideal place to raise a family.

Earlier on their wedding day, I had helped Salem to load the cart that would take them to the house that we had prepared for them. Furniture that he slowly accumulated was already in place waiting for them.

* * *

The cart stood ready waiting for the bridal couple. On the back, the wooden chest, filled with trousseau and clothes, was already fastened down with strong ropes. Before Manouch was helped up on to the cart by Salem, she turned one last time to look at her mother and aunt. They stood on the side of the path, watching them with family members, who gathered to wish Manouch on her way. A feeling of sadness came over her knowing she would not see her mother again as she was leaving the next day, to go back to Australia, taking with her, her own childhood. Then she felt his strong hand holding her arm, and nothing else mattered but him.

Chapter Six

Fifteen months later their first child, a son, was born, and thereafter at approximately two year intervals, another child followed. There was always a baby on the breast, and one on the lap. Salem and Manouch glowed in their bounty, as they watched and laughed, at their brood.

Salem was a loving father yet firm in his guidance, and Manouch never questioned his authority. She was a beautiful woman who was always well groomed, and Salem loved and cherished her, beyond all boundaries.

Eblen, Salem's brother, was a regular visitor, and was always treated with the utmost respect, and happiness. He, Eblen, shared in the happiness of his brother and his family. Salem's family was also Eblen's family, and that was how it always would be.

* * *

He was short, and wiry, black as coal and cleanliness shone like a beacon around him. His short white trouser was snow white as was his shirt.

He carried only a small bedroll with him. His bare feet were firmly planted on the ground as he waited his outcome.

A journey, which took him from Algoa Bay, where he worked for Paul Kruger, the then President of the Transvaal, and later for Pietie Joubert, another leader, had reached its end. He, much like Salem and Eblen, had decided to seek his fortune on the goldfields, and so found himself in this east rand town where mines, were sprouting up like wild flowers. He soon realised he would not be able to do the underground work in the mines, and instead, became a houseboy for a Lebanese family.

Now another Lebanese family wanted him to work for them and he waited patiently for the outcome, of the decision, being made by the two men talking.

Alfred knew about this other man who wanted to take him. He knew he was a fair man and hoped that he was going with him. A smile broke on his face as Salem indicated to him to follow him. He knew in his heart he would be happy.

He saw she was still a young woman, and a baby was on her lap. He also saw a toddler playing nearby, and one crawling at her feet.

Alfred stored his bedroll under a table, next to the coal stove, in the lower kitchen, and started straight away by stopping the crawling child, from falling down the step that separated the top kitchen from the section below, where the stove and washing up area was. And just like that, he became a part of the family. It was as if he had come home.

That night, when everyone was settled in bed, he took out his bedroll and rolled it out in front of the warm stove, and lay down to sleep.

Still dark the next morning, he unlocked the door and went outside to the tap in the yard, and washed himself after taking off his shirt. When the family awoke, a new fire was burning and water was boiled ready for tea.

The family only spoke Lebanese although Salem could speak English. There was no other way for Alfred but to learn the language.

He was always nearby helping with the wagon or the children, or whatever needed to be done and this was pretty much everything, and anything. Never was he treated as anyone other than a member of the family and the smaller children accepted him as their grandfather. They climbed all over him as they played and he smacked them when they were naughty. He became an integral part of the household and his advise when asked, was gratefully received whenever a problem presented itself.

Alfred learned not only to speak their language but also their culture. He asked for no payment, and none was given. When he accompanied Salem to the market, where he sold his fresh vegetables and fruit, he was given a coin, which he put carefully in his pocket, to put away when he got home. His clothing needs were minimal and when Salem bought clothes for the children, Alfred always got a shirt or a trouser, as well. He never needed shoes, as he never wore them, winter or summer. Food was always shared with the family although he preferred to cook his own. A small steel dish with meat and potato was slowly cooked in the oven till tender, and eaten late at night, when everyone was settled in bed.

Sometimes one of the boys would secretly help themselves to this tasty meal only to be met with a smack, which did not deter them from doing it again. Manouch depended on Alfred not only as a helper, but as a friend, who gave her advise when she needed it and she trusted him with her children, knowing he would take good care of them. This was his home, his family, and destiny had brought him to this place.

*   *   *

Chapter Seven

'Manouch, come here, hurry!'

She quickly went out to where Salem was.

'Look at Tonius.' He said.

She laughed as she saw how their eldest child clung to the horses' mane riding bareback.

'Hold tight!' Salem shouted as horse and rider galloped past them.

Manouch held her stomach, big and rounded with child and laughed till tears rolled down her cheeks.

Barely nine years of age the boy, tried everything. When Salem packed the wagon he was right there, and when he was in the garden, he was there as well, as he followed his father around.

His brothers Peter and Dawood, who were playing a bit further on, goaded their brother as he galloped past. Fear was plain on his face as his hands clung tight to the mane of the horse and his scream for help was not only filled with panic.

Salem waited for horse and rider as they passed again and expertly flung a rope around the horses' head and pulled it tight. As horse and rider stopped he took the boy down and hugged him briefly before the boy ran to his mother.

Peter and Dawood came running to their brother, and Salem now stone faced, called them together.

'You must be careful, you children, you know I need this horse to work.

I don't want you to do this again. Next time, a good 'shellacking' he said slapping his hand on his thigh, to show them how it would be done.

Laughing the three boys ran away. Salem smiled and shook his head, they were a handful but he loved them with all his heart. Then he took Manouch by the arm and together they went inside.

Depression was like a cancer eating away the very fabric of humanity.

It took pride and honour and discarded it like chaff in the wind. The camps of unemployed people grew daily on the outskirts of towns.

Salem was not the only one that packed his wagon with fresh vegetables and fruit to take to these people, no he saw other men doing the same, and when they passed each other on their wagons or carts, they would raise their hats in silent acknowledgement. Most of them were also stretched with heavy burdens but nevertheless found something to share with these desperate people. These men on their carts and wagons went home and thanked God for their bounty, however meagre it was, a roof over their head and a warm stove to help with the cold.

* * *

Waiting on the wagon outside the market, the boy let his thoughts wander as he usually did, while his father was busy inside the market.

My name is actually Anthony, although everyone calls me David.

I don't mind them calling me David, in fact it makes me feel important. I am the number one child of the house of David so it's fine. I love my father with a passion and learn all his ways so I can be just like him when I grow up. I love my mother as well, but there is always a child on her lap, or on her breast, so her attention is always with the youngest, whoever it is.

Sometimes I forget their names, and I know my father also does, because he calls me by another name, but I always respond anyway.

And there he is, my father coming to the wagon where I am waiting and I wave at him and he waves back and my heart nearly bursts as he throws me an apple. I catch it expertly like I always do. The wagon creaks as he climbs up and takes the reins in his calloused hands.

On the way back we stop at the abattoir where my dad selects a freshly slaughtered lamb. Lamb, he tells me is the best meat, tender and tasty.

* * *

Salem carried the lamb over his shoulder and lay it down on the kitchen table where Manouch had spread a clean cloth. A big wooden board with a sharp knife was also waiting. The task, of cutting up the carcass, was always done by the two of them. They worked in unison separating the carcass into sections. The legs were for making 'kibe' a delicacy of raw lamb cut into small pieces, and then stamped on a hollowed wooden block, until very fine. Crushed wheat and greens were then added and re-stamped, after which salt and fine black pepper was added. The mixture was smoothed, with hands dipped in cold water, on a flat serving plate and oil was drizzled over it. This dish was eaten by tearing off pieces of the thin soft bread, scooping out bite size portions. Everyone ate from the same dish, placed in the centre of the table.

The ribs would be grilled over the open fire on the stove and served with chillies and rice or sometimes roasted in the oven with potatoes.

Portions of the carcass would be finely chopped to use in the filling of grape leaves or cabbage rolls from their own garden. Preparation of meals for the family took up most of the day and everything was carefully apportioned.

Sounds of chattering and laughter spilled out into the street, as the children crowded excitedly around the table where their parents were busy cutting the meat.

Eagerly they waited for Salem to hand them small bits to taste. They loved it when their parents worked together like this. There was always laughter and joking going on with the occasional smack from their parents as they tried to steal a piece of the meat.

The kidneys were carefully taken out of the carcass and kept for later to be shared by Manouch and Salem after they had seen to the children. This was a special delicacy and due to the size of the portion was not given to the children. Once everything was cleared away they would sit together and enjoy it. First they would remove the thin layer of skin, from the kidneys, and cut them in halves. Then the membrane was removed and the kidneys were chopped into small pieces. Salt, pepper and chopped chillies were on the side and it was eaten with the traditional bread.

An absolute delicacy and each mouthful would be savoured to its fullest.

Sometimes if Eblen was there, it was shared with him instead of Manouch. His presence was always welcomed and the children adored him. Eblen came on Sundays and stayed for lunch and afterwards they all sat together on the veranda where it was cool.

Lamb is used in many of the traditional dishes like 'piselle' made with finely cut lamb and onions and brazed till nicely browned and the onions transparent, then shelled peas are added with grated tomatoes and spiced with salt, black pepper and cinnamon and slowly simmered to lock in the taste.

Vermicelli rice is served with this meal. First the vermicelli is broken off into small pieces and fried in butter till brown and then the washed rice is added and fried before water is added with salt and pepper and slowly cooked till done. Grape leaves were picked from their own vines, while the leaves were still young and grew on the adjacent land among the vegetables and fruit trees.

The leaves were carefully chosen for size and had to be blemish free, and was washed in cold water. Finely cut lamb was mixed with washed rice, salt, black pepper, cinnamon and butter and this was used as a filling for the leaves folded into little parcels and tightly packed in a pot with grated tomatoes on top. A plate is then placed inverted over this to keep the parcels from separating. Water to cover the contents is then poured in and slowly cooked till the rice is done.

One could go on and on like this forever, with cabbage leaves, and baby marrows or bringals and sheep intestines and stomachs, with each dish more tasty, than the other.

David left his siblings around the table and went out into the yard. He picked up an empty string bag where it was packed in the corner and walked to the railroad on the rise.

With the bag in his hand he started picking up coal that had fallen off the coal train as it passed their property. He and his brothers and sisters did this twice a day. On good days, they nearly filled the bag, which meant it would be enough to keep the stove going for the next day. Although the bag became heavy, he carried on until all the coal along the tracks was picked up. His arms were paining when he dragged the bag home, but this did not stop him from his task.

'Good work son.' Salem said when he saw him. 'Go wash your hands and come and eat.'

David felt so proud that he could do this task for his father, and his mother as well of course, but he stored the praise from his father deep in his heart.

School was a place he never liked and only went because he needed to learn to read and write. So he did go until he mastered the art and felt he did not need it any more. His duty was to help his father and to make sure the younger children did attend school so that they could find work when they were old enough. With figures David was particularly good. He could add and subtract faster than anyone he knew, and he learned to negotiate, and deal in business from an early age. After all, he was always at his fathers' side learning all the while. Being the eldest child was not only a position of power or privilege, but came with responsibilities. This was what his father was always telling him and he took his position very seriously. For now David knew he was still a child, but one day he would be a man, with decisions to make and duties to perform and he had to be capable.

* * *

Sitting in the sun Manouch was peeling potatoes for the evening meal.

Badeo was stirring a big pot on the stove brazing the chopped cuts of beef for the curry they were making. She always helped her mother, as did Amiro, who was busy making tea. These two sisters were close friends and were always with their mother who depended on them to help with the children. They helped to get them ready for school in the mornings and then they all walked to the convent a short distance away.

This in itself was already a hefty task. The boys walked a few yards behind watching the girls who were not allowed to speak to anyone.

The girls in turn watched that their brothers did not misbehave and the brothers knew this also.

Many times these groups, brothers and sisters, would complain to their mother when they returned from school. She would listen patiently and then chastise the guilty party in a stern manner. This complaint was then later passed on to Salem. If he deemed it necessary he would take further action, but mostly he just smiled at their antics. After all, children had to learn to settle their own differences.

None of the children wanted to disappoint him and dreaded that they ever would, so a warning usually kept them in line.

Now looking at Badeo and Amiro busy at the stove, her eyes Manouch took in their beauty. Badeo, a tall girl, with a slim body had her black hair tied loosely in a knot behind her head. She was beautiful with a face shaped like a heart and big brown eyes, which glowed like warm amber, from a face flushed with the steam rising from the pot she was stirring.

Amiro, younger and shorter than her sister was also an attractive girl but really still a child. Her long black hair was thicker and fanned in a bush around her face. She was a serious child, who loved school with a passion. The nuns also gave glowing reports of her work at school.

Yes! Manouch thought, they had a truly handsome brood, and her and Salem could not be more proud than they already were.

Then her gaze dropped to the floor where Finnie was playing with a rag doll. Josephine was shortened to Finnie, by her siblings, and so that is what they all called her. Before long she would be helping her sisters but for now she was happy to be a child. Manouch smiled at her as she looked up. Outside she could hear the boys playing. There was always a lot of noise from them, and Manouch knew Alfred would be nearby, keeping an eye on them, without them even realising it. He was her right hand and he loved the children as if they were his own. In fact, he believed they were his children, and they knew it and accepted it loving him in return.

Chapter Eight

Just as David was always with his father, so Badeo was with her mother.

Her name was actually Johanna, and she was called, Joyie by her friends, and Badeo, by her family and she always had one or two children with her. Her mother depended on her, and like David, she stayed in school just long enough to master reading and writing. There was so much work in the household with all the children who were always either in an infant stage or crawling, or running around. Alfred helped a lot as well and the older brothers were usually with their father but it was the little ones that needed the constant supervision and care, and then there was still the cooking to help with. She knew she had no time to waste by being in school. Once all the children were settled at night she was so tired she could hardly get to her own bed that she shared with her younger sisters.

Morning always came too soon when the whole process started again to get the younger ones ready for school and making sure they had a breakfast of toast and jam, and a hot cup of tea, which Alfred made. No lunches were given to take to school where a feeding scheme was in place to feed children. Many, many families had no food at home so sent their children to school so they could have something to eat, however meagre.

It was always a relief once the school going children left and they could concentrate on the little ones. Bathing them and feeding them took most of the morning and then it was time for the others to get back from school. Weekends were less strenuous and Badeo looked forward to Fridays when she could sleep a little later.

The downward trend in the economy worsened and there were always more mouths to feed and bodies to be clothed. The government did what they could but the future became bleaker and bleaker.

On the days when rations in the form of coupons from the government were given out at the market, they all went while it was still dark, to stand in the long rows outside to wait for their turn. Unsifted flour, sugar and butter were issued by the government to help the poor and destitute, and there were thousands.

Shivering in the cold morning air they waited in their thin jerseys pulled close around them, if they had one, and bare feet went unnoticed.

Many lived in the tents along the roads or under a bridge or in a gully and depended not only on the government rations, but also on the generosity of others, to get through the days.

Badeo washed out the bags where the unsifted flour was in, to cut and sew them into shirts, or petticoats for the children. They hated this, especially when some of the writing was still visible on the fabric, but they had no choice. It was the only clothing available except when the nuns at the convent handed out warm jerseys that they received from donations. All the clothing in the house was worn by everyone, whatever fitted, or in many cases too small, or too big, was used. Feeding and clothing a large family was a full time occupation and needed careful planning. Badeo took care of most of this with her mother and Amiro. If one of the little ones were ill, Badeo kept them with her, so her mother would not be infected and so infect the baby, whoever he or she was at the time, and there was always a baby just about to be born or, like the little girl at her mothers' breast, barely three weeks old.

Yvette, named after the saint, was a lovely baby, with her olive skin and black hair.

Content in her mothers' arms she suckled noisily. When she was done feeding Manouch handed her over to Badeo to place in the cot. The cot, was well used over the years and never stood empty, at times two occupants filled it.

The cot stood against the one wall of the bedroom with the beds of Salem and Manouch side by side and two closets and a dressing table, filling the room.

The sound of babies or small children crying always filled the background. Its intensity was measured to assess the urgency of the cry, which usually stopped as abruptly as it started, if it was not serious, so no notice was taken unless the crying persisted.

The bearing and rearing, of children, had done nothing to tarnish the beauty of Manouch. Her body had become more rounded and mature but she was still attractive and Salem loved her more than life itself.

* * *

Chapter Nine

Black water fever was what they called it. So named, because the fever, turned ones' tongue black, before death set in. Burials took place daily and few families were spared. A pall over the country kept families close together, too afraid, to be among others. Sailors embarking were kept separate from the locals to avoid spreading the fever. Schools were closed and a hand sewn sachet, filled with garlic hung from a ribbon around each ones' neck. Hands were dipped into water with disinfectant added before eating anything.

Although the house was usually crowded, Manouch made sure her family kept to this ritual, and watched them carefully. Hoping all the while that the curse would pass them by, but they were not spared and when the first signs appeared the doctor was immediately sent for.

Busy as he was, he made time to see the sick child. When he stopped his cart, Manouch was waiting for him on the veranda, having heard his approach. Next to her, stood her eldest daughter Badeo who could speak English.

The doctor knew he was constantly at risk and wore a white gauze mask when he attended to his patients, and tried to help as best he could. It was difficult as medical supplies were scarce, and in many instances outdated, when he eventually did receive it. This fact was never spoken of to anyone and he was the only one who knew it. What would it matter anyway? He also knew that he was not the only doctor dealing with this problem. There just was not enough medication for all the sick people so they did the best they could with what they had.

Slowly he got off from the cart and took his worn black bag.

He had gotten to know Manouch and her family over the years and knew her as a good and caring mother and he had the highest respect for her.

They entered the house and he followed. The room, a small one on the side of the house, had a narrow bed and nothing else. Dark hair fanned over the pillow and the girl of about eleven or so was burning up with fever. The pillow was damp with the sweat seeping into it and sweat glistened on her forehead. No one was to be allowed into the room, except Manouch and Badeo. There was no space in any hospital so patients had to be nursed at home.

He first rubbed his hands with alcohol, which he kept in a flask with him, and then he put on rubber gloves. He pulled the white gauze cover over his mouth as he bent down.

Before he had even touched the girl, he knew what the outcome would be. Nevertheless, he filled the syringe that he took from his bag, and injected the fluid into her vein.

"Wipe her forehead with a cool cloth and give her soup and don't let anyone in the room.'

A large bag of fresh vegetables was handed to him as he left which he took gratefully. Many families he went to had nothing to pay with but that did not stop him from his duty.

He put the bag on the cart and climbed up. This was his last stop of the day and he was going home to wash himself and his clothes thoroughly in disinfectant. Death was all around him and he knew that within hours he would be called back to declare the girl dead and issue a certificate. He would also have to report this to the local authority. The room where she lay would then be scrubbed down from ceiling to floor and all the bedding burnt on a heap in the yard. Having very little, or anything at all at these times, made this a harsh requirement, but there was no way out. Everything had to be burnt to stop the infection from spreading.

Being right in his estimation it was late afternoon the following day when he got the message.

This time, there were three people waiting for him on the veranda. Salem was flanked by his eldest son David, and Phillip, one of the younger ones.

Manouch and her daughter Badeo were in the room washing down the body of the young girl whose dark hair was still fanned over the pillow.

Her body looked thin and translucent and he saw her breasts were beginning to bloom. He felt sad at the thought of the premature death of this once vibrant girl.

After his precautionary ritual he examined the girl for the last time and wrote out the certificate. A freshly slaughtered chicken was handed to him by Salem when he left and his own voice was hoarse when he thanked him.

Only the family attended the funeral as fear of infection kept people away. Manouch and Salem were grateful for this as refreshments for people were unaffordable at this time and it spared them the embarrassment of not being able to provide for them in an adequate manner. A pal pervaded the once happy home, and the children whilst playing, hardly made any noise.

Manouch sat at the table in the kitchen and now looked with sadness as Badeo and Joe took over the cooking for the family. Joe was young but thought nothing of helping with the cooking, in fact, this was where he felt most happy. He knew his parents were grieving as he did, but he knew their pain was more intense. Placing a cup of tea in front of his mother she looked up and smiled at him and his heart nearly burst with happiness. He thought he would never see her smile again and tears welled up in his own eyes as he turned away.

* * *

Chapter Ten

I am the firstborn. It is like the bible says. The first child that is born, is special, and a great responsibility rests on their shoulders. True though it be that the younger siblings should respect you, it is not always easy when one has so many brothers who are bigger than you are in physique. The girls are not a problem, but brothers are more difficult.

School was a torture for me. I was always cold and knew my brothers and sisters were as well. Learning to read and write was difficult but I knew I had to master this, so I persevered. English came easily and so, to my surprise, did Afrikaans. Many of the children were from Afrikaans homes even though they were at the convent, and I made friends easily.

My brothers Johnny, Dawood and Buddy (whose given name was actually Peter) and I were always in the same group and nobody dared to even say anything bad to us. We were like an army, the four of us, and trouble, was another story altogether. Dawood and Johnny had tempers that were plain scary. The nuns sent messages home with the girls to tell my parents when they fought, but the girls never passed it on. They, the girls, were too afraid of the repercussions from their brothers, so said nothing.

We dropped out of school one by one, us brothers, as we mastered reading and writing and felt we had learnt enough, and found ourselves a job.

I love nice clothes and turned my charm on and soon had a position in a clothing store in town.

I was surrounded with upmarket clothing for men and I was happy and I knew my boss was happy as well, with the increase of sales.

The pay was not a lot but it helped in a small way to relieve the expense of my upkeep and this made me happy.

* * *

The nice thing about a big family is that you don't need other friends. You can play rounders with a plank taken from a tomato box, and could organise your own adventures or games whenever you wanted to, that is of course when there was a bit of spare time, which was not really plentiful with all the chores we had to do, like picking up coal along the railroad, or watching the younger ones.

The bad thing about a big family is that you don't always get enough food to quench the hunger pains, and clothing is also a problem. By the time the smaller ones get anything, it has been mended many times over and the fabric was thin from all the washing. Then there is the problem that I am smaller in stature than my brothers which meant the trousers would be too short for the next brother, or not fit at all, and this meant the seams would have to be let out and the turn-up of the trousers were let down leaving a distinctive mark where this was folded over. It was also difficult to have your voice heard, especially if you were one of the younger ones. Washing oneself was one of the biggest problems. The water started being warm and thereafter it got colder and colder and then it was just plain cold. There was only one alternative and that was to find your own nest, and move out. This was my goal and I was working on it.

* * *

Nobody ever called me Johanna although that is my given name. My friends call me Joey and my family call me Badeo. I am the eldest girl and never really had a childhood of my own. Instead I looked after my younger brothers and sisters from an early age. It was always 'Badeo, Badeo where are you? See what is wrong with the baby. Badeo help your brother, Badeo bring me some tea' and on and on it went.

The only time I had for myself was when I was at school. Once I knew how to read and write I knew I would have to leave to help at home. I dragged this out as long as I could but in the end the outcome was plain, my mother needed me and depended on me to help her.

Cooking was a full time duty. It started early in the morning before the younger ones left for school. Alfred, bless his soul, made heaps of toast on the open fire with a grid on top of the hot stove giving off a smoky taste which lingered and made the toast all the more enjoyable. Jam without butter was the only spread on the toast and this never varied. He also had a big pot of strong tea ready and poured it into mugs for us.

Amiro, my younger sister and I were friends. She helped me as best she could until she became ill. When she died I thought I would also die. It was like a part of me was cut off from my body. My parents grieved for her and nobody saw my pain but it was there like a severed limb. At night I cried myself to sleep and in the morning I was in the kitchen again.

Finnie, my younger sister, now became my shadow. She tried to help as best she could and I let her. I do need help but I have to get her used to doing more things.

I am already taller than my eldest brother David who is probably five feet and six inches and I was not as tall as Buddy who must be at least five feet and ten inches tall although it was only a guess. My figure is slim and when I go anywhere with my mom, people especially the young men, notice me. My dad, when he is with us, watches them carefully. He knows that they are interested and quickly puts a stop to this by grilling them about their future plans. What work do they do? How would they provide for a family? Usually a few questions would have the men re-think their options wondering if they were actually ready for such a commitment. This strategy worked in most cases but had no affect on Dawood, my cousin. His mother and my father were brother and sister. Any marriage between cousins is frowned on by most nationalities but somehow was encouraged in the Lebanese people.

Why this was so I don't exactly know, but accepted it as it was.

He was shorter than I, and this put me off in the initial stages, but he persevered, turned on his charm and became a regular visitor. What I never considered, now seemed possible, and the very thought of getting married and leaving my home filled me with uncertainty while at the same time I was excited.

The relationship between my mother and myself, changed in a way that she became more of a friend instead of a mother. My brother Joe and Finnie took over much of the cooking and Yvette was also roped in to help although she was still very young. My mother went shopping with me and my trousseau slowly expanded. Fine cotton sheets and soft blankets and the most beautiful bed covers were bought. She also had some dresses made for me by a local seamstress and I felt special. My father was always talking to Dawood and I liked that. My brothers were also happy for me and I was happy.

And then, finally, the day arrived that I was to be married.

The night before, the women were all present when the washing of the bride took place. They sang to me and showered blessings on me and my husband to be, who was I knew, with the men at another house. My mother and sister Yvette rubbed fragrant oil over my body and washed my hair in scented water and Finnie helped with packing my clothes.

I was a queen and they were my helpers. My mother cried and I cried with her. My dress made from soft silk hung against the wall and my shoes stood ready. My body was relaxed from the warm bath and oils, and I succumbed to sleep almost as soon as I lay my head on the pillow.

This was my last night with my family and although the thought saddened me I was excited to begin my own life.

A feast was laid out for the families, after the church service was concluded, on long tables under the roof of the cool veranda.

What a day it turned out to be. Laughter, talking in loud voices and children crying made for a noisy afternoon. We were not going far away, in fact, the small detached house, we found to rent was a walking distance away.

My uncle Eblen waved at me when he saw me and I could see how pleased he was for me. He was more like a second father to us children and we loved it when he was there.

This was good that we would not be too far away, and meant my mother could take a walk on a nice day, to visit. It was comforting to know this because although I had worked hard for my family, I loved them all, and would always want to be near them.

He looked so handsome dressed in his wedding clothes and when he smiled at me, my legs turned to jelly. I knew I also looked beautiful because he never stopped looking at me and I was happy.

I looked at my father and mother where they stood next to each other and love filled my heart with hope that we would be as happy as they were.

* * *

The strain of a house full of children of whom boys were dominant meant ultimately that more demanding needs had to be catered for. The selling of fresh vegetables, and household goods, was no longer sufficient for their growing needs. After another unsuccessful trip, Salem sat down with Manouch, and together they agreed to diversify their business to bring more money into the household.

The plan was not a new one, and there were other families already practising it, but for them it would be new. The selling of hard liquor to brown people, was totally against the law, although it was done nevertheless. With the mining compound nearby it could work, although there would be risks to be taken. Manouch listened to her husband and knew they had to find more money and she trusted him in his judgement. Being Lebanese also posed constraints, as they were not allowed to buy from a bottle store.

Stock would be supplied, Salem said, from a connection, which he knew about from a family friend.

* * *

Chapter Eleven

Vegetables and fruit were still taken to the market as usual but the home scene now changed to allow for the new business to be included. Flat wooden benches were erected in the yard where the clients could sit and music played on a radio nearby. Word spread quickly and before long the yard was abuzz with laughter and loud talking. They, the men, were dressed in mining overalls and heavy boots, and knew the rules of survival that were laid down to them. Behind the house, in the open field, the grass grew tall and lush, which could hide one easily if the need presented itself.

In the kitchen, sections of the wooden floor boards were loosened where bottles could be hidden. There were also other places scattered around the house for this purpose. The universal language of the mines was a dialect called 'Fanagalo' and although Manouch never learned to speak English, she picked this dialect up quite easily. The men respected her for serving them in an equal manner. They never felt that race was an issue and felt welcome. They also felt that they belonged there and would, if necessary, defend Manouch or her children with their lives. Salem, when he was home on the weekends was like a king as far as they were concerned. They knew of his generosity to all races and the fair way in which he dealt with people, and so respected him not only as a father and a husband, but also as a person who cares for his fellow men. They saw how Alfred was part of the family, and they knew he was loved by all.

The girls together with Alfred helped their mother serve measured tots of brandy into metal mugs, as well as the opening of bottles of beer.

The atmosphere was jovial while at the same time the mood was constantly closely observed. Whenever someone started to get out of hand he was led away without causing a scene. Once it looked like someone had too much to drink, he was asked to leave in a friendly manner. No one took offence and returned the next day without any complaint.

The younger boys now had another duty. They were lookouts perched high on the rise at the back of the house and in front near the road. If anything suspicious were spotted, a shrill whistle would alert those in the house.

In seconds the yard would be cleared and all the bottles hidden so unexpected visitors, such as detectives, or police, would come across a peaceful scene of normal housekeeping. Some of the law enforcement men were more understanding than others, and even at times, sent out warnings of planned raids beforehand. Their service never went without reward. The problem was that teams from other towns, were sometimes deployed, of which they knew nothing beforehand.

Risk was always an issue but Salem knew that survival was what one did in order to provide for your family and they were survivors. He and Eblen often spoke about the dangers and also about the benefits and they realised that their way of making a living had changed over the years. Yvette was now at a stage where she got in everyone's way trying to help. David was married in what seemed like a stormy relationship and would soon be a father. Buddy, Johnny and Dawood were all good looking young men and Salem knew they would soon be settled as well. Joe and Phillip on the other hand, were content at home and Salem knew they were not eager to leave just yet. The house was crowded, and nobody, could blame the older boys, wanting to leave. In fact they, the older boys very rarely slept at home. Salem knew they were most likely at a girls' house and did not ask too many questions. Children slept everywhere at night with three or four to each bed and there was no privacy for anyone. The bathroom was also a problem with so many using it and Salem saw the boys using the outside toilet which he built for Alfred on a regular basis. He himself did just that when the girls took too long washing their hair or some other things which he knew Manouch took care of.

* * *

Looking at his wife across the table as they were having dinner one evening Salem saw the telltale flush on her cheeks and the pulse flickering in her neck. He knew the signs without her even telling him, that she was pregnant. This thought made him happy and sad at the same time. They had eleven children, counting their daughter that died from the fever, and each one was precious to them.

He saw her now as he looked at her as the most beautiful woman he had ever seen and when she looked at him and smiled his heart wanted to burst with pride. Their love for each other was bound together not only with their children but in their very being where each breath taken by one was shared with the other. Their eyes were filled with this joy. There was not one moment, from the time that Salem had laid eyes on Manouch, that he had looked at any other woman.

To him there was no other to compare with her.

* * *

Manouch did not tell Salem right away about her being pregnant for a reason she did not even know why.

She somehow felt he knew even though he said nothing, and so she left it for later.

It was as if something held Manouch back in sharing her news with others. She was happy that she did this for when Badeo and Dawood came to visit with the good news that she was pregnant with her first child, Manouch could share in her daughters' happiness. She felt she would let Badeo enjoy the feeling of importance for a while longer, before telling her about her own pregnancy.

* * *

Without warning they were there. A team of men rushed through the house pushing aside those who stood in their way. It came when there were fewer lookouts and those that were there did not see the unmarked van approaching.

Manouch stood with a bottle in her hand and fear was on her face. Their clasp was strong and fast and she hardly had a chance to cry out.

The two men held her arms on both sides and she had no chance to get away.

When the younger children saw their mother dragged to the van, by the men, they ran to her grabbing at her dress and cried.

'Mommy, Mommy.'

A quick backward glance was all Manouch could do before the doors of the van closed.

* * *

Salem was there with Eblen his brother, and a lawyer. They tried without success for bail and were not even allowed to see her. The courts' decision the next day was swift and merciless. Jail with no other option was the outcome. The children cried, Salem did all he could but to no avail and Manouch was led away to the cells to begin her sentence.

* * *

The house felt empty although the rest of the family were there. Manouch was the presence that made the house a home and she was no longer there. Yvette as young as she was, and Finnie, together with Joe saw to the preparing of meals and Alfred made sure the children had breakfast before leaving for school. The older brothers went to work and Salem filled his wagon and went to the market taking along Phillip and Jimmy. On Sundays Salem was allowed to visit his wife in prison and looked at her with a heavy heart. He knew she was suffering, being pregnant, with no loved ones around her. This was more difficult to bear than anything else, and he saw the pain in her eyes.

Not once did she complain. Instead she prayed incessantly for the well being of her family. Unable to communicate with anyone she kept to herself. She understood English but did not speak it. The narrow cot in the cell was like a bed of torture for Manouch as her belly grew with the child she was carrying. Did she know it was to be her last?

Shortly before her time was due to give birth the courts relented and she was released.

At home she was met with tears as the children clung to her. She cried as much as they did and Salem kept his face averted to hide his own tears.

The midwife wrapped the baby in a soft blanket and handed him to his mother. The birth went without incident much like the others, although without anyone realising it, it would be her last. The mother did not know it at the time and neither did anyone else. This was the last baby she would suckle on her breast. There would be many babies on her lap from her children but this was her last.

When Salem joined his wife their eyes locked and the happiness that shone from each was tangible.

'Ah! Manouch, we have done it again. Thank you.'

Manouch smiled at him and nodded her head before looking down at the child. 'He looks like you Salem.'

He laughed softly touching the little hand. 'Do you really think so?'

'More than anyone, just look at his eyelashes.'

Salem looked at the scrunched up little face and shook his head. 'Where are the eyelashes, I can't see them.' But he did, he saw the eyelashes on the soft skin and kissed the baby on his forehead. "I have to go, rest now, we will talk when I get back.'

Salem turned away and left the room. He did not have to be anywhere but a feeling of great sadness had come over him as he looked at his wife and child and he knew he had to leave before Manouch sensed it. When he had looked at the little face of his son, he thought he saw tall grass swaying in the wind and the sound of a train clattering on its rails. Then he shook the feeling from him and walked into the kitchen.

'Alfred, what do you say?'

Alfred chuckled softly 'he looks fine to me, just a bit small.'

'He will grow strong like a cedar.'

'He is not a tree' came the reply.

Salem now laughed. 'Oh! He will be, you just wait and see. Promise me you will always look after them.'

'Why, where are you going? Alfred asked.

'Nowhere now, but in case I am not around, promise me.'

Alfred waved his hand at Salem as if he wanted to shoo him away.

'Ag, go do your work, you know I am always here.'

Manouch put her head back on the pillow and tucked the baby in the hollow of her arm where they both fell asleep.

Later that day Eblen came to see the new arrival and he loved the infant instantly as if it was his own. He had never married although he lived with a good woman who looked after his needs. No, his family was here with his brother Salem.

When Badeo and her husband arrived later to see them, Badeo bent over with difficulty, to look at the little bundle wrapped in the soft blanket. Her due date for her first child was only a few short weeks away. She picked up her new brother from the bed when he began to cry and rocked him in her arms making little soothing noises. Soon she would be holding her own baby and leave her sisters, Finnie and Yvette to take care of him. She held him for a while and then put him back in her mothers' arms. This was no longer her duty and she knew her sisters would help her mother to take good care of him. They stayed a while and Manouch asked her whether all her preparations had been made for her first birth.

Manouch was not worried knowing that Badeo was well experienced in looking after babies, and for this Manouch was happy.

Badeo did not look at her mothers' face as she turned to leave in fear of feeling as if she had abandoned her. Her time was now for her own family. Dawood took her by her arm as they left and she knew he understood.

* * *

The boy Badeo delivered was not the first grandchild, although that is how it felt for Manouch and Salem. David, their eldest child had fathered a daughter, but his marriage was short lived, and the child stayed with her mother, so they the grandparents, never saw her. To them, this boy, born from Badeo and Dawood, felt like their first grandchild. When they came to visit the two boys lay side, by side, uncle and nephew. Manouch held her grandson on her lap and loved him like her own. She nuzzled the little boy and he gurgled with pleasure. Nearby his mother was changing her baby brother. They were just two mothers with their babies.

With Badeo out of the house, Manouch lingered with her infant. True she had given birth to babies many times before, but this felt different.

Evenings when the other children were settled in bed, she and Salem sat together looking at their son who lay asleep wrapped securely in his blanket, and they were happy.

The closeness that was always between them, had somehow intensified.

Neither Salem nor Manouch spoke about it, but each clung to the other in silent recognition. Being away from home in jail, made them realise how uncertain life can be. If they were afraid, they never mentioned it to each other for fear to say the words out loud, in case it should become a reality. Life without the other, they knew, would not be a life at all.

* * *

The two little boys grew up together, uncle and nephew, both of the same age with only a few weeks marking the difference in age. If they thought they were brothers, it was quite understandable, besides, nobody told them otherwise. It was only when they were older, that they would understand their relationship to each other. When Manouchs' little boy started walking with uncertain steps, to his mother where she sat, and found her lap occupied already, the little boy cried in frustration. He wanted to sit on his mothers' lap, why couldn't he? Clinging to his mothers' dress and crying, he waited for her to lift him on her lap with the other one who was his nephew.

Soon Badeo and Dawood had another child. This time a girl and they were happy. What this meant, was that Badeo did not visit as often as she used to, and now finally, the young boy felt, his mother was his own.

She sat like she so often did, at the kitchen table. In a bowl in front of her the fresh beans lay rinsed and ready for docking. Expertly Manouch broke off the one end and pulled the vein down to the other side before breaking the bean in three sections. She had done this so many times before that she could do it with her eyes closed she thought, and with that thought, a cold feeling settled on her heart. Why did she think of it in such a way?

She shook the feeling off and carried on with her task. Before long her mind wandered again and this time it was David, their eldest child, who came to mind. Of course his real name is Anthony, but everyone calls him David. It's probably because he is the son of David and so he is called David although to her he will always be Anthony or rather Tonius as they called him. Manouch shook her head as she thought how terrible he behaves with women. He flirts with every woman he meets and then treats them with disdain when they respond. Not at all like his father who always treated his wife and his daughters as well, with respect. Whatever was going on with the young people of today baffled her. Her mind, clear again, calls to see where the children are.

'Alfred, Alfred!'

'What is wrong?' He comes instantly to see what he must do.

'Where are the small ones? Can you see Jimmy? He always runs away. See where they are.'

Alfred turns around to go and find them, and is back shortly. 'They are playing in the yard. Don't worry.'

'Watch them Alfred, don't let them go far.'

Then Joe comes into the kitchen and suddenly it is as if the sun fills the spaces. Manouch playfully slaps his hand away from her shoulder where he places it as he bends down to kiss her cheek. She always does that, although she loves it when he kisses her. He is her golden child. The one child that sensed her feelings, before she even did. Manouch knew that she loved all her children with a passion, and knew Salem did as well, but Joe is different from them all. It is not only his gentle manner, and loving nature with his parents and his siblings, but because of a special quality emanating from his very being. He is she felt, like a guardian, looking out for all of them.

Joe loved working with food and he cooked for the family on many days, not as a duty, no, more like a passion. Even cakes were baked, and he revelled in their enjoyment, of his labour.

'I see the beans are nearly ready.'

'Yes, you can take it' Manouch said handing him the dish.

He took it from her in a flourish, making a low bow and she laughed at his antics, shaking her head. This is how he always was. To him, life was a song that had to be sung each day.

He was tall, and handsome, with a hint of plumpness due to his love of food, and always dressed impeccably. His black hair had a natural curl and he combed it to the side but an unruly curl kept dropping down on his forehead. A pencil thin black moustache lay neatly on his upper lip. There was no doubt about it, he was good looking and he had a manner about him that made him stand out from any crowd. Where his brothers were more olive skinned, he like Badeo, had a fair skin with a flush of pink on his cheeks. A son all mothers could only dream of having is what Manouch thought, as she heard Joe singing at the stove where he was stirring a big pot from which a delicious aroma filled the kitchen.

The toddler, playing nearby, is expertly caught before falling down the high step and laughs when Joe swings him around, before holding him close to his chest. He loves this little one. Small for his age, his chubby legs now dirty from playing on the floor, was loved by all. 'Don't let him go out. ` Manouch shouts. 'Don't worry Mom Alfred is outside he will watch him.'

'No bring him to me I want to hold him a bit.' Joe gives the wriggling boy to his mother who nuzzles him with her nose until he laughs.

Content the boy settles on his mothers' lap and soon falls asleep. Seeing this Joe takes him gently from his mother and lay him in his cot. After covering the child he returned to the kitchen.

When Salem returned from the market he carried in two boxes of olives.

Phillip and Jimmy also carried two each stacking the boxes one on top of the other on the kitchen floor.

'We were lucky today. Green, and black olives and at a good price.'

Manouch kissed Salem on his cheek. 'Well done, my husband.'

The table was immediately cleared and a clean cloth draped over it.

Big dishes filled with water were placed side by side where the olives were separated into black and green. This was the first wash, and later would be covered in fresh water overnight before the preparation took place for preserving them in big jars.

Once the children were seen to the next morning, that is those that went to work, and those that went to school, and those that needed to be fed, the preparation began in earnest. Many hours would pass before the olives were ready to fill the big glass jars. The jars, once filled with olives and chillies and herbs, were then left unopened for at least two weeks, before it was ready to eat, but the work was worth it. The taste was so special that one licked ones' fingers afterwards.

Chapter Twelve

Phillip was busy in the garden picking ripe tomatoes for his mother when he saw his little brother coming towards him. The toddler walked unsteadily to his brother waggling from side to side on his bare feet. A stone made him trip and Phillip scooped him up before he could fall. The child put his arms around his big brothers' neck and laughed. With the toddler in his one arm he picked up the dish where he was dropping the ripe tomatoes into with his other hand, and went inside.

'Alfred' he said 'you must watch Norman. He was outside, just now he walks away and we wont know where to find him.'

'I was busy and I did not see him go outside.' Alfred said as he took the boy from Phillip.

Phillip put the dish of tomatoes on the table and sat in the chair his mother always sat in where she could look out of the window. He looked out as she usually does, at the open velt stretching up the bank to where the rails of the trains were, and he was just going to shift his gaze back to the kitchen, when a change of scenery took place before his eyes. It was not the tall dry grass from the velt that he saw, but shadows of figures hiding amongst the grass. Alarmed he got up from the chair and leaned nearer to the window trying to get a clearer view, but he saw nothing moving. Without saying a word he got up from the table and walked out of the door to the open velt and through the tall grass. He stood still for a moment while his eyes scanned the area from where he was right up to the embankment. All he saw now was the grass moving in the wind and he shook his head as he turned around to go back inside. But something made him hesitate so he walked a few paces and quickly turned around. His heart skipped a beat as he thought he saw a shadow again, and once again, he walked through the grass and as before saw nothing. A chill crept over him, and instinctively he crossed himself. What had he seen that was not actually there? He went back to the chair overlooking the yard and the velt beyond, and peered through the glass but now saw nothing. He sat for a while longer and then went to his mother where she was busy in the bedroom. 'Mom, are you all right?'

Manouch looked at her son and was unsettled by the look in his eyes.

'What is wrong Phillip?' 'I don't know Mom its just a strange feeling that I have, are you sure everything is all right?' Manouch hesitated before answering her son. In truth, she herself had felt uneasy for a while, but had not told anyone about it and she smiled and assured him she was fine. When she saw the relief on his face she knew she had given the right answer.

Later that afternoon David came to visit. The door stood open as usual and he walked straight to the kitchen where he knew everyone would be. Manouch was busy at the stove and Alfred was feeding Norman who was sitting on the step leading down to the bottom part of the kitchen with his little legs dangling down, while Alfred coaxed him to eat. Phillip was sitting at the table looking intently out of the window, and Finnie was setting the table, with Yvette helping her. David loved the scene before him and his heart swelled with a feeling of happiness. Phillip saw him first and greeted him with a smile, and then Manouch turned around smiling as she did so. 'David! How are you son?'

'Fine Mom, how are you?'

'As you see, thank God.'

David pulled a chair out and sat with Phillip. Yvette started to get tea cups ready when she saw her brother, and before she had even poured the tea Salem arrived, and Jimmy and Joe followed behind him. The mood in the kitchen was noisy and happy as the men sat around the table while the women served them.

Manouch filled a serving dish with spaghetti and meat and Joe took it from her to put on the table. This scene was similar each evening except for the faces that sometimes changed. Some days it was Johnny sitting where David was now sitting, and some days it was Dawood, and very rarely it was Buddy. Phillip was usually there, and Joe was always there as was Jimmy, with Finnie and Yvette helping Manouch with the serving. Norman was usually with Alfred who looked after him while the family had their meal. This was a happy time of the day and Salem and Manouch cherished this feeling of togetherness with their family.

* * *

David looked around the table where they sat and felt his own importance. He was the firstborn and although he no longer lived at home with his parents, it changed nothing. Anything of importance was always discussed with him before his parents shared it with the rest of the family.

He was his fathers' right hand and he knew his mother depended on him. Salem taught his eldest son well, and he now had a good job with the clothing store in town. He was a good salesman and Salem was proud of him, although he did not approve of the way David treated women. Oh, he heard how David liked woman and there was nothing wrong with that he supposed. He had spoken to David on many occasions about this, and he had promised in return that he would be more understanding. Salem hoped so. Women were to him as important as men were and needed looking after. He himself had never treated Manouch in any disrespectful manner and cherished each moment with her.

Much like Salem, David was respected among the community.

He not only knew all the owners of all the shops in town but knew their families as well. In fact, most of the owners knew his own family, the brothers and the sisters as well as Salem and even Manouch, who never really went into town, except to go to the movies where she went as often as she could and this in itself, was her only entertainment, as she was amazed at a story depicted on a big white screen. Usually a few of the younger children went with her although she sat a few rows behind them, so she could make sure they did not misbehave. The children were well aware that she was there but they also knew that within a few minutes she would be engrossed in watching the screen.

They heard his voice even before he came into the kitchen.

'Salem, how are you?'

Salem rose from the table to greet his brother with a hug. The children all came to take their uncles' hand and kiss it. They loved this man and knew he loved them as well. When the younger ones came, he turned slightly, so they could put a hand into his jacket pocket where he had the sweets he brought for them. They each took one and went back to their places. Now the mood in the kitchen was festive, and laughter and happiness, was like a shield around them. Manouch put a plate in front of Eblen and he helped himself to food from the dishes on the table. Manouch looked at the two brothers Salem and Eblen with a smile and wished she could always see them in the way they were at that moment. Alfred came in from outside and seeing Eblen went to him, and they shook hands.

'How are you Alfred?'

'Thank God I am well, how are you?'

'You know I am always happy to see you here.'

The kitchen was crowded but nobody minded. They were where they wanted to be and it was paradise.

Before the evening ended, Eblen would have spoken to each of them individually. He wanted to know how they did at school and what happened in their lives, and each one would receive some form of advise on how to deal with any problems they had. The children felt at ease with their uncle and kept all their problems no matter how small, for when he came. Once they spoke to him about whatever bothered them, he made them see it in another light, and just like that, the problem was solved.

David was no different, and waited till last, before approaching him.

He hoped to spend more time with his uncle, and even though Salem was his world, it was his Uncle Eblen who was his confidante, and David like the others, always valued his uncles' advise. He never made him feel as if he was letting anyone down by having problems, and he knew he would not discuss their conversation with anyone else.

When Eblen left, David went as well, and the house became quiet as the children retired to bed. In their bedroom, Salem held his wife close to him feeling content and happy. They stood like that for a while in silence, each savouring the nearness of the other.

*   *   *

For some reason there was never the exuberant pleasure when Johnny came around to visit and he knew it instinctively. It was as if a transparent shield hid their feelings but he never let it worry him. He felt this feeling of reserve even with his parents. He put it down to a feeling of inferiority from their side and in fact it made him feel as if he had somehow risen above their upbringing.

To tell you the truth I was happy to leave home. I love my family but was now more content visiting than staying. I rented a room from an aunt who lived closer to the furniture factory I was working in. I was indentured as an apprentice for cabinet making and my wage was very low and transport was costly. The room was clean and a plate of dinner went with it. True nothing ever tastes the same as when ones' mother makes it, and when I did go to visit, I enjoyed indulging in that luxury, but one did what was necessary to achieve ones' goals. I was determined to make a success of my life and nothing was going to stop me. My father is an inspiration to all of us and we do not want to disappoint him in any way and although my father, taught us what we knew, it was always David at his side. My brothers Dawood, Buddy and me Johnny, were only helpers. We carried the crates and loaded the cart and unloaded it again, but it was David who sat up front with my dad. True my dad never favoured the one from the other, and expected each one to fulfil their duty, and we all knew that, but still it was always David making sure he was right there next to my dad. The three of us, Dawood, Buddy and myself were taller and bigger than David, but David never saw that as a threat. He was the eldest and commanded respect and we gave him that. It was my mother who pushed me to expect more from myself.

'Look to the future Johnny, take up a trade. That way you will always be able to provide for your family one day.'

She was right of course, times were changing, work was scarce and we knew we had to fend for ourselves sooner than later, besides I enjoyed working with wood. It had a life of its own and once the item was finished and varnished, it was a feeling of immense satisfaction that made one proud. In actual fact, I did not plan to ever go back to my hometown any time soon. The hub of a big city was more to my liking and the people around me were friendly. No sir! I have definitely moved on with my life, and I see a whole other future for myself. Besides, there was also another reason why I preferred not to stay at home. My temper and that of my brother David, did not go well together at all.

He was way too dominant, and that got to me. Besides, Phillip and Jimmy were also flexing their muscles, and as far as Dawood was concerned, I give up. He attracted trouble like a magnet, and us brothers were drawn into the thick of things, time and again.

No, it was better that I was far away, and only heard these things afterwards. Besides, there was this girl I met, and I think she is really nice, so I try to keep out of trouble. Just thinking how violent us brothers can be when we land up in a fight amongst ourselves, makes me worried, like when Phillip and Jimmy was fighting and my mother had to hit Phillip with a pan on his head to let go of Jimmy. Man, it got ugly, and this went on all the time, it was either David and Dawood or Dawood and Buddy or myself with one of them, but it was always someone fighting with someone. Men and growing boys, needed to show their strength, and we all understand that, but it is still scary.

I know that I am good looking, and it is not only the mirror that tells me that, but the guarded glances from young girls cannot be ignored, and it is not only my confidence and good manners, but the whole package, which girls find attractive. I know this because I see them looking at me trying to attract my attention. I keep my face clean shaven meaning I have no moustache like my dad, or Joe or Phillip or my uncle Eblen and I like it like this.

As far as strength is concerned I know that none of my brothers could beat me in a fight. I knew it for certain and they suspected it and did not want to test it. Not that any of them were weak. No sir! They were pure dynamite, except for David who was smaller in stature than any of us but out of respect we would never challenge him. Of course I am not talking about the younger ones Jimmy and Norman who were still small and did not count yet. Besides each child knew that he or she had to respect their elder siblings, which they did most of the time.

Chapter Thirteen

After that day when I saw the images in the grass in the velt behind the house I saw it once more and then not again, even though I constantly looked out of the kitchen window. I hoped I never saw it again, because it made me uneasy and somehow afraid. I know that I am the favoured one. I have my fathers' looks and am taller than him by about three inches. My black hair has a natural curl when I comb it back and my thin moustache is always trimmed neatly. Unlike Joe, I have a slim body and a barrel chest and good shoulders. My brother Joe and I are good friends. We enjoy the same movies and when we are together girls try to impress us. Like Joe, I am always around my mother, who is the light of my life, and I always try to help wherever I can. Like my father, I enjoy working in the garden and growing vegetables. There is something in our hands that make things grow. If a crises arises, it is my name that is called, 'Phillip come quickly, Phillip talk to your brother, Phillip this and Phillip that.' I don't mind, I like to be there when they need me. I am also the protector for the younger ones, when they, are bullied by my older brothers. I am not aggressive like Dawood and Johnny or as vindictive as David, but they, as well as myself, know the reckoning will be ruthless, if I got to know about anything. Yes, I am their shield, and when they have been naughty, they run to me for protection. When Amiro died, I watched over my mother, knowing she was in pain. Her pain, is my pain, I will do anything for her just to see her smile. Like David, my oldest brother, I prefer working in sales and he got me a job at a clothing store in town. The pay is not much, and barely, covers my own needs but a small portion is given to my mother to help with expenses, but I think she saves it for me. She did this with my older brothers so I think she does the same for me. My older brothers David and Buddy, don't usually go out with us. Dawood, Joe and myself are always together but I know if we need the others for anything they are always right there beside us. Johnny keeps to himself and seldom mixes with us. He likes to think he is better than we are, and we joke about that, but he says he does not want to get into trouble, and you can't blame him for that, although Joe and I never look for trouble. No Dawood is the one who just can't resist a fight.

Actually Johnny, and Dawood, although two totally, different characters, get on very well. My brother Dawood, is one of a kind, he is the joker of the family. He lives hard, drinks hard, and fights whenever the opportunity presents itself and loves girls. Not that we don't all like them but he is in his own league. School was a torture for him so once reading and writing was mastered he never went back. No apprentice indenture either and not cut out for sales, he opted for manual labour. A body strong like an ox and a character loved and feared by all. Friends from every walk of life and every nationality were loyal to him and he, like myself protected the younger children, who loved him but never got in his way, especially when he was angry and that you could easily see when his eyes bulged and his nose flared like a bull. Dawood and Buddy, were usually with my father, helping him with the packing and loading of the cart with David or sometimes Alfred giving orders.

Now my brother Buddy, although usually with Dawood, is in character more like Johnny. Reserved, not loud like Dawood, yet built in a similar way as Dawood. Taller, than David or Dawood with a strong body, he seldom showed any anger, much like Joe and myself. He was sure of himself, and confident when dealing in business, even though like Dawood, schooling was limited. He knew what he wanted out of life and was determined to get it. His actual name, Peter, keeper of the keys, was the peacekeeper for us brothers, especially for David and Johnny who were always at loggerheads.

Buddy never used his fists to settle an argument but rather talked the problem through. Why anyone had to revert to violence Buddy could not understand, after all, once you discussed a matter, it usually sorted itself out. Well, for him it usually did anyway. Phillip knew his brother Buddy was just biding his time to flee the roost like Johnny and David. He didn't blame him with all the noise of the children shouting and crying and running around. Leaving was the only way to go, although Phillip knew he himself, would never leave his mother and he knew Joe also would not, unless they got married like Badeo, which they were not planning to do any time soon.

It was a Saturday afternoon, and Joe and Manouch had made Lebanese mince pies earlier. It was one of those special dishes that took long to complete, and although many dozens were made would be eaten up the same night, with a strong cup of tea, to wash it down. Mince and potato with chopped onion was spiced to perfection with salt and black pepper and cinnamon for flavour and cooked till nicely browned then placed on flattened rounds of dough and covered over and fried in deep oil. Each batch was like a special delivery and savoured to the fullest. The younger children stood around with big eyes and when nobody was looking they quickly grabbed a pie and ran away.

Manouch and Joe smiled at their antics and pretended not to notice.

It was a day like so many others and they loved working together.

* * *

When Alfred spoke, Phillip jumped with fright. He was so caught up in his own thoughts looking out of the window, that he completely forgot where he was.

'Why did you do that Alfred? You nearly, scared me to death.'

'I called you but you didn't listen.' 'Your mother wants you.'

Manouch was in the bedroom dressing his little brother Norman. The boy was laughing as his mother tickled him. Phillip stood looking at the scene for a few seconds enjoying the happy moment, before he spoke.

'Alfred said you wanted me.'

'Yes, I want to go to Badeo, will you walk with us?'

Phillip carried his little brother effortlessly in his one arm, and carried a basket with pies, his mother had prepared for Badeo. Joe made lovely mince pies and the smell from the basket wafted up to them. Phillip could hardly wait to get to his sisters' house to have one. Manouch walked easily beside him, chatting as they walked, and he was happy just being alone with her. It was for him just he and his mother, the small boy in his arm hardly counting as a person yet, and he loved being with her.

There were always so many children around her that one got lost in the bunch.

Before they even got to the house, Manouch was calling her daughter who heard her mother from inside the house, and quickly went to open the door.

'How are you mommy?'

'All well, how are you all, how is the baby?'

'Sleeping, thank goodness, I was up most of the night with her.'

'How are you Phillip? Is that for me?'

Phillip put the basket on the kitchen table, and Manouch took out the covered dish. Soon the kettle was boiling and they sat around the table enjoying the pies. Badeo put four in a small plate and covered it, to keep for her husband, to enjoy later when he got home. Norman, and Badeos' little boy, played in the corner of the kitchen with small cars. One hour became two, and when the baby woke up, Badeo brought her to her mother to hold. This was a scene that took place at least two or three times a week, and the women were happy to be together. Phillip had left them after they had tea and went to visit his cousin who lived nearby. He knew he had at least two hours free before walking home with his mom again. Life certainly was pleasant he thought, and he knew he could go on living like this forever.

* * *

Although the big platter stood in the centre of the table heaped high with mince pies that evening, Manouch watched that the younger children did not take too many. Sometimes they hid their one hand clutching a pie, behind their back, and took another.

Not that she minded, she just did not want them to waste anything.

She heard Salem's voice at the front door and her heart leapt with joy.

His rough timber voice sent a tingle through her body making her blood feel like liquid caramel. Then she heard Eblens' voice as well, and she smiled to herself.

Salem must have let his brother know to come for supper knowing how much Eblen loved pies. Eblen kissed Manouch on the cheek where she sat at the table, and she smiled at him.

Like always when he arrived, the mood became light and happy. Everybody loved Eblen, and they all knew their father and his brother loved each other unconditionally. In fact, Eblen was as comfortable in his brothers' house and with his brothers' family as if it was his own, and hours soon passed before he left.

Much later when the house became quiet again, Salem sat with Manouch at the now cleared table. They just sat there looking at each other not needing to say anything. Salem put his hand over hers, content in their love, and then a feeling of such sadness washed over Manouch that she thought she would die. She dropped her eyes as she dared not look at her husband for fear he would see the pain in her eyes. Slowly she freed her hand from his rough hand and without looking at him, went to the bedroom.

She stood against the cool wall with her one hand over her heart and prayed silently. When she heard Salem approaching she turned to him and smiled, but he did not return her smile, instead he put his arms around her and whispered in her ear.

'God is with us. Remember always that I love you more than life itself.' A sob escaped her lips and he stilled it by placing his fingers on her mouth.

Chapter Fourteen

His crying woke Manouch and she went to the cot to pick her son up.

She felt his fever even without touching his forehead. She lay him down on her bed, and woke Salem up.

'Salem, watch him, I am going to get a wet cloth, the boy is burning up with a fever'.

He stood in his long underpants holding the boy who now had stopped crying, making weak whimpering sounds. A vice gripped his heart as he held the child close to his chest.

'Please dear God don't let it happen again, please spare him.'

When Manouch returned to the room she had a basin with water and a cloth. Salem lay the boy down on the bed and undressed him so Manouch could sponge him down. The child started crying again when he felt the water on his body. The sound was more like a wail, and then Finnie was there, and shortly after Joe as well. Manouch did not dress the boy again but wrapped him in a soft blanket. Finnie took the baby from her mother and rocked him slowly until he stopped crying. She held him a while longer and then lay him down in his cot.

'You must sleep mommy, if he cries I will take him, tomorrow we will bring the doctor.'

Manouch lay on the bed and Salem put his arm around her. They did not sleep but prayed softly until the first light filtered into the room.

The child had not cried again, and this worried them even more.

Finnie and Joe left to fetch the doctor before the sun had fully risen. They waited outside his house for a while, before knocking on the door. They knew that he also needed his sleep but they wanted to get him before he left for his early rounds. When he opened the door, he was already dressed, and when he saw them he picked up his bag from the floor in the hallway without a word, before following them. It was a short ride and Salem was waiting outside when they arrived.

The doctor took his time checking the boy and then covered him again with the blanket. 'He has to go to hospital, it is diphtheria. We will take him with us.' Manouch turned to Salem, who looked at her, before he nodded. Manouch wrapped her son tightly in the blanket again and picked him up.

'Finnie, you stay here, I will go with Joe, make sure the others are taken care of.'

Salem helped his wife and child to the car and watched them ride away.

This time there was no bag of vegetables. Somehow Salem never even thought of it, his mind was so clouded with worry. Later he would remember this oversight and leave a bag on the doctors' veranda.

When he turned to go inside, tears dropped on his hands, and he did not even notice it. He had work to do and needed to look after his family.

The kitchen, now filled with the morning rush, was like salve on an open wound.

'How is he Daddy?' Jimmy asked.

Salem looked at this son of his, a good boy and intelligent beyond his years. He expected big things from him. Like his brother Johnny, he liked to work with his hands, and everything he did needed to be perfect.

He looked at the boy and could not help smiling sadly. 'You must promise me Jimmy that you will always look after your younger brother.'

'I promise Daddy, you must not worry, I am sure he will be fine.'

'I know but I depend on you to look after him. Now go and get ready for school.'

Alfred placed a cup of tea next to Salem with olives and goats' cheese with two slices of toast. This was his usual breakfast, and he ate it without thinking. He had to leave but could not tear himself away from his family, somehow it became very important for him to make contact with all of them. Was it the fear that he may not see his son again? He did not know what to make of this feeling of dread and called those that were at home.

Finnie was in the kitchen getting Jimmy and Yvette ready for school when he called them over. 'Finnie, Jimmy, Yvette come here to me.' They looked at their father in surprise and went to him immediately. Something in his voice put them on their guard. His calling them was a most unusual request, as he always left after having his tea.

They stood before him, Finnie in the back with Jimmy and Yvette in front. Salem pulled Jimmy and Yvette towards him and put his arms around them. 'Remember, all of you, that we love you very much even when we are busy. I want you to promise me that you will listen to your older brothers and sisters if your mother or I am not around. Do you hear me?'

'Yes Daddy.' Came the answer from all three.

'Your brother is ill but I am sure they will take good care of him. Your mother will be tired when she comes back with Joe from the hospital, so you must let her rest. Always remember, that it is important to do well at school. Your future depends on what you know. Now go before you are late.' The length of his conversation and the importance of it made the children silent on their way to school, and for once they did not argue over anything.

*   *   *

On the way to the market Salem stopped first at the men's outfitters where Phillip worked. His son saw his father as soon as he entered the shop, and excused himself to go to him. 'Is everything all right Dad?' 'Your little brother is in hospital. The doctor says it is diphtheria. Joe went with your mom.' Salem's voice was flat when he spoke.

'Oh! Dad I am sorry, will they keep him there?' Phillip felt his heart beating faster and knew he had to comfort his father who he could see was upset.

'Yes, the doctor says he must be in hospital for treatment.' 'I will go after work and see him.'

'You must not worry Dad, the doctor will take good care of him.'

'I know my son, but I wanted to see if you are well.' Phillip gave a lopsided smile and took his fathers' arm.

'You must not worry too much Dad, its not good for you.'

Salem took his sons' other arm and when he spoke a cold feeling ran down Phillip's spine and for a fleeting moment he saw the velt behind their house and saw the shadows flitting through it. Then he smiled at his father and saw the love that shone from his fathers' eyes.

'You must promise me Phillip, that you will look after your mother and the younger children, when I am not around.'

'Why, where are going to Dad?' Now there was no smile as he looked at his dad.

'Nowhere, I meant if ever.'

'I promise you Dad.'

'And another thing, look after your work, it is not easy to get a job these days.' Salem pulled his son toward him and hugged him then he turned and left.

Phillip stood watching his father walking away for a short while thinking how tired his father looked, then he went back to what he was doing, before his father came. But an uneasy feeling had taken hold of him and he decided to ask his employer if he could leave a little earlier than usual so he could first go to the hospital before going home. He chided himself for sleeping out the night before as he sometimes did and that he was not there when they needed him.

* * *

David was saying good-bye to a customer at the entrance of the shop when he saw his father. Surprised David excused himself to walk towards the approaching figure. When Salem saw the look on his eldest child's face his own spirits lifted.

'How are you my son?'

'Very well thanks Dad, but lets go inside, this is a surprise. Is everything all right?'

'Your baby brother is in hospital.' Salem replied.

David stopped walking for a moment, and then carried on, as thoughts rushed through him. Is it serious, he wondered, it must be, otherwise his father would not be here, and his heart grew heavy. When he spoke again his voice was low.

'What is wrong with him Dad?'

'Diphtheria, the doctor says he must stay in hospital where they can treat him.'

'Can I get you some tea Dad?'

'Yes, thank you, I am thirsty.' Salem sat down on one of the chairs grouped in the centre of the store, where clients could sit down while trying on shoes. He waited for his son to return, and looked around at the shelves of clothing. He knew his son was a good salesman and was respected by the owner, an elderly man, who pretty much left everything up to David to look after. Salem was proud of all his children and David being his shadow when he was younger, filled him with confidence knowing that what he had taught him, had made his son a good salesman.

David brought their tea and turning a chair around, sat opposite his father. They were comfortable, in each other's presence, and conversation flowed freely.

'I want you to know my son, that I value your help and assistance very much.'

David made to answer, but Salem held up his calloused hand to silence him.

'Let me finish first. There may be a time when your mother, or myself cannot be here, and I want you to look after your brothers and sisters, especially the little ones, as if they are your own. Which, in fact they are because we are a family that looks after each other. Do you feel that way as well?'

David hesitated before answering such an important question.

Yes, he looked on his brothers and sisters as his own, but he knew for a fact, that Johnny and Buddy were not of the same opinion.

'You know I will look after them Dad.'

'That is good, I am not worried about the older ones, who can take care of themselves. It is the younger ones that I worry about.'

'Why are you talking like this Dad? Are you OK or is something else wrong?'

'No, I just want to make sure.' Standing up Salem put his empty cup on the chair. 'I am late, look after yourself.'

When Salem reached the door he turned around and looked into his son's eyes. 'You are the best son that any parent can ever have, I want you to know that.'

David stood still and a feeling of sadness came over him. When he spoke his voice sounded hollow to himself. 'And you are the greatest father that any child can have.' Salem smiled and left.

David watched his father walk away and for some reason he could not take his eyes off the figure growing smaller. He knew something was not right but could not put his finger on it. When he could not see the figure any longer he went back to doing what he was busy with but his mind kept drifting away. Eventually he gave up and went outside the shop to light a cigarette. He watched the smoke as the wind blew it away and stood there until the cigarette was finished before he went in again.

* * *

It was late when Salem started his deliveries but he felt he had to do what he did. An inner peace was in him and once he was on his way a prayer of thanksgiving was said. How can any man expect more from life than he had?

When he stopped at his first client, he was his cheerful self again and laughed and chatted as he usually did. If any of his clients saw the sadness in Salem's eyes they said nothing.

Chapter Fifteen

The kitchen was noisy with all the children there. Badeo was there from the afternoon to help with the cooking, knowing her brothers would all be home in the evening to find out how their brother was. Although it was a lot of work she enjoyed it when they were all together.

Bickering and laughing, and pulling each others' leg was rife when the brothers got together. Finnie and Yvette were helping her with Joe for once sitting with his brothers around the table. Manouch was quiet and said little while Salem revelled in the presence of his sons and smiled often as he looked at them. Looking at Finnie, Badeo thought her sister looked very pale. Well, no wonder with everything going on in the house, she thought and left it at that.

It was late when those that lived away from home had all left and the table was cleared. Badeo had left earlier to see to her own family and now it was only Joe and Phillip sitting at the table. Salem and Manouch had retired to their room as well as Jimmy, and Yvette was in the bathroom. Finnie was packing the last dishes away when Phillip looked up and saw her fall to the floor. Like an arrow from a bow he jumped up with Joe close behind him shouting for Yvette.

Finnies' eyes were bulging and foam bubbled at her mouth. Her deathly pale skin felt pallid to the touch while her body was making jerking movements. On instinct Phillip gripped her tight to his chest and slowly her body relaxed and only when she became still, did he lay her on the floor. Her eyes were glassy and he took the cloth Yvette held out to him, to wipe his sisters' face. Then they were all there, Manouch, Salem and Jimmy and between them they carried the girl to her bed where they covered her with a warm blanket.

'She is overtired.' Manouch said as she rubbed her daughters. wrists to warm them

'Bring the basin with that cloth Yvette' Salem said 'keep her forehead cool, and Phillip, stay with your sister. Joe will come with me to fetch the doctor. Manouch, I want you to go and rest, everything is under control, I don't want you sick as well.' The room where Finnie lay was very small and two people filled the room. Phillip sat on the only chair and Yvette knelt on the floor with the basin of water and wiped her sisters' face. Manouch went to her room where she closed the door. She sat on the bed for a while just staring into space not daring to think about anything, then she slowly got up and unhooked the rosary hanging from the bedpost, and her fingers moved from bead to bead as she prayed. She was still praying when she heard Salem and Joe return and then she heard the doctors' voice.

She did not get up but waited for her husband to come and tell her what the outcome was. Her body was weary and tears were near but she held them back. There is no time for tears now she said to herself.

The bedroom door opened and Salem stood there with the doctor behind him, and then they entered the room, and closed the door behind them.

'She is not ill' the doctor said 'she has a condition which is epilepsy. It is not life threatening but is life changing. This condition is sometimes brought on by the hormonal changes in ones' body. An attack can occur at any time and she must always be with someone. She must not be upset as this can trigger an attack. I will prescribe some tablets that she has to take every day. I have given her an injection so she will sleep for a few hours. Let her stay in bed for the next two days. I will come again tomorrow to check on her.' Salem translated as the doctor spoke so Manouch could understand clearly what he said. When he finished she got up from the bed and took the doctors' hand and held it with both her hands.

'Thank you very much doctor, you are a good man. Please look after our children.' Again Salem translated so the doctor could understand. The hour being late, Salem left the room with the doctor to take him back.

Jimmy was waiting at the car where he had already placed a bag of vegetables and fruit. A white muslin cloth was also on the seat with Lebanese pies.

Conditioned to all situations, the doctor was now filled with gratitude for these people who worked hard, and tried their best for everyone. He knew it would be difficult for him to wait until he got home to have one of the pies knowing how tasty they were.

* * *

Morning came with sunlight washing over the bed where Finnie lay. Her eyes were open and she could not remember how she got into bed. Her body felt sore and lethargic. She heard voices in the kitchen but somehow could not get up, and then Yvette was there, with a cup of tea and some toast. Finnie realised she was hungry and tried to sit up but the movement made her head turn and she fell back again.

'Don't get up Finnie, the doctor said you must rest.'

'What happened to me?'

'You took a bad turn and fainted. You must stay in bed for a few days.'

'Is mommy ok?'

'Yes, she is at the hospital to see Norman, Joe is with her. You must try to eat something.'

'You can leave it, I will eat later.'

Yvette left and Finnie closed her eyes again.

Everything felt different but she did not know why it was, she just knew.

* * *

Eblen was in the kitchen waiting when they returned from hospital.

Yvette had made him coffee in the small pot and a plate of olives and goats cheese stood nearby.

'How is the boy doing?' he asked

Salem was happy to see his brother and smiled. 'Thank God, a little better but he has to stay there for a few days.'

The brothers sat for a while without talking and Yvette brought another cup for her father. Her hands held the cup carefully. She was always a little nervous when serving her father and she knew it was because she did not want to disappoint him. She knew he loved her, but when he looked at her, in that stern way of his, she was extra careful.

Eblen waited till Yvette was out of earshot when he spoke again. He did not want to alarm the children any more than was necessary and the past few days were trying.

'Are you sure you are alright Salem?'

Salem smiled faintly at his brother and in that moment felt a rush of love wash over him. They had together experienced many hardships but having each other was what helped them to survive.

'Just a little tired, it's the children, they have me worried.'

Eblen knew his brother better than anyone else and although he accepted his brothers' explanation he was still concerned.

Manouch when entering the kitchen was happy to see Eblen there with Salem. Earlier she had noticed that her husband seemed pale and knew he was concerned about the children. Now looking at him she felt afraid. and after greeting Eblen, walked past them out of the door, into the yard for no reason at all. She knew she needed fresh air and without thinking she went to the garden where she picked some fresh tomatoes and chillies. Her actions were out of the ordinary as she always asked Salem or Alfred to pick what they needed, but for some reason she felt she had to do it. He needs to rest a bit she thought, they demand too much from him. She must remember to tell Joe to help more.

When Salem saw Manouch with the fresh vegetables he was surprised.

'I could have done that Manouch.'

'I know, I just needed a little air.' She looked at him and smiled and he looked at her tenderly.

Eblen stayed a while and the two brothers discussed the market trends and problems they experienced.

When Eblen finally got up to go he drew his brother to his chest and hugged him.

'God is good my brother, he will look after all of us.'

'You are right Eblen, I must leave everything in his hands.'

'I will see you later tomorrow Salem. I have some business to take care of first in the morning but I want you to promise me that you will rest a bit.'

'I am tired. Salem said. 'I'll ask Joe to give me a hand. I first want to go to the hospital before I go to work.' The two brothers walked out to the car and Salem stood at the open window of the car where his brother sat at the wheel. As Eblen started the engine, Salem put his hand on his brothers' shoulder. 'Promise me you will look after them Eblen, I mean just in case I cannot.'

'You know I will Salem, why won't you be able to?'

'Oh! I will, but just in case I have to go somewhere, you never know.'

Eblen looked up at his brother and he stretched his hand out of the window to touch his brothers' face. 'Remember always where we come from Salem. Remember the Cedars and how majestic they are, and how they look out over the sea. That is how God looks after us.'

Eblen pulled away slowly and watched his brother, in the rear view mirror, until he could not see him any longer. His heart was heavy, knowing his brother and his wife were under great strain with the children and he was happy that he had no children. He knew that children brought much happiness, but with that came the fear of not being able to look after them all the time. For him the price would be too high, so he chose to keep things simple and not complicate it with a family. Better to be an uncle than a father was what he thought and he knew in his heart that he had made the right choice.

* * *

Finnie felt much better the next morning, and was up and dressed before her parents even woke up. She went to the kitchen to help with getting breakfast ready for the children and they were all happy to see her up and about. Manouch and Salem had explained to everyone what was wrong with their sister and that they were not to discuss it with her. Instead they had to carry on as if nothing had changed but at the same time, they had to keep an eye on her in case she took a bad turn. It may never happen again, but if it ever did, they had to act fast to prevent her from hurting herself. The children did not quite understand the problem but listened intently and nodded their heads to their parents. Now seeing her back in the kitchen made them happy and they went about as if nothing had happened.

Chapter Sixteen

At the hospital everything seemed in order. Norman was getting better and Salem felt relieved. He went to the market and filled his cart to go about his daily tasks. He still felt very tired and put it down to the worry of the children. When Eblen had left the night before, a feeling of peace had flowed through him as he hugged his brother to his chest, and he still felt that way. He was right to leave everything in God's hands, he knew that now.

A flash of pain in his chest made him pull the cart over to the side of the road where he sat very still, waiting for the pain to subside. Beads of sweat formed on his brow but he made no attempt to wipe his face. He was not concerned, because he had on occasion felt this pain before, and knew it did not last long. So when he felt better, he gave a pull on the reins, and the horse started up again.

* * *

Salem finished his rounds early and when Manouch saw him she was concerned at the drained look on his face but she said nothing and smiled at him. She had gone to the hospital with Joe and knew Norman was better. The staff there told them that Salem had been there early in the morning so she said nothing to him. Together they sat at the kitchen table and enjoyed a cup of tea.

Life had in a fashion returned to normal, or so they thought.

Salem could see the tall grass in the velt outside, from where he sat next to the window, and for a fleeting moment, thought he saw someone in the high grass. He rose from his chair to take a closer look through the window, and saw something like a shadow weaving in the grass and then it was gone. He sat down again but his thoughts were distracted, and when Alfred spoke to him he was startled.

'What is wrong Alfred, you scared me.'

'We need more tomatoes, must I fetch some?'

'No, it is alright I will go, I want to check how the green peppers are.'

Salem picked up a small round dish to put the tomatoes in and went outside to the garden. He passed the velt on his right and felt the urge to walk through the long grass just to make sure there was nobody hiding there but he shook the urge from him and continued to the garden.

He chose the reddest tomatoes knowing they would have the best flavour and placed the dish on the ground so he could first check his green pepper plants. He heard the screaming from the road and turned to see who it was. He saw his cousin Rosi, running and screaming towards the house and he wondered what was wrong with her, and then a strange feeling that somehow made him feel light like a feather in the wind, made him smile.

Rosie did not see him in the garden as she was heading for the front door of the house, but the wind carried her words to him where he stood beside his plants. 'Oh! My God, what happened, they say Norman is dead.'

A vice clamped around Salem's heart and a pain like fire coursed through his veins. Slowly he sank to the ground. The wind that had come up blew softly through his hair.

Manouch went out to meet Rosie when she heard the scream.

'What is wrong Rosie? Take it easy come and sit down, he is in hospital but he will be fine.'

Manouch hoped it was the truth as she crossed herself.

A cup of tea was put in front of Rosie who crossed herself before taking a sip.

'I was so worried Manouch, I heard only today and came as quick as I could.'

She wiped a tear from her cheek 'such a sweet lovely boy, are you sure he is alright?'

'Yes, yes, you must not worry yourself Rosie, the doctor says he will be fine but they have to keep him for a few more days.'

As Manouch uttered these words she crossed herself again as a cold shiver ran down her spine and she looked through the window to see if she could see her husband, but saw nothing. 'Alfred, go see where Salem is. Tell him to come inside Rosie is here.'

Rosie spoke again but Manouch took no notice. A feeling of intense and utter desolation had taken hold of her and she stood still just looking out of the window at Alfred walking to the garden and then she heard his cry and she started to run.

* * *

The sound she made was not human and sounded more like a wild animal in its last moments of life.

She flung herself down over her husbands still body on the ground and lifted him up in her arms holding him to her chest.

Then, she was gently pulled away by Joe.

'Wait mommy, let me see.'

He saw the lifeless eyes that bulged from their sockets and knew instantly they would not be able to do anything. Tenderly he closed his fathers' eyes and kissed his cheek before he lay him gently on the ground. He got up and wrapped his arms around his mother who was sobbing and wailing. They stood like that for a second before Manouch tore herself away and fell over her husband once again. 'Get the doctor, I will stay with him.'

Phillip was also there now and he stopped Yvette who heard the scream and came running to see what was wrong.

'Leave them' he said 'just leave them. Go back to the house and wait for me.' His voice was hoarse and he could hardly get the words out as sobs racked his body.

Finnie who was in her bedroom when she heard the wailing saw her father on the ground and thought he had fallen. She quickly took the blanket that was folded at the foot of her bed and went outside where she handed it wordlessly to Phillip. He lifted his mother up and covered his father with the blanket and then the doctor and Joe was there.

The men took the blanket off their father and the doctor examined Salem. When the doctor rose they lifted Salem onto the blanket and carried him inside where they lay him on his bed and closed the door.

The crying was like a river that broke its banks. Badeo was there and held her sisters close to her. Jimmy, sat on his own, on the step in the kitchen, and kept very quiet. Rosie, now silent, sat at the table with tears running down her cheeks as she hit her closed fist to her heart in unison with her prayers.

Alfred was nowhere to be seen. Phillip and Joe were with their mother in the room with the doctor, where the door was still closed.

When the door opened and Manouch came out, the girls rushed to her and put their arms around her, and together they cried, until Manouch loosened herself from their grip, and spoke in a voice that sounded as if it came from a hollow tunnel. 'Go, wash your faces and your hands, there is a lot to be done, we cannot disappoint your father.' Reluctantly they went with Manouch following her to the kitchen where she spoke to her children that were there.

'All of you must listen carefully.' She folded her arms on her breast and gripped her arms on both sides.

'Today a Cedar has fallen, and we were blessed to have it in our own garden. There is work to be done and I need all your help. Jimmy find Alfred see if he is alright then come to me so I can tell you what to do.'

Jimmy felt important that his mother needed him and he left to find Alfred.

He knew where he would find him, so he went straight to the garden. A strange feeling made him stop on the path leading to the garden. Shadows now enveloped the plants and he hesitated. He knew Alfred would be at the far side where he sometimes went to escape the noise in the kitchen so he called instead.

'Alfred, Alfred, we need you.'

'Go away.' Was the answer that came from the shadows, beyond the rows of vegetable plants.

'Please Alfred can you come, my mother needs you.' Jimmy waited where he was until he saw the slight figure walking towards him, before he turned to go back inside.

* * *

When Eblen arrived, Phillip took him to the room where the door closed again behind them. Manouch and David were also in the room, but Eblen saw only his brother on the bed. He went straight to the bed and fell on his knees resting his head on his brothers' chest and his tears fell onto his brothers' already drenched shirt. They left him like that for a while and then David gently took his arm to lift him up.

'David, you must let the children come in one by one, to see their father.

Take your mother out of the room and give her some tea.'

Manouch did not want to leave but knew Eblen was right. The children needed to see their father so she went with Eblen to face the people who had already gathered to offer their sympathy and help. When she looked into Eblens' eyes she saw the pain she felt, and knew he suffered, as she did. It was only when someone asked her about her son in hospital that she remembered where he was.

Soon the house was full of people who sat on the chairs arranged on the veranda. Men sat outside and women sat inside. Manouch sat on a chair in the lounge and the people filed past bending down to take her hand sympathising with her, but their faces were all a blur to her. David, Buddy, Dawood and Johnny sat outside side by side, to also accept sympathy. Joe, and Jimmy helped Badeo, Finnie and Yvette in the kitchen preparing and carrying trays of tea and small cups of black coffee, while Phillip moved between the people and gave orders to the kitchen. He knew the situation could change at any time and he watched Finnie carefully hoping she would cope. The stream of people was endless and Alfred kept the dishes washed with the maid and the girls drying. This was the first night and already more and more people came, soon the house was full and the men spilled from the veranda on to the street.

* * *

At the hospital late that evening, Eblen spoke to the ward sister on duty, who gave him the good news, that Norman was much better. His temperature was dropping but they were keeping him for a few more days.

Eblen told her what happened and said it would be better for all in the circumstances. He was only able to see the boy through a glass partition and looking at the boy, he knew he would be fine. He waved at him even though he knew the boy did not see him, and left knowing Manouch was waiting to hear from him.

* * *

She looked into his eyes and smiled. 'Thank you Eblen, God be with you.'

He held her hand just long enough for her to know he shared her pain.

Earlier he had gone with David, Buddy, Johnny and Dawood to make all the necessary arrangements for the funeral. Manouch stayed at home knowing she could leave everything in their hands. She in turn made sure that Joe, together with Badeo and Phillip had everything in hand at home where people arrived and left throughout the day. It was not only refreshments that were offered but the children had to be fed and the close family as well. Big pots on the stove were constantly stirred releasing pleasant aromas that nobody noticed as they went about their labours.

* * *

That first morning had come as a relief after the agony of the night before as sleep eluded most of the family members. Thoughts, of dark shadows clouded their minds and crying was heard from room to room.

The lounge now cleared of all ornaments looked bare and the table in centre had a cloth over it where the coffin would be placed, when the undertaker brought it.

They stood in a row with the oldest first and Manouch right at the end as the coffin was carried into the house and placed on the table in the lounge. They waited for the undertaker and his assistant to leave before they gathered around the open casket to say their last words to the man they loved so dearly.

Phillip and Joe held Manouch on each side as she bent over to touch her husbands' cheek.

'Oh Salem my husband, my love, why did you leave me? Look at your children, they need you and I need you.'

The two brothers did not let her stay long and led her to a chair. Each child now had a turn to speak to their father for the last time with the girls first. Then the boys each took their turn.

The air was charged with emotion that was like a thick mist enveloping everyone. Manouch sat there with the children as they said their last good bye, then they left her alone. She got up and stood next to the table and covered her husband's cold hands with her own.

She was calm as she stood with her husband in silence. Her thoughts like soft gossamer petals and each one filled with happy faces of children laughing.

It was much later when Alfred came. Manouch left him alone with Salem and slowly walked through the garden where she looked at the vegetables her husband tended. She knew Phillip would take care of the garden so she did not worry about that. No, it was the lonely feeling that clung to her insides that made her weak. How she would carry on without him she did not know, although she knew, she would have to. He was her strength and her happiness, and now he was no longer with her. She stayed in the garden for a while and then realised he would soon be taken away so she ran back to the lounge so she could once more hold his face between her hands.

* * *

She stood on the veranda watching, as his coffin was carried to the hearse.

Her eyes never left him, even when the black car rode away. Today she said good bye to her loved one, today her life changed forever, from today she was in charge of a future that promised that her endurance would be tested beyond all human strength. Her name is Manouch. She is the widow of Salem, her youngest child barely three years of age is in hospital and she has a responsibility of raising her children to be respectable and happy.

She saw him sitting quietly on the low wall of the veranda at the far side where he watched the car leave and knew she was not alone.

'Come, Alfred, we have a lot to do.'

*   *   *

Part Two

Chapter Seventeen

Months followed weeks and turned into years. War was raging globally and food was in short supply, not only countrywide, but worldwide. What vegetables could be grown were used, and many days would pass without meat on the table. Under garments like petticoats for the girls and vests for the boys were still made from the washed flower bags.

No white flour was available and many mornings saw the whole family, mother, and children, stand in the long queues at the market with food vouchers for butter and other basic foods.

Now it was Manouch, who loaded the cart with household goods of blankets and pots, and other supplies, like material and sheets and undergarments for men and women. Her journey could take a few days visiting the mines, where she sold her goods to the miners. She always took one of the younger boys with her to interpret although she would have preferred it, if they could rather attend school. She had no choice leaving the others with the older ones, and Alfred was always in charge of all of them in her absence. He in turn, was checked by Joe and Phillip. Each one needed the other to survive and that is what they were doing, surviving. Manouch worried when she left them knowing she had no choice if they were to have any kind of future. She was not the only person plying this trade and found herself having to travel further and further away, which meant she was away from home, for longer and longer periods. Sales were also less in demand and she knew she would have to look for another form of income.

When returning from one such journey, with hardly anything sold, she knew it was time, and dreaded the decision she had to make.

* * *

Trials and tribulations were commonplace in the household where so many children were boys. Siblings always disagreed and many fights had to be quelled and in extreme cases, either David or Johnny was called in to help. Dawood and Buddy were seldom approached to settle problems, and Phillip usually shied away, not wanting to hurt anyone, although he kept a watchful eye to step in if need be. Manouch was the spill around which everything turned and Alfred was her informer and adviser. Nobody, no matter who they were, would harm her, and the children in turn, were protected and loved by all.

David was now the appointed head of the family and took his duties very seriously, while Johnny, Dawood and Buddy stayed out of his way not wanting to challenge him out of respect, and the younger ones, although respecting him, feared his wrath. Manouch depended on him a great deal especially where the younger children were concerned, and listened intently to the advise he gave, when she asked for it.

* * *

Evenings, when the older brothers came visiting, was Alfred's best time of the day.

Hearing the laughter and joking and the occasional argument made him smile where he sat on the step in the kitchen. He knew Finnie and Yvette would make tea, and later one by one, the brothers would come to him for a little chat. This was his family and he loved them all, especially the youngest. Thinking about the boy made his eyes soft. He loved Joe and Phillip and Jimmy but nothing could equal his love for Norman. This was truly his child. He had brought him up. He played with him and watched over him at all times. He was his joy. Later, when everyone was gone he would eat his food waiting in the oven in the now dented and chipped metal dish, slowly baked to perfection. He knew the meat would be tender and the potato would be crisp and juicy. Afterwards when he locked up, he would take his bedroll from under the table, and roll it out in front of the warm stove. This he packed away again before dawn touched the sky, and washed himself in the yard with water cold as ice. Winter or summer, he never deviated

Afterwards the stove would be freshly packed and lit, and tea and toast was always ready for the children when they got up. He lived for the sounds of the people whom he loved, with all his heart, knowing they loved him with the same passion and that they all belonged together.

Chapter Eighteen

'You know the dangers mommy, and yet you want to do it again.'

'What else can I do Tonios, we need money to survive.'

'We can all try to help you mommy.'

'You know I appreciate your offer, but you hardly have enough for yourself.'

'I still don't like it, but if you must then you must.'

David was alone with his mother and although he did not approve he knew their position was critical. He could barely look after himself with the salary he was getting, and it was true that they had no future without selling goods to the miners, but her decision worried him. If she was caught again he knew her sentence would be severe.

And so with all the dangers known to them, they began planning. Once again they would make use of their previous supplier, and once again areas for possible hiding places were earmarked, but above all, safety measures had to be in place.

Although Eblen's visits became more irregular with his brother no longer there, and Manouch often being away selling goods, he made a point to at least be there once a week, usually on a weekend.

On such a day, they sat on the cool veranda, and his mind went back to another time, when he and his brother paid a visit to a cousin on a cool veranda, so long ago. It was as if it had been in another world all together. He felt lonely without his brother and missed him most when he was with his brothers' family. He looked at Manouch and marvelled at her still beautiful features. Always well dressed with her hair shining, and brought together in a loose chignon behind her head, she looked smart. He knew she was a good businesswoman and well respected in the community and everybody knows her as fair and honest and kind to a fault, fiercely proud of herself and her children. He spoke to her about this very thing on more than one occasion, that is the kind part, but she always had an answer ready why it was necessary to do what she did, and he accepted it. He knew his brother had been very happily married and had basked in the love of his family and had also realised all his dreams. He, on the other hand, knew that although he was content, he had lived his brothers' dream and somehow fell short of his own, but he had accepted that long ago.

When he saw Norman coming towards him he put his hand in his jacket pocket and took out a handful of sweets. Norman took it and ran to share it with Jimmy and Yvette. He watched the boy as he ran away and felt sad that his brother was not there to see the younger children as they grew up. He hoped that his brother could see them through his eyes as he closed his eyelids to lock in the moment.

Manouch told him about her decision and he listened without interrupting once. He knew how difficult it was to make a living from selling goods to miners these days and her needs were much more than his own.

'If there is anything I can help you with, you only have to say the word.' 'I know Eblen, and I will if I need to.' was her answer.

On his way home his thoughts were milling around thinking of the dangers that lay in store for Manouch. He worried about her and her family even though he knew the older brothers kept things pretty much in control.

It was late when he arrived home and more than ever the loneliness, lay heavy on him, as he went through his ritual of retiring. He always expected to see his brother sitting on the opposite bed as they did when planning their future, and he smiled because he somehow knew he was not alone.

* * *

Weekends were busy in the yard. Talking and laughing and the usual swearing came from the men with music playing in the background where they sat in their working clothes with mugs in their hands. Lizzie, the domestic helper, moved around like a barmaid, topping up where needed and when the pitch grew too high, cautioned them to talk softer which they did for a short while, before it picked up again. This was where they, the black miners, relaxed among others like themselves, and enjoyed a drink. Alcohol was not permitted to be sold, to any person of colour, but here, in this yard, close to their compound, they were not black, but people entitled to enjoy themselves, and they were happy. Yvette and Finnie helped and they, the customers, respected them. Not one of them would ever dream of harming any of the family and it was not because they were afraid of Joe or Phillip or any of the other brothers, no it was because they all knew and respected Manouch, and her kindness to everyone. Sometimes Alfred joined in and drank a little too much, and knew he would be scolded by Manouch. He hated to disappoint her, and when it did happen on occasion Manouch would shake her head and point her finger and threaten him with the prospect of dismissal. They knew it was never going to happen but played their roles as they always did.

Outside the boys were playing cricket, but their eyes constantly scanned the roads on all sides. Further along on a sandy outcrop, sat a figure gazing over the roofs of the buildings for any movement. A car was parked on the top road and Phillip sat there so he could have an overview of the row of small houses below. The lookouts were all in place as business was carried out below.

The profits were good, although the risks were high. Manouch was not only able to support her children, but helped them save a little for when they decided to marry. Life was good. Yes, there were times when everyone had to scramble to hide the stock and clear the yard leaving everything to look like a busy kitchen, but they were used to this. There were of course the times when a 'plant' tried to break through, but he was soon detected or pointed out by another customer, and quickly removed.

This activity of informal liquor sales was not one of a kind. No, in fact there were a number of similar places within a small radius, which sometimes led to jealousy when customers were lost or if they were just being plain vindictive, and then the police would be tipped off by a rival to close down such a gathering.

If they were fortunate to receive a warning of such an impending visit they were grateful, and quickly made the necessary arrangements, which included some kind of payment for the officer who alerted them. However, there were the out of town detectives, who did not share in the local fraternity, and they were the ones to look out for.

Salems' vegetable garden was still tended to a degree, by Phillip and Joe, although the rows of vegetables were less now. The serving of clients were taken care of by Finnie, Yvette and Lizzie and the replenishment of supplies, was carried out by Manouch and Phillip. Joe was happiest when he could cook and bake, and he worked on and off, but never stayed at one place for long. This habit of his really made David angry. David was a loyal and conscientious employee and could not understand why Joe was not the same. Phillip still worked at the outfitters where David got him a job and Johnny lived in a suburb further south where he rented a room close to the factory where he worked as a cabinet-maker. He was engaged to a girl he met at church and planned to marry her as soon as he was able to. David was still at the same place where he started many years ago and he now held a senior position. He had married again after playing the field for a few years when he divorced his first wife and was soon to be a father again. Dawood, who left home as soon as he was able to, stayed in the same town as Buddy, further east. Buddy had married a girl from another Lebanese family and they had two children, a boy, and a girl and expected another baby soon. Badeo still stayed were she moved to when she got married, and now had three children a boy and two girls. Finnie was at home as well as Jimmy, Yvette and Norman the youngest, who where all still in school. Jimmy was an intelligent boy, easily conquering each grade although he seldom attended school except for when exams were written. He shorter than Phillip and was more powerfully built than David and looked nothing like his brothers, Phillip or Joe. If one looked carefully he probably resembled David the most. There was a slight slant to his eyes and his siblings nicknamed him 'Chinaman'. His manner was more like Buddy, Joe and Phillip, always being in control of his temper while David, Johnny and Dawood differed from them by being very short tempered and raised their fists for the slightest thing. Like Phillip, Jimmy protected his sisters and Norman when the older brothers chastised them, taking a stance in front of them to accept any challenge that could occur.

Jimmy would of course never lift his hands to his older brothers, but this could change if he had to protect the younger ones. He was fearless, sometimes unnerving the challenger before him. His presence was usually enough to let anyone back down hiding their smile from their young brother. This was the way they were used to things around the house and it was all a matter of testing the mettle of each other. Alfred watched and rarely intervened unless he thought it was absolutely necessary.

* * *

'Life is what you make of it. What you put into it is what you get out of it.' David said to Joe where he was at the stove stirring a pot.

The kitchen felt cosy and warm. Rain was falling from early in the day and kept the customers away. David was happy about that. He hated the idea of selling illegal alcohol to the black community although he knew his mother depended on the extra income. That is why he wanted Joe to take more responsibility. Why can't he just stay and persevere in one job?

David had arranged many of these jobs that only lasted for a short while before Joe left, making David look a fool again. He had just about as much as he could take and promised himself to stay out of it and let Joe find his own job. Yes, that's what he would do, exactly nothing, that way his mother could see how lazy Joe really was. Oh, he knows Joe is his mother's favourite, and frankly he did not care, but fair is fair and he should contribute to household expenses. He had taken on the responsibility of being the head of the family very seriously, and his mother depended on him a lot. Being so much older than the younger ones, he knew they were afraid of him, and that was also good. Not having a father did not mean they had to grow up wild, no he would see to that, after all, his father did ask him to do just that. Oh yes, he knew his mother and Alfred looked after them very carefully but they had to know that he was watching. Jimmy was a clever boy, and David expected great things from him. He was aware that his brother seldom went to school but he also knew that when the end of year tests came around, he passed with flying colours. He smiled to himself just thinking of Jimmy who did not have the privilege to be with his father like he did. Jimmy was also not like Phillip and Joe who needed to be around his mother all the time. In actual fact, if he really thought about it, Jimmy was pretty much a loner. He could not even think of any friend of Jimmy that he knew about. The boy lived his own life in a quiet way usually playing with Norman and Yvette when he was not on lookout duty. That David felt was another issue, the lookout duty. The responsibility that the children had was a burden that they should not have to bear, and yet he knew of no other way they could survive.

Manouch sat at the table in her favourite chair where she could see out into the yard. Rain obscured her view and a chill made her pull her cardigan closer around her breast.

'What are you thinking about son?' David loved it when she called him son. He never heard her call any of his other brothers son, only him. He looked at her face thinking how tired she looked.

'Are you all right mommy? You look a bit tired. What is wrong?'

She knew she would have to tell him even though it would cause a row.

'Its Phillip, he joined the army.'

David looked at his mother with a stunned expression on his face. 'Who told you that?'

'He did. I told him it was a bad idea but he went ahead anyway.'

David sat still for a while before speaking. 'It may not be such a bad idea mom. He needs to get away from you to stand on his own feet and this may be just the push he needs.'

'How he will cope not being with his family, I don't know.' She replied.

'Well, mom, he will soon find out. Don't worry, he will be fine, he is a big boy now.'

And she smiled at her son. He always knew just what to say to help her.

Of course he is right, she worries too much, Phillip is capable of looking after himself.

When he stood in the doorway, resplendent in his army uniform, he looked absolutely fantastic. When Manouch saw him her heart filled with pride.

He looked like a movie star, and she could see, he himself felt good. The children ran to him, when they saw him, and he warded them off, not to touch his clothes.

'Whoa, take it easy, everything must be perfect.' They laughed and he laughed, and if it was a little wistfully, nobody noticed. This was his family and he knew he was going to miss them.

He did not stay long and when he kissed his mother on her cheek he had to hide his emotion. She made his life worthwhile and he was going to miss her more than anything.

'Jimmy, come here.' Jimmy now a gangly teenager came to his brother who stretched out his hand. 'I am depending on you to look after Finnie and Yvette and your brother Norman. I know Joe will look after them, but when he is not here, it is your duty. Will you promise me that you will do that?' Jimmy took his brother's hand that he held out and turned it with the palm facing down, and kissed the top of Phillip's hand.

'I promise, but you have to promise me that you will look after yourself.' Phillip looked at his younger brother and wondered if the boy knew what a responsibility had been bestowed on him.

'I promise' he said and left. The kitchen went quiet, as everyone kept their thoughts to themselves. They knew they were going to miss him but did not want to say it out loud.

Alfred was waiting for Phillip on the veranda and without a word took Phillips hand in his.

'Look after yourself, there will be no one to do that for you. Don't worry for the family, we will look after them.' Phillip knew that Alfred was right and bent down and kissed him on the top of his head.

Where before Alfred would have shooed him away, he now stood still and then he pushed him away. 'Go, you are a man now.'

They missed Phillip a lot in fact, especially Manouch, but she never spoke about it. Now and again they had a telephone call from him and everything sounded fine. That was until two months of basic training was complete and then a demon appeared. A frantic telephone call came from Phillip.

'I am going to be posted out somewhere overseas and I don't even know where.'

'Well Phillip' Manouch said 'surely you knew that this would happen sooner or later?'

'I didn't think they would, they said we might be posted near to home. I don't want to go mommy.'

Manouch knew there was no alternative. He joined and belonged to the army and that was that.

Manouch told David about the call and he only shook his head. 'I told him but he would not listen. I will see what I can do but I promise nothing.'

It was still dark when Manouch heard the knock on the front door. She put her cardigan over her shoulders and went to the door.

He stood there, in uniform with a lost look in his eyes. 'I cannot go away mommy, I just can't.' She took his arm and pulled him inside then closed the door. Now she knew they really had a problem and she would have to get hold of David as soon as possible.

Joe left early to catch David before he went to work. David was livid.

Did Phillip not think this thing through before he started with this nonsense? He knew, it was probably the uniform, more than anything else that had attracted his brother. All he knew, was that not only was Phillip a wanted absconder, but he had put his family at risk for harbouring him. Did anyone know just how trying it was to look after such a large family? He didn't think so.

They were in the kitchen the next evening when the military police came for him. Jimmy saw them first and ran to alert his family and Phillip quickly ran to the bedroom where he hid in the wardrobe where they found him and took him away.

Her heart was heavy as she watched them one on each arm, escorting her son, to the waiting army vehicle. Yvette and Norman clung to her and she put her arms around them. Phillip was their hero. They loved him more than anything. Further on the veranda Jimmy stood watching with Finnie by his side. Joe was not there when they came and heard all about it later.

They were allowed to see Phillip in confinement. He looked pale and worn with fear in his eyes.

There was going to be a court martial and the outcome looked bleak. The country was still at war and the crime was serious.

You have to give David his due. There is no doubt that he is a marvel. How he does it, is a mystery, but once his mind was set, he let nothing stand in his way until he reached his goal. A buy out, and a dishonourable discharge, was the best he could do in this case. The financial burden was heavy, but Manouch managed with help from David, to put the money together.

When Manouch looked at Phillip where they sat in the kitchen she smiled, and when he looked up, saw the love in his mothers' eyes. He gave her a lopsided grin and promised himself, that he would make it up to her one way or another, if it was the last thing he did. All he knew was that he learnt a lesson that he would not easily forget.

Chapter Nineteen

The mood in the back yard was filled with tension and fear. Sporadic gunfire could be heard further away at the mine compound. Faction fighting had started the day before and the police were powerless. The men fighting with each other were enraged, and their intervention just aggravated the mob. The mine manager had called in the police and they had called for re-enforcements, but still the fighting went on. Fires were burning on the outskirts of the compound and bodies of men lay strewn everywhere. The rubber bullets the police fired did not deter the mob in any way, and in fact only worsened the situation so the police formed a cordon around the compound to prevent the fighting from spilling into the streets.

There were not many customers on that day and those that were there, looked with fear at each other. In the yard however, total control was being maintained by Joe with Finnie and Yvette. The family stood no nonsense, from anyone and it was uncanny how the young children managed to control them. Manouch gave short instructions in 'Fanagalo,' the language that they all understood, and the children did what she told them to do, without arguments. Jimmy as always was the lookout at the back making sure everything was safe.

Today they knew all the members of the police force were occupied, and the only danger was that fighting could erupt, from the very people who sat together in the yard and who were today, closely watched. Strangely the family felt no threat from the violence a short distance away, even though they saw the orange flames in the trees and heard the gunfire.

David was there earlier cautioning them to be careful. News about the unrest nearby, was all over the radio, and the police had blocked the roads around the compound.

'Rather close up Mom, it looks like its getting worse.'

'We will be careful. You must also take care.'

'Joe, I told mom to close up.'

'I know David, but these men are safer here than there.'

David threw his hands in the air.

'What is it with you people, cant you see how dangerous it is?'

Then he walked out to his car.

'Perhaps he is right Joe.' Manouch said.

'We will just wait a little while then I will tell them to go.'

They came running, three bedraggled, bloodied men, and Manouch hearing their screams, went outside to see what was going on. When she saw them she called to Alfred to come and help. 'Alfred! Alfred! Come, bring water and a cloth. Yvette get an old sheet so we can tear strips for bandages. Hurry, Finnie come and help me.' She took the shivering men into the kitchen where she made them sit on the floor. Finnie and Yvette helped as Manouch washed their wounds and wrapped the torn sheet over their wounds that were mostly to their heads.

She spoke to the men in Fanagalo, the universal language of the mines.

'How many dead?' She asked them

'Too many.' They said

'What is the police doing to help?'

'They are helpless, they tried but they themselves are also getting killed.'

When she was finished binding their wounds she called Joe. 'Come with me and don't say anything.' When he saw what she planned to do he held her fast.

'No, mommy, you are not going, I won't let you.'

'Then stay, I will take Jimmy.' Fear gripped his heart as he saw her take a short stick from behind a kitchen cupboard. He knew, he had no choice if it was between him and Jimmy, who was just a boy.

She strode purposely with the stick held high in her hand with Joe a step behind.

He stayed that way so he would not be seen as a threat but only a support.

The police saw their approach and watched in amazement at the slightly built woman brandishing a short stick walking towards them. What on earth has got into her? Surely she knew how dangerous the situation was? When they came nearer two policemen tried to stop her but she brushed them away. 'Joe, tell them to let us through.' When he told the police they were going in, they did not want to let them through until their officer in command came forward. He listened to Joe and told his men to let them through but to be on alert. They all knew Manouch and her children, and how they made a living, but they also respected them, knowing their kindness to all who asked for help.

When they came to the outskirts of the compound, Manouch stood still for a moment, looking at the carnage in front of her. Joe stood a few paces behind her. He carried no weapon. Then she moved forward lifting the stick above her head into the mass of men with kieries and pangas. She hit them left and right with the stick and they opened a path for her and Joe.

'Why do you want to die? Look at yourselves, dead and bleeding, stop! I tell you, stop.'

Through the mass of bodies covered in sweat and blood, she moved forward, until she was at the centre of the crowd of men where she stood still and lowered the stick. The smell of their bodies was even stronger than the smoke of the fires on the outskirts. Fear and anger was a palpable force that promised certain danger. She turned slowly to all sides and spoke calmly.

'Let us move the dead and injured to the front so they can be attended to. I want to speak to every leader now.' Her voice, when she spoke in fluent 'Fanagalo' was strong although her heart was pounding in her chest.

She saw Joe watching every movement while keeping a calm expression and she knew he was afraid as she was but would do nothing unless it became necessary. Men pushed themselves forward from the mass and stood in front of her.

Their bodies were pressed close together, in the small circle, and were almost touching her, and she saw their eyes yellow with rage and anger, as she raised her stick again above her head.

'You have families who depend on you. If you are dead or injured they will have nothing to eat. Why are you fighting? Let us talk like men and sort it out. While we are talking let your men remove the injured so they can be attended to.'

The police watched from the outskirts and saw the bodies being carried out from the crowd. On one side the dead were placed in rows while the injured were brought to the front. Smoke from the fires made the men look like eerie ghosts appearing, and for a while, the police just watched in awe, before they signalled to the ambulances, waiting a distance away, to come nearer. The police while still keeping their distance, helped to load the injured into the ambulances. There was a hush among the men, and the police watched and waited, till they saw her come out of the crowd with her son behind her. She walked with her head held high and her stick kept low. The crowd now calm, stood still as if waiting for a sign and when she reached the clearing she turned around and raised her stick once more.

'Go now, wash yourselves and eat some food. The injured and the dead will be taken care of.' She waited until the men turned and dispersed before turning her back to them.

When Manouch and Joe reached the police cordon, the men took off their caps and held it to their chests as she passed them by. Nobody said a word but their respect was like a tangible force that carried her and Joe home.

Nothing was written in the papers and no medals were issued but every person for miles around knew what took place that night and her name when spoken of was always done so with the greatest respect

When David heard what had transpired he went into a rage and very nearly broke everything in sight. How could his mother be so reckless?

Did she not care for the safety of herself and her family? He stayed away for a whole week to cool down but the incident festered in his mind.

Chapter Twenty

What made Joseph, or rather Joe as everyone called him, different from his brothers, was first of all his complexion. While they were more olive skinned, his complexion was fair. His eyes were gentle and more amber than brown and changed instantly with feeling. Slightly overweight from his love of cooking, tall like Phillip, and good looking like Johnny made him stand out in any crowd. A pencil thin moustache accentuated his black hair with a natural curl that kept falling over his forehead. Where the difference was really noticeable, was his nature. Loving and gentle, never getting cross with anyone, or ever saying anything bad or nasty, made him the envy and hero of his siblings. No matter how they taunted him, he never retaliated, and this sometimes really got them worked up. What he did not like was to be away from home. No, Joe preferred to be busy at home, making sure there was always food on the stove and the younger ones were fed and looked after. When he baked biscuits or cakes, the younger ones crowded around the table and started eating the biscuits as they were taken off the tray. He loved being able to spoil them and his mother when he could. She was his universe and he knew her every mood.

This relationship irritated David, who unlike Phillip never understood Joes' love to be with his family. Phillip and Joe were usually together and hardly ever mixed with their older brothers who had different expectations from life than them. Jimmy was a teenager who never mixed with his older brothers and Norman was still a child. They looked to Joe as their confidante and protector. It was only when he was not around that they approached Alfred or Manouch for help. Joe was the one who understood their needs more than anyone.

Manouch loved to have Joe helping her with the younger children or in the kitchen. She felt content knowing her older children had made a life for themselves working and planning for their future. Of course she knew Joe should get a permanent job, although she knew he was happy just looking after the household. She tried to explain this to David and to Johnny but they did not agree with her. They wanted to help her and felt Joe should be earning some sort of wage so he could help with expenses, and to this end, arranged for interviews for jobs whenever they could. True, Joe did go to the interviews, and sometimes even started working, but it never lasted long before he was back in the kitchen cooking and baking, which to their minds, were plain and simple laziness. Buddy was seldom around and Dawood did not care either way, and as for Phillip, he was not concerned knowing that Joe took care of the family. Besides, Finnie was never to be left alone, having the medical problem she has, and Phillip was not always around which really left only Joe. No, it was David, with Johnny, fanning the flames that got tempers flaring.

As for Joe? Well, he knew their feelings and understood them trying to help him, but when he thought the time was right, would find his own job, one that he could enjoy and had nothing to do with sales or working in a factory, so he went about his cooking and baking and sang while he was busy.

His strong beautiful voice made Manouch smile where she was busy in the bedroom. How she loved this son, who was like a breath of fresh air, in a world filled with tempers flaring up for no reason at all.

Sometimes, just sometimes, she thought to herself, the boys became too overwhelming. She missed Badeo more than she realised. Yes, there was Finnie of course, and Yvette but they were younger and did not share the companionship she had with Badeo.

* * *

How does one know when your last day is given to you? Do you wake up and look in the mirror tracing all the lines in your face and dress into something special? Do you smile at everyone or are you nervous? Do you feel a tremor in your body or is it calm? How does a mother know to look at her children locking their faces in her mind on that particular day?

Do you hide your eyes for fear of showing your pain? What is the feeling that nags at you? Does the fact that you drink this cup of tea for the last time, or eat this piece of bread or hug your mother, or your child, for the last time warn you? How do you know so that you can be sure they know how much you love them? In truth, you never know. There may be a heavy feeling making you depressed, or it may even be a feeling that makes you feel on top of the world that morning, you just never know for sure.

Does the fact that a soft rain was falling outside, making clicking sounds on the windows, have anything to do with the outcome of the day? No, like a thief in the night it waits until you are off guard and then it strikes.

Like a coward it waits . . . . and waits . . . . and just when you are feeling safe, it pounces.

* * *

Manouch sat at the table drinking a cup of tea, her mind drifting away to a time when Salem, with the fresh lamb over his shoulder, came into the kitchen, and a smile played over her lips as she listened to Joe singing. He had such a lovely voice, deep and rich, and now and again he made a dance step to the side and twirled the dishcloth like a flag. He was not only her son, but her sun, giving off rays to warm all who were around him.

An aroma of slow fried onions and tomatoes emanated from the pan on the stove where Joe was preparing a sauce for the spaghetti. The smell was so delicious it made your mouth water. He was singing as he worked but stopped as his brother David walked into the kitchen. The front door always stood open except at night and everybody just walked in without knocking.

David bent down to kiss his mother on her cheek where she sat at the kitchen table. Her smile grew bigger when she saw him.

'Tonios! How nice to see you. Come and sit, Joe bring your brother some tea and some of those lovely biscuits you made. How is the family?'

'All well, thank you mommy, how are you keeping?'

Did she see a glint of steel in her son's eyes or was it the light that made it look that way?

Joe put a cup of tea and a plate of biscuits in front of his brother.

'Thank you, Joe. What happened to the job interview you were supposed to go to?'

Joe looked at his mother before answering and for a moment thought he saw a flash of pain in her eyes, and then a cold shiver ran down his spine.

Chapter Twenty-one

Joe saw her look, indicating he should be respectful, which he usually was, but for some reason he felt afraid, so he chose his words carefully.

"They already hired someone else.'

Joe saw his brother's nose flaring at the opening, and stood a pace back.

'I told you to go yesterday. Why did you leave it so late?'

Joe stood still for a moment then he returned to the stove to stir the pan he was busy with. He could see his brother was upset, so he moved the pan to the side of the stove where the heat was less. Then he saw his brother moving towards him. He knew him only too well and waited for the blow which he knew would come. Joe would never retaliate out of respect for his oldest brother and he took a step backward as the blow fell.

'Tonios, leave your brother alone!' Manouch shouted, but anger had already overtaken David as he hit his brother again with his fist on the side of his head.

Joe turned and ran out into yard, but David was quick behind him, hitting him with his fists on his back. Joe turned and held up his arms to shield his face, while the rain made little rivulets in the blood on his cheeks. David was even more enraged now, and did not let up. The rain falling made the men wet and their feet slippery where the sand had made mud puddles and Joe swerved and ran into the outside toilet realising too late that it was a mistake, as David rammed him up against the wall. Manouch was now behind David pulling him by his shirt to stop. 'Stop it! Stop it! It's not his fault.' She latched on to

David' s arm but the area inside the small building made it difficult and they kept slipping on the wet surface.

Joe tried to shield his face with his elbow but an undershot from David caught him on his nose and he felt his legs giving way underneath him. Joe glanced at his mother behind David and the look she saw on her sons' face, was not one of pain, but a plea for forgiveness. Her scream of agony rose above the crack of bone on the metal cistern of the toilet, as Joes' head hit it, and she fell to her knees on the wet ground hugging her body, rocking back and forth.

As his body fell awkwardly in the confined space, the realisation hit David like a hammer. Blood gushed from his brother's nose spraying it all over, drenching the bottoms of David's trousers. He stepped back and turned to his mother to lift her up from the ground. She pounded on his chest crying in a hoarse voice 'you killed him, you killed him, you killed my child.' Then Phillip was there lifting his mother up from the ground, and David turned and ran.

* * *

He ran into the velt and did not stop until he reached the train tracks.

The wet grass, rose up as he flung himself down, pounding his fists on the hard ground, until blood flowed from the broken skin. His howl, though silent filled his whole being. He David, his fathers' son, the guardian of his fathers' family, he the chosen one, he the murderer.

And he prayed and begged to be released from his body unto death, and time stood still, as rain fell on the shivering body laying curled up in the grass.

* * *

He lay there till his brother Phillip came to take him back to the house.

When they entered the kitchen he saw many people there. They were his own family, but he did not recognise any of them, and greeted nobody. His mind was blank, a great void was now where his heart once was, and all he heard was the crying. Jimmy grabbed him and hit him and then Dawood was rushing at him like an angry bull, his eyes protruding from his head, but Phillip was quicker this time and grabbed the raised arm of his brother shielding David. His voice was low but filled with steel. 'Stop it, you are all like animals, the next one will feel my fist and you all know what that means. Let us through and stay away.'

David made no attempt to shield himself and stayed behind his brother who pushed open a path for them. He kept his eyes down and when he put one foot before the other, he saw the blood on his trousers where the rain had turned it to almost black.

Women were crowded around the bed and Phillip pushed them aside.

'Go and wait in the kitchen.' They kept their eyes down and as they passed David, they made the sign of the cross.

Manouch was sitting on a chair in front of the bed. A basin was on the floor next to her, filled with bloodied water. The cloth she was wiping the face of her son with, was red as she bent down to rinse it in the already bloody water Tears streamed from her eyes as she kept repeating the words 'Hail Mary full of grace, hail Mary full of grace, hail Mary full of grace . . . .'

Phillip gently touched her arm and she looked up. When she saw David behind Phillip, she got up and pushed Phillip aside and flung herself at David. She started pounding David on his chest crying 'you killed him, you killed him' her voice grew softer and became a wail as David put his arms around his mother, and held her close to him. He held her like that until her sobbing grew weaker then he led her to the other side of the bed where he lay her down next to his brother. He took a blanket that was folded at the foot of the bed, and covered her, and sat on the edge putting his arm over her. He looked up at Phillip and now his eyes were two black holes that showed no life. 'Have you called for the doctor?'

'Yes he is on his way.'

'Call Badeo and Dawood in and close the door. Let nobody in but them.'

Phillip returned with Badeo and Dawood, and Badeo took the basin of water and put it under the bed to empty later.

Dawood took another blanket from the wardrobe, and put it over his brother' body on the bed, leaving his face uncovered.

A calm had settled over them as they waited for the doctor.

Badeo's husband was waiting outside for the doctor and when he arrived he led him to the bedroom. He opened the door and closed it again after they entered.

The doctor saw the man on the bed nearest the door under a blanket and a woman on the other bed. Were they both ill, was the first thought that crossed his mind, but then he saw the pallor of the man and his heart gave a lurch, knowing he was too late. He stood still as seconds passed and then Dawood spoke.

'Thank you for coming doctor, there has been a terrible accident.' He did not look at the doctors' face as he spoke but kept his eyes instead on his brother's body covered with a blanket. 'My brother fell. There was a bit of a scuffle and he slipped and fell. We tried to help him, but he must have hit his head.' Then he looked the doctor full in the face and their eyes locked for a moment.

Silently, the doctor bent down, and removed the blanket His movements were slow as he took out his stethoscope. He listened for a heartbeat knowing he would find none, and gently raised an eyelid with his fingers and closed it again. Then he drew the blanket over the man again still leaving the face uncovered. Rising, he went to the other bed to see to the mother.

He knew Manouch and her children well, and always had the greatest respect for her. Her eyes were tightly closed, but he knew she was not sleeping and called her name. The pain he saw in her eyes when she opened them was like a dagger in his heart. In his profession he dealt with many extremely sad cases, and many days he wondered why he had chosen the profession he had, not finding an answer. He took her pulse and listened to her heart. He knew she was diabetic and worried about the shock she had, and took out a syringe from his bag.

'I am giving her an injection for the shock. She will sleep for a while but not too long. It will give her body time to recover.'

'Thank you doctor' Dawood said 'We really appreciate you coming.'

The fact that it was Dawood that took charge when he knew David was the eldest, did not escape the doctor, as he followed Dawood out.

Phillip stayed in the room and watched his brother Dawood and the doctor from the window. The doctor got into the car and he saw him bend down to take something from the glove compartment of the car. Then he saw him take out a pen from his jacket pocket. He handed Dawood a paper, which he folded, and put into his pocket, and then he waited until the doctor drove away before returning to the house. He went to the bedroom and closed the door behind him again, before he gave the note to Phillip, who after reading it, gave it to David who slowly read it, and handed it back to Phillip, then David dropped his head into his hands and wept. The heading on the note was 'Certificate of Death' and the writing said 'death by accident' with the date filled in below next to the signature of the doctor.

* * *

Phillip took David by the arm as they made their way between the people to David's car that was parked in front of the house so many lifetimes ago, and opened the door on the passenger side, for David. He went to the driver's side and took the key that David held out to him.

Once David tried to speak, but Phillip held up his hand to stop him, and David did not try again.

When they stopped at the place where David stayed with his wife and family he got out of the car and walked with David.

Phillip held up his hand again as David's wife opened the door and he followed David inside. 'Don't ask any questions now.' Phillip told her. 'Get him cleaned up and let him lay down. Give him something hot to drink and make sure he eats. He must not leave this house until I come for him. Do you understand everything I say?'

She knew something bad must have happened, and only nodded her head, as Phillip turned and left.

* * *

Later Phillip returned for his brother who had changed into dry clothes. The brothers said nothing as they rode in silence.

There were many cars parked outside the house now and men stood around on the veranda in the dark. Light filtered through from inside making the men look like ghosts. Phillip walked in front with David close behind him. Nobody stopped them as they walked straight to the bedroom where the door was still closed. Joe was no longer there, having been taken away by the undertaker.

Manouch was sitting on the bed with Johnny, Buddy, Dawood and Badeos' husband. David went to his mother to put his arm around her, but she turned away from him, and he stood back.

It was Buddy who spoke first. 'We are not here to fight with you because the outcome will be even more tragic, and mommy has already had enough of that.' He indicated for David to sit on the only other chair in the room while they all stood. David did this knowing it would be futile to make any excuses or to ask for any forgiveness. He felt like an accused in court and waited for them to speak. He was at their mercy and he had no defence. It was Johnny who now spoke. 'What you did will be your punishment forever. Not only yours, but you will carry the pain of your father, your mother and brothers and sisters with you.

You will never, not even once, lift your hand to any of he younger children ever again. If we find out that you do, it will be your last day.'

Johnny gave a sigh as if the words were too heavy to bear. 'It will take time for everyone to give you any face, but that will only be among ourselves. We have told the doctor and the people that he fell' and here his voice broke and the next words were hoarse when he spoke them 'and hit his head.' Now Johnny was crying so much that Dawood took over.

'I will find you if you even lift one finger and you know that I will kill you without blinking an eyelid. We know you did not mean to do what you did, but it did happen.' David sat stone faced, his eyes on his mother, where she had put her hands over her face while her body shook from her sobbing.

Phillip knelt next to her, holding her body against his chest. Tears ran down David's face knowing he was the one that caused her pain, and he made no attempt to wipe them away. He was made of stone, his body was breathing but he was not even aware of it.

Badeos' husband walked to David and touched his arm to follow him.

They walked out to where the people were, and now hands of sympathy were extended to them, when the people saw them. 'Please accept my sympathy for your loss of a brother.' 'God is good, he will help you, please accept my sympathy.' And so it went on. David shook the hands and accepted the kisses on his cheeks and nodded his head. His head felt as if it was bursting open from the intense headache that enveloped his whole being. How would he ever survive this ordeal? Did he want to survive, was another thought that ran through his brain. He felt as if his body was one great pain from his head to his feet and he slowly made his way away from his brother-in-law, and disappeared into the dark. It was a long way to walk home, and Phillip still had his car keys, he knew he wanted to be alone more than anything. After walking a short distance he sat down on the ground with his back against a strange building and cried and cried till no more tears could come, and then he got up and walked the rest of the way to the house he shared with his family.

He knew his wife would be waiting for him, and a small flicker of hope rose within him.

Chapter Twenty-two

The sun shone brightly on the people gathered around the family grave where Salem was buried, years before. Although the writing was in Arabic his name was written in English on the polished slab. A life size figure of St Joseph in an alcove at the head of the grave watched over the mourners, while four small angels in white marble, mounted on the four corners of the family plot, looked on sadly. Amiro was not buried in the same grave but rested further down in the older section of the cemetery, in an unmarked grave. There are no words that could possibly describe the feelings at the funeral on that day. Death is always expected from the old and weary but when a young life is lost, it is more difficult to understand. Word had quickly spread that Joe was dead as a result of an accident, and being the popular person that he was, meant that there were many mourners. The family had closed ranks and the same reason when asked about his death, was given by all. He slipped, and hit his head, a tragic accident. The fact that they kept their eyes downcast was not found strange, after all, one tended to hide ones sorrow from others.

After the coffin was lowered alongside his father, and the final blessing was made, the family members stood in a row to receive a handshake or a kiss on the cheek, from those attending, expressing their condolences. All he brothers and the sisters were there, as well as their wives and husbands, except for David, who stayed at home with his mother, who after the shock, was told to stay in bed for a few days.

He sat next to her bed, and spoke to her softly.

'Mommy I am so very sorry, you must know that I did not mean for this to happen. You know I love you with all my heart and would never do anything that I thought could hurt you. It will take time, I know, but if you can one day forgive me, for being the cause of your pain, I will be the most grateful son any mother could ever have. Your well being is the most important purpose in my life.'

Her eyes were dull with pain and sorrow, and tears had dried on her cheeks. She lost not only her son, but the sun, in her universe. How can anyone know that pain? How was she expected to survive?

His voice was soft and full of pain and she knew, as much as her suffering was, his was greater. She did not know how she knew this, but she did, and her heart felt his pain as well as her own.

'Please forgive me mommy. Please can you ever do that?'

Manouch said nothing for a while then a deep sigh escaped her lips. When she finally spoke, her voice was clear. 'I forgive you my son.'

David went on his knees in front of his mother where she sat on the bed, and he cradled her in his arms. She rested her head on his head as they both wept.

They stayed like that for a while, then he kissed her forehead 'come, you must get up, the people will be here soon.'

He helped her up and fetched the comb on her dressing table and combed her hair, then holding her arm, they went to the lounge where chairs were arranged along the walls. He settled her into an armchair and fetched a light rug from the bedroom to put over her legs. Although the sun shone outside, there was a chill in the cool lounge. Before long, they heard the bang of a car door closing, as the first cars arrived and then people were spilling into the house.

Her daughters took their places next to Manouch, while her sons sat outside on the veranda, with the men. It was the daughters-in-law who went to the kitchen to see to the refreshments. With all the people around her, Manouch's searching glances went unnoticed, as she looked between the figures, hoping to catch a glimpse of Joe.

*   *   *

Time was somehow irrelevant. To Manouch it did not matter whether it was day or night, or cold or warm. When she put on her black dress, it was because that was how she felt inside. The sun never penetrated her inner being, and although she answered when someone spoke to her, she forgot what it was about almost immediately. Alfred was always nearby with a cup of tea, or a small plate of olives and cheese. If she ate any of it, it did not register with her. She knew he was also in pain and yet she felt powerless to help him, with her own pain like fire in her heart. When the children came she smiled at them, and asked about their health, and they smiled back, but the smiles never reached their eyes. Nobody ever spoke about the tragedy, and as if by mutual agreement, Joe's name was never mentioned in her presence. The only measure they did not resort to, was taking down the picture painted of him, which hung alongside that of Johnny, on the wall in the lounge. These two paintings were done by the same artist, and showed off their handsome features, that could outshine any Hollywood actor.

Alfred sat on the low wall surrounding the veranda, and waited for the children on their way out. When they left his words were few.

'Tell David to come and see his mother.'

'Where is your son Badeo? Bring him to see his grandmother.'

'You must come tonight, Finnie and Yvette is cooking something special.'

'Come and fetch your mother and take her for a drive.'

They listened to him, not because they loved him, which they did, but also because they knew he was wise, and so the stream of visitors never stopped.

Before he woke the children in the mornings to get them ready for school, the smell of toast made on the open top of the stove, would fill the air. Tea would be drawing in the big teapot and sandwiches with jam were ready to take to school. He kept his mourning to himself as he went about his duty, to lovingly care for his family.

*   *   *

Life as they knew it, slowly settled into a routine again. Manouch seldom sat in the kitchen at the table where she liked to be. Instead she spent more time in her bedroom just sitting on the bed, where she could see out to the front of the house. She only went to the kitchen when she joined her children for a meal, and then she enjoyed the bantering between them, hardly ever looking towards the stove, or out of the window facing the velt. Her brood was growing up and it was only Jimmy, Finnie, Yvette and Norman now living with her. Phillip was still a daily visitor and Badeo came whenever she could. Johnny only came on weekends and David sometimes stopped in after work for a little while. Buddy hardly ever came, and Dawood was unpredictable. If anything urgent or important cropped up, the family came together at short notice, but all in all, they were growing up, and working on their own future.

Finnie, a real beauty with her long black hair, hoped her family would relent and let her marry, but she doubted it. She knew her condition could erupt at any time and did mention this to the young man who was keen to know her better. If he said it did not matter, one could understand, only because he did not see what effect it really had, which if he had, would make him change that statement without any doubt, or that is what her brothers told her. Between her and Yvette, with Alfred helping, as well as Lizzie who cleaned the house, they looked after the serving of the customers in the yard. Norman now a gangly boy, was usually outside on surveillance duty, where Jimmy joined him when he was around. They all had their duties to perform and accepted this, complaining often, without receiving any sympathy. This was the business that fed and looked after them all, and this they also understood.

Weekends were busy with crates of beer and boxes of brandy being delivered and stored in the hidden places, while clients socialised in the yard, where an argument would break out now and again, and just as quickly be quelled by whoever was serving. If anything looked suspicious, a loud whistle by those on surveillance duty, was enough to alert those inside, and within seconds all evidence, as well as clients were cleared. Hiding places were constantly changed and if a brother or two were visiting, boxes were kept in their cars, so they could drive away to a safe place waiting for the all clear message, to reach them.

Raids by the local authorities still took place at regular intervals, and although a warning was sometimes given, the unexpected was always waiting to pounce.

Chapter Twenty-three

One thing the brothers all had in common, were their appreciation for a beautiful woman, and this in many cases, was not limited to their wives.

Oh, they loved their wives, and were good to them, well, most of the time anyway, but their charm and good looks were like a magnet. Manouch was well aware of their weaknesses, and warned them constantly to be strong, and they were, most of the time anyway. After all, she was the person who was most important in their universe, and they did not want to disappoint her. The wives knew this of course and accepted it, well knowing that if the need arose, Manouch would be their best ally.

Buddy had settled in a town further east where he made a life for him and his wife among the community. Like his father, he was an outstanding businessman, and carefully and determinedly, built up his own future.

He bought a building a few blocks away from the main road and opened a fish and chip shop. What could not be seen from the outside of the shop was the area at the back, where a pergola offered shade to the clients sitting at the tables on comfortable chairs. A low-key buzz among the clients, while they enjoyed their beer, was like the sound of a beehive. He knew the business from experience, and with some improvements, offered a good service.

The house, he had bought stretched from block to block, on the main street of the town, and was a mere few blocks away from the city hall. He clearly had a large family in mind to occupy all the rooms, and went about doing just that.

Johnny settled more to the south, so he could have easy access to his work, where he soon obtained a senior position in a furniture factory. An upstanding member of the church and the community, made him, and his wife well liked and respected. A gentleman by all means, that is until his path is crossed, to the peril of those in his way. A bull of a man, with a temper that had to be kept under control at all times, which granted he mostly did.

Dawood had married a woman from the town where Buddy stayed. She was a gentle woman, although she stood her man when the need arose, which seemed to come around quite often. They settled not far away from where his mother lived, on a mining property where he worked in the mine. There was speculation between the family of who was strongest between Johnny and Dawood but nobody was prepared to place any bets. One thing was certain, Dawood was a force to be reckoned with, and nothing stood in his way.

Like a horse would be harnessed, he wrapped a halter around his chest, and pulled the carts filled with ore, deep in the mine. His body was strong and nobody dared to challenge him for fear of being demolished. School was never his friend when he was young, so once he could read and write, he did not go back and found himself a job where it mostly involved manual labour. The mine paid a fair wage, and a house with very low rental went with it, so that is where he worked. Respect was what his co-workers had for him, and they had no desire to get on his wrong side. Loyalty to his friends, who knew they could depend on him for anything, went without question. He lived, played and drank hard, and when he was angry and his eyes bulged out of their sockets, it was best to run very fast and very far to survive.

As for Badeo, she was content to raise her family, always expecting her mother to visit regularly being a walking distance away. If she was unhappy with anything or anyone she did not show it, and mother and daughter drew strength from each other.

To say that Phillip looked like a film actor, when the same could be said for Johnny, may sound farfetched but it was true. His tall frame with barrel chest and slim hips was noticeable in any crowd. His natural curling black hair was combed to the back, and a pencil thin moustache completed a pleasing package. When he smiled, his lips curled at the ends like a frill on a collar, and a twinkle lit up his velvet brown eyes.

Oh yes! The girls all wanted him to notice them, and he did.

When Phillip saw her that day, it was as if he saw her for the first time, although he had seen her many times before. She was petite with a full bosom, and maybe this was what made him take a special interest. Who knew for sure? After all, he knew her family well, as her mother and his father were brother and sister making them first cousins. She was born in The Lebanon and had travelled with an aunt whom she looked after. She had hoped for a new life, and hopefully, a husband.

She saw her cousin look at her that day quite differently from the times before and a tingle ran through her body.

If there were any misgivings about the relationship, it was never aired, and soon a wedding was being planned.

And Finnie, what about her you may well wonder. A beautiful girl, now a woman, cursed with an affliction that made her family refuse proposal after proposal, for fear of her health. How sad that happiness shared with someone, would never be experienced. Surely she could have enjoyed married life, even if it would mean not having any children. On the other hand, there was probably more wisdom in their refusals, than one gave them credit for. So there she was, a most popular woman, respected and loved by many friends, knowing she would never reach her full potential. Bitter perhaps in some ways, but accepting the decision nevertheless.

And if over time she gained some weight it could be understood.

Jimmy, well you see, Jimmy was always a loner. Not much interested to have friends, his passion was only work. He had a brilliant brain, blessed with a natural affinity for engineering. Shorter than his older brothers Buddy, Johnny, Dawood and Phillip and more compact in his build, he did not stand out in a crowd, choosing to avoid visiting or getting together with anyone except his own family. He had his own mind and his sights were set on engineering.

The only other interest he had was women. He felt comfortable in the presence of a woman, and as his brothers, his charm did not escape them. Of all his siblings, he loved his youngest brother the most. He looked after him and protected him, and anybody had to first get past him before they could touch his brother, who followed him around like a shadow.

School was a breeze, although attendance in class left many gaps. This however did not stop him from attaining top marks for science and maths. The exams at year-end were written and passed even though no notes were written in any books. Finding a position, as apprentice fitter and turner was easy for him.

Knowing what he wanted and being good at what he did, his ability did not go unnoticed, and the usual four years of apprenticeship, were covered in two, as he proved his worth.

He loved his mother as much as any of the others, but rarely showed his feelings. Handsome in his own way, he did not resemble the film star looks of Johnny or Phillip or Joe. His eyes, although brown, did not have the luminous colour of his brothers and were hidden by his eyelids that turned up at the sides, giving him a slightly Asian look. His strength was carefully controlled and nobody wanted to test it. They knew it was there and that was enough, and to his younger brother he was a god. When his older brothers came to visit in the evenings, he listened and rarely contributed to the conversation, just enjoying their presence.

True to his nature of not wanting to attract attention to himself, he brought the first girl home to meet his mother, not as a girlfriend but as his wife.

Yvette was a beautiful young girl. Her olive skin had a feint blush to the cheeks much like Joe had, and her long black hair, combined with her slim figure, made many young men seek her attention. Her brothers were naturally protective towards her, and each suitor was scrutinised and tested, and usually declared, as not suitable. And still they came to seek her out and offer proposals, one after the other.

He was handsome with curly black hair, and a twinkle in his eyes that caused little lights to dance, and his smile was pure bliss, and yes, the pencil thin moustache, was also there.

He was definitely not recommended, and in fact, was most vehemently rejected by the family, as totally unsuitable and from the wrong family.

No, no, no, they said, and what about her? Yes, she said, he was the man she wanted. Yes, she knew they did not approve, and yes, she would elope with him if she had to. She loved him and that was all that mattered, so they got married and he took her away to his parents' house not far away.

Youngest of the bunch, and never knowing the love of a father, having instead many father figures, giving him orders and looking after him, his whole world was centred round his mother. She was his sun, and he loved her with a passion. Not excelling in school like his brother Jimmy, he focussed instead on sport. First it was boxing, where his eldest brother David showed a keen interest for his achievements, pushing him to limits that were sometimes unbearable. He loved being in the ring with a good opponent, and what he lacked in strength, he made up in heart and prided himself that he could not be put down, and no opponent was feared no matter his strength or size. When a boxing match left him severely battered and bruised, his brother David went with him to explain to their mother why he looked the way he did. His mother, when she saw the state he was in, stopped him going back for fear of permanent damage. It was rugby in high school where he felt most at home. Although he was neither tall nor well built, his speed and agility secured a position for him in the school's first rugby team. Blessed with a heart that did not recognise fear he drove through the pack with the ball firmly in his grasp, brushing his opponents aside with his other hand. Olive skinned, with the biggest brown eyes one could imagine that gave off a luminous glow, and eyelashes that were totally wasted on a male, made him very popular with the girls in school. His black, oiled hair was combed into a ducks' tail at the back of his head with the front carefully coifed complimenting his appearance. The other thing he enjoyed besides rugby and girls was nice clothes. The total combination was very pleasing to the eye. He was popular not only with the girls, but had many good friends. Sadly those same girls drove him to distraction from the sport he loved. At sixteen he left school to work in the furniture factory where his brother Johnny managed to get him an apprenticeship as a cabinetmaker. He worked two years of agony in cabinet making, hating most of it, and looked for a way out. With the help of his brother Jimmy, he changed to engineering as a machinist starting his training all over again. He was happier even though Jimmy was in many ways, worse to work with than his older brother Johnny, who he had found to be a tyrant at work. Many were the days that he complained to his mother when he returned from work, but her only advice was to keep quiet, and learn as much as he could from his brother. He knew she was right and endured the daily pain of working with his brother knowing that he had no choice if he wanted to achieve any worthwhile career.

Chapter Twenty-four

On a day, like many others, found Yvette crying in the bedroom that she shared with her husband and baby, in the home of her in laws. She was by herself, not daring to show any discontent when anyone was with her.

Not only was the baby crying all night long, but she was left alone at home again, as always. Her husband had a job that took him away most days and nights as well. A well paid job, on some days, and not so good on others. It was horse racing on race days and cards in the clubs at night. Oh, he was good! Everyone knew that. In fact, he was a professional at the game of gambling. So some days he was in a good mood and others not so good. Did she dare to say anything? Would a good wife do that? She did try once or twice but the result was such a disaster that she rather said nothing at all, and she did love him very much, which was also a problem of a kind, with him liking women, the way he did. Her unhappiness was kept to herself mostly, not daring to complain to her mother, who would have told her to be a good wife, which she was. She cleaned the house they shared with his parents, and cooked, and made sure his clothes were washed, and looked after the baby who just kept crying all the time. When she could take it no longer, she sent a message to her mother, who went with David to see what could be done to help her. Yvette and Badwa with their baby came to stay in the small house next to Manouchs' house that consisted of two rooms and a small kitchen with no stove and no bathroom, but they were content. Here they could be alone together, building their family.

Cooking was what Badwa loved to do more than anything, except for gambling of course, and now there was a man in the kitchen again, with the gift of turning anything into a gourmet meal.

Manouch sat at the table once again, enjoying the company, while the children played nearby. She was content hearing the children crying and playing together with Alfred shouting at them when they were naughty. To her, these were the sounds of life, and she sighed as she though of the times when her own children, were small.

It was still dark one morning when Manaouch was woken up. It was not so much the noise coming from the kitchen, but the aroma of meat grilling on an open flame that woke her. She smiled to herself. He must have won, she thought, as she lay for a while with her eyes closed. It was always like this. If he won, he brought a fresh lamb from the market just like Salem used to do, and made breakfast for them no matter what the hour. If he lost, his mood was foul and he went to sleep until it was time to get ready for the horse racing. Manouch knew he was not an ideal husband for her daughter, but she liked him even so, besides he never treated her without respect, which although she knew was the right thing to do but she appreciated it nevertheless.

She never interfered when there was an argument between husband and wife, and always stood up for him no matter what. After all a good wife, should always respect and listen, to her husband. Yvette did love him and her mother had explained to her that if the moon is yellow and your husband says its pink, you agree with him, because he is the man in the house and he must be respected at all times.

Manouch dressed slowly and then went to the kitchen where laughter met her.

The table was already laid out with a wooden board in the centre, on which small pieces of meat were still sizzling, straight from the open flame on the stove. Next to the meat, freshly cut chillies were on the side, with little heaps of salt and fine black pepper and fresh Lebanese bread. She smiled when she saw the pile of notes lying on the step. She knew this would be counted after everyone had eaten, so she first went to the bathroom at the other end of the kitchen to wash, before returning to sit at the table where a plate was already laid for her. Yvette brought her tea and just like that, she was absorbed in the joy of her family.

Chapter Twenty-five

When he came into the room, Manouch smiled at her son. He was her baby, although no longer a baby, but a young man. His light grey speckled jacket was fashionably long with padded shoulders, and the charcoal trouser, pressed to a fine edge, hung loose from his waist and narrowed to the bottom. The collar of his charcoal shirt stood straight at the back of his neck and his black hair was oiled and combed in a coif. Black patent leather shoes with white tips, completed his outfit. There was no doubt that he was good looking, that was for sure. She knew he always had girls with him, although he never brought anyone home to meet her. He was young and had no inclination for a permanent partner as yet, enjoying his life.

Trouble was always just around the corner when he was nearby, and he had to be bailed out more than once, by his brothers.

'Be careful, stay out of trouble.'

'Mommy, you know I will, stop worrying.'

'Don't be late. I will wait for you.'

'I know you will, but it won't be early.'

'Don't get into any trouble, promise me.'

Instead he leaned over and kissed the top of her head and left.

It was a short walk to the station where he waited for a train to take him into town. Town, meant Johannesburg, where everything was happening.

It was a Saturday and the long awaited movie was starting at the Plaza theatre not far from the railway station, close to the centre of town, so everyone made use of trains to get where they wanted to be.

Crowds of teenagers filled the pavements close to the theatre, with the local police having a hard time to keep them off the road where cars made swishing noises as they drove past. The hum of voices rising from the crowd was palpable, as every new arrival was sucked into the heart of the mass of people. The boys, all without fail, had hair swept to the back with their fringes coifed. Some had jackets on and some had tight tee shirts showing off their muscled arms, while some wore black tight trousers with leather jackets filled with studs. Girls had either wide skirts with starched petticoats and a wide belt around their waists, or tight cropped pants also with wide belts, showing off their figures. Most girls had soft flat shoes on, almost like a ballet shoe. And while some girls had their hair falling to their shoulders it was mostly ponytails that flipped back and forth as they moved their heads from side to side. The era of enlightened youth had arrived, and it was plain scary. Where parents had the power to quell their teenagers before, they were now faced with a dilemma where their children had a will of their own. A new breed of youngsters emerged from the staid and reserved forties. When the music was first played on the radio, an outcry of banning immediately went out. What on earth possessed the radio stations to play such music? But a new dawn and a new breed could not be stopped, as boundaries of music performers, broke through the narrow confines of controlled airing. It was bigger, much bigger, and it swept the youth into a crescendo, as the outcry from the prim and proper, was lost in the frenzy.

Today was the opening matinee of the film making waves all over the world, and it was called 'Rock Around The Clock.' Young people started arriving from early morning, to make sure they got a ticket to the show.

He was greeted from all sides as he approached, and was quickly absorbed into the mass of bodies. Smiling, he greeted friends as he made his way to his cousins, who he spotted at the far side. Joe and his brother Paulie, stood nonchalantly against a wall smoking, and greeted him with a smile. It was still early, and the ticket booth had not opened yet, so they just stood around waiting, checking out the girls around them. They made a good looking trio, and girls watched them covertly waiting for some kind of recognition. Well known among the young people, their reputations, for pretty girls, preceded them. A look of interest, and a quick wink, was all that was needed to entice a girl away from her partner, if she was with one, and the pretty ones usually were. There was just something about these cousins that the girls could not resist. The fact that they were Lebanese, was a contributing factor, and gave them some kind of a mysterious attraction, setting them apart from the boring crowd. While the girls were intrigued, the young men who were with them, carefully watched in case they had to step in to look after their girl friends. And still the crowd increased until everyone was practically standing up against each other.

Police vans were parked at strategic points in case the crowd of young people got out of hand, but so far, everything was still under control, and they relaxed while talking to their colleagues.

* * *

It felt like someone behind him tried to put his or her hand into the back pocket of his trousers, and his reflexes were instant as he swung around and hit the person, who he saw was a man, just before his fist connected. That was all it took, as bedlam broke out. It was as if the gates to a boxing arena had opened to a free for all, and it caught the police off guard. Fighting whoever was nearest, not caring who they were, boys and girls screaming and shouting and swearing, made the crowd more excited.

As the fighting snowballed, sirens filled the air and policemen started running with batons in their hands, hitting the youngsters left and right.

Traffic was jammed in the street, making it difficult for the police vans to get closer, and it was only the centre of the road where the trams ran on steel rails, that were clear, and then he saw a rattling tram approaching, and once again his reflexes kicked in, as he ducked below a group fighting with each other, and jumped on to the step of the moving tram. He hung onto the handrail with his jacket flapping in the wind, and looked back at the carnage he had started. His heart raced in his chest, as he made his way to an empty seat and sat down. Slowly he made the sign of the cross by touching his forehead, and then the centre of his chest, left shoulder then right shoulder, and then his lips. It took a while for his heart to get to a slower beat, and then he smiled to himself.

'Are you all right young man?' The old lady behind him leaned forward, and he turned to her, still smiling.

'Yes thank you mam, never better.'

She shook her head and sat back in her seat. What a nice young man not like those hooligans she saw fighting back there as the tram passed.

What she did not see was the grin spreading on his face as he took a packet of cigarettes from his pocket and lit one, heaving a sigh of relief.

* * *

Manouch was happy to see him home early, and when Phillip came to visit later, it was even better.

Front page, news the next day, showed pictures of the crowd getting out of hand in the street in front of the theatre. 'Police used fire hoses to quell the crowd of youths. Banning of film called for. Many arrested.'

Yes! Trouble was his second name, and he smiled as he put the newspaper down, after he read the headlines where he sat in the café. Well, lucky he was not there, he could have been hurt or arrested even, you never knew.

Then he wondered how Joe and Paulie were, and if he should go around to check on them.

* * *

Days were for working, and nights were for going out, and weekends? Well anything could happen on a weekend, after all, this was the time of revolution for young people. Gone were the days of oppression and total parental control. This was a new dawn, and anything and everything, even when not allowed, was done anyway. And it was time to cash in.

The old warehouse was on the top floor of a department store and offered plenty of parking in the street below at night when the store was closed. The train station also made it ideal for youngsters from other towns to get there. Besides both his sons were musical and played the drums and his youngest son was a very good singer as were their cousins Joe and Paulie so the business was ideal. Anyone who knew anything made a plan to get there and business was booming.

* * *

Music blared from the lit up building next to the railway station. Cars and motorbikes were parked all over the roads and the pavements. There were people inside, and outside, and everywhere. Corner House, was well known to everyone, and being well placed right next to the railway station was easily accessible. Many of the youngsters who frequented the place were too young for a drivers licence or could not afford their own, car so made use of public transport if friends could not take them. Even though parents were mostly just scraping by and pocket money was limited, they found a way to be there on a Saturday night.

Not only did they come for dancing, which everyone enjoyed, but to meet other young people, and with a bit of luck, a fight could be thrown in just to make the night perfect.

Girls in particular, were on the menu. This was not where you went to find a wife or a husband, but rather to have a good time, and the place was pumping.

Quick to make the most of the present trend was Badeos' husband Dawood who everyone now called Dave, offering not only a venue of enjoyment, but a whole new level of entertainment. Bands playing 'rock 'n roll' music sprung up overnight, and talent was exploited to its fullest. They came from everywhere, in cars or on trains or motorbikes, or by whatever means they could, to be there where the action was.

And there were many groups, not really gangs but friends, who found security and pleasure in each other's company. Many were from neighbouring towns and supported each other whenever the need arose, which happened pretty much each weekend. These groups were easily distinguishable by the clothes they wore and the way they spoke.

There were those from 'Fitas,' a rough part of Johannesburg, with their tight black tee shirts, showing off their rippling muscles, and wide trouser bottoms, called floor sweepers. They were dangerous, with steel knuckledusters, in their pockets, and steel tips on their shoes and were best left alone. They usually kept to themselves, drinking and enjoying the evening with a girl on their lap. Outside their Harley motorbikes, some with sidecars attached, were parked in a line with someone always nearby keeping an eye on them.

There was the crowd from Boksburg, on the east rand, always ready, and looking for some action, but all these groups, paled against the Lebanese, who usually were not in a group preferring the company of a pretty girl on their arm, but would come together in an instant to help each other, if the need arose.

For anyone not knowing each one by sight, and thinking the other was alone and flexed their muscles, could have a result of enormous proportions facing him. But worse of all was when discord broke out among themselves, as no other groups liked to get involved when fighting took place within a group, and rarely if ever, gave a helping hand not wanting to take sides.

It was late on the warm Saturday night, and music was blaring out into the street below, when the fight broke out. The whole thing started when Norman was chatting to a pretty girl. He stood with a glass of brandy and coke in his hand, and turned his head as he heard someone call the girl. 'Stay' Norman said to her and he saw the uncertainty in her eyes. 'Stay, don't go to him.' She looked at the other man who was now walking towards them. The man was bigger than Norman and attractive and had an overpowering way with women that they found difficult to resist. Norman put his glass down on the counter and was ready when the man came near. The unexpected blow caught the man on his chin, making him stagger backwards. His brothers were there like a flash and knowing that support would soon be mobilised, dragged Norman outside between them and took him away from the noisy crowd to a quiet ally.

All this happened very fast and in a way that did not cause undue notice.

Norman never got home that night, and in the morning Manouch sent for Phillip and David.

On Sunday mornings town was quiet, and it was mostly churchgoers who were on the road.

First they went to the club where the jive session was held the night before, and found it locked with nobody around. Only one car was parked in the street. They knew the car, and fear gripped their hearts as they began their search.

They scoured the whole area, but did not find Norman, and got back into their car, to go to their cousin's house, to see if they knew where he was.

As they turned into the main street of the town, they saw him. Stripped naked and fastened to a pole. Blood had dried on his face and battered body, and his head was resting on his chest. They both panicked, and David was out of the car before it came to a standstill, and ran to his brother. Phillip was quick on his heels.

Relief washed over them when they saw he was alive, and they quickly untied him from the pole. Between them they carried him to the car and took him home to his mother who was waiting anxiously for news.

Gently they lay his bruised body on the bed and Finnie ran to get a basin with warm water and a cloth to wipe him down. Yvette brought a glass of water and held his head up, to let him drink. The liquid stung his broken lips, and ran down his chin, as he tried in vain to swallow. She covered him with a blanket, and left the room, not wanting her family to see the tears in her eyes, as she looked at her brother's battered body.

She was worried for her mother and what this could do to her.

Yes he was trouble with a capital T.

Chapter Twenty-six

Life went on in the household as before. Nothing changed as old wounds faded and Finnie and Yvette had turns with cooking, with Badwa taking over when he was home. The grandchildren were getting bigger, and naughtier, and the yard was still filled with customers, enjoying a social drink.

Alfred went about his tasks in his own way, now looking after the grandchildren.

His hair now consisted of tight white curls on the sides of his head, with a bald patch from his forehead down to the back of his head. There were also some teeth missing from his mouth, but this did not seem to worry him. His feet were leathery and crunched up like dry prunes, and a light mist covered his eyes, but the smile was always there. He faithfully rolled out his blanket at night in front of the stove where it was warm, and ate his baked food late, when everyone was in bed. This was his family, this was where he belonged, and here he was happy, especially when the brothers came to visit their mother. He knew they always came to him in the kitchen just to talk. He listened carefully to what they said, and although his words were few, they usually found their mark.

'Alfred, why did you not leave me some potatoes? You know I like them.'

'When you pay me what you owe me I will keep you some. Where is your wife, why don't you bring the children?'

It was always like that, and each basked in the others' presence.

Whenever she could Manouch still went to a bioscope. She loved watching most anything. If it was funny, she laughed wholeheartedly, and although it was in English, or sometimes in Afrikaans, she followed the story easily. This was where she escaped to whenever she could, walking briskly into town where the theatres were with one or two children in tow.

Her family, as diverse as they were, were her lifeblood, and she was, as always, an integral part of their lives. Sundays her sons usually came and brought their wives and children with them. In the evenings, after work they also sometimes dropped by, and then did not stay long, except if they came later in the evening with their wives who then helped Finnie in the kitchen, making strong tea with hot milk, which they served on big trays. Not all of them came together at the same time of course. Phillip was there as often as he could be, and David popped in occasionally for a short while during the day and always on a Sunday. Dawood usually on his own came in the evenings when Jimmy was there with his wife. Finnie was always there as was Yvette, and Norman who went out later.

They all loved this time together laughing and joking and sometimes discussing their problems with each other. Manouch never spoke much when her family was there except to reprimand them when the teasing got out of hand. Their voices felt to her like a warm drizzle on a hot day and she tried to keep them longer when they prepared to leave.

The grandchildren were usually running about if it was not too late, so the house was always busy and this was how Manouch liked it.

She was still attractive, her hair now grey, was always freshly washed and rinsed in washing blue, softening the grey, and her body although fuller, was always neatly dressed.

On her feet were soft felt slippers, with shiny pom-poms.

When sugar diabetes was diagnosed years before, the children kept a careful watch on her diet and made sure her medicines were taken as prescribed. Manouch was not really concerned about this and went about her tasks as she always did.

Saturdays were always busy. Crates of beer were delivered early in the day by their connection supplying them, and the yard was abuzz from early in the morning, till late afternoon.

The accident happened on such a Saturday afternoon while they were busy moving around to help the clients.

It was just after payday, and the men in the yard were in a good mood, singing and joking. Finnie worked at the nearby vegetable shop on Saturdays, and was paid with fresh produce, which Manouch shared out among the children. The vegetable garden, that Salem tended to so carefully, was now left fallow, since that terrible day that was never spoken about. Phillip was there on that Saturday, and was helping Lizzie and Alfred to serve the men in the yard. Manouch, although not directly involved in the selling, having a record already for that offence, was only helping in the background. When the brandy bottle was empty Phillip called to his mother to fetch another one from the hiding place. She brought the bottle and put it on the table so she could ease the cork out with her thumb, a task she had performed many times before. She bent forward just as the cork shot out of the narrow neck of the bottle, straight into her eye. The force of it blinded her, and she screamed before grabbing at her eye. Phillip heard her cry and ran towards her, calling for Lizzie to come and help, leaving Alfred to look after the customers. Alfred had also heard the scream, causing his heart to lurch, and although he wanted to be there, he knew he had to stay.

Between Phillip and Lizzie, they helped Manouch to the bedroom, where they lay her on the bed. When Phillip gently removed his mothers' hand covering her eye, his own filled with shock. The whole eye was covered in blood. 'Lizzie, look after her, I am going to phone the doctor.'

When he got back to the room, he told Lizzie to fetch a bowl of cold water, and a clean cloth, and then to go and help Alfred, while he waited for the doctor to come.

* * *

After he put a sterile dressing over her eye, the doctor sat down and wrote a note that he gave to Phillip. 'The injection I gave her will make her sleep for a while. This is a letter to an eye specialist. I will go to the office where I have the number and let you know when you can take her.

It is urgent, but I have to first speak to him.'

'When do you think it will be doctor?'

'Tomorrow if possible, otherwise Monday, but I will telephone you with the details. Better get hold of David and your other brothers and sisters as soon as possible.'

Phillip sat on the chair next to the bed where his mother was sleeping and the muted sounds coming from the kitchen sounded very far away, almost like a dream. He took a blanket from the cupboard and covered her sleeping body then he closed the door and went into the lounge where the other telephone was. When he completed the last call, he went to the kitchen where he knew Alfred and Lizzie were waiting anxiously for news.

* * *

Four of them were with Manouch when they arrived at the specialist the next day.

David, the eldest with his brother Buddy, and Yvette with her husband Badwa.

David went into the consulting room with his mother, while the others waited out in the reception area. David explained to the doctor what happened, and the doctor took Manouch by the arm to help her on to the examination chair, where a nurse was already waiting. David stayed with his mother while the doctor examined her. He did not allow any thoughts to take hold in his mind, not daring to think of anything. When the doctor completed his examination, he left Manouch on the chair where she sat with the nurse watching over her, and motioned to David to follow him, and closed the door behind them. He spoke to David as he closed the door wanting to prepare the family. 'The news is not good'. David looked straight into the doctor's eyes and what he saw there made him afraid.

There were only two chairs for visitors to sit on in the doctors' office so Buddy and Badwa stood behind the chairs while Yvette and David sat down.

After sitting down behind his desk the doctor looked at each one. His gaze spoke of strength and calmness and they knew what he was going to say was the only way to help their mother. Slowly they dropped their eyes and waited. 'There is no other choice, the whole eye is shattered and will have to be removed.' Tears fell onto Yvette's hands folded in her lap and she opened her bag to take out a hanky. It was Buddy who spoke first and his voice was hoarse. 'Is there nothing you can do to save the eye?'

'I am afraid not. We can, after a while, put in a glass eye but now we have to remove the eye so we can repair whatever damage we can. If we don't do this, the eye will continually bleed into the brain and she will die.'

David stood up 'I will go and speak to my mother.' He turned to Buddy and they both went into the other room. Yvette was sobbing now and Badwa put his hand on her shoulder. He was also close to tears.

It was his mother-in-law but he had grown to love her, and he knew she loved him also.

Chapter Twenty-seven

Like the other challenges in her life that Manouch had faced, she overcame this one as well, although it took longer, seeing her face in the mirror each day.

She knew it was only having the children around her that carried her through each day. Her sugar diabetes had escalated, even though, her diet, was closely checked by her children. It took a lot of willpower to make any plans at all. She lived for evening visits from her sons and sometimes their families, even though she hardly ever joined in their conversations. It was enough for her to have them with her. And the grandchildren, running around screaming and shouting during the day, was to her like the sound of a waterfall flowing from a crevice in a mountain, filling her with sounds of life. Was it her imagination or was the light getting dimmer? Shadows seemed to be everywhere and she had to concentrate to keep figures in focus. Well, she knew it was going to be difficult, and she just had to be patient.

* * *

They were all excited. Manouch was dressed and waited for Yvette and Badwa while they were getting dressed in their home. Finnie left earlier with Phillip and his wife, as did Norman. Manouch saw again how good looking Norman was all dressed up in the black suit that was hired by Buddy. There were going to be twelve groomsmen and twelve bridesmaids and the wedding party had to be there early so they could make sure all the arrangements were in place. Phillip was also a groomsman and was dressed exactly as his brother was, and all the other groomsmen. Jimmy declined the invitation hating the thought of being all dressed up.

He was unlike his brothers, and preferred instead to be on his own. Manouch even had her doubts whether he would show up at the wedding. That would be a pity, she thought to herself as she knew his wife enjoyed dressing up. Truth be told, she was always dressed in the best clothes and looked more like a film star than anything else. When Yvette walked in, Manouch was speechless. A special outfit was bought for this day and suited Yvette very well. She was beautiful without any doubt, and Manouch felt her heart swell with pride. If Salem could have been there, she knew he would feel the same seeing his children as she did.

The drive to the house was about thirty minutes away. Badwa was a skilled driver and she watched as he confidently chatted as he drove. Manouch sat in the front passenger seat and Yvette sat at the back. Whenever they took Manouch with them it was like that, although she often objected, they insisted. She was glad she was in the front today as they got nearer to the house. The spectacle reminded her of a Holywood movie set. Although the wedding was still hours away, traffic was blocked at both ends of the main road leading to the city hall. Badwa had to slow down and waited for the traffic controller to speak to him as he reached the front. 'Your name please sir.' When Badwa gave his name it was checked on a long list that the traffic controller had. When he found the name on the list he smiled, and waved to let Badwa through. Further along, another controller showed them to a place that had been reserved for them to park the car. There were people everywhere. To Manouch it looked like thousands, although she was sure it was less than that. She knew it was going to be grand, but this was much more than she had expected.

The property comprised a whole block. The house stood in the centre of the plot with wrap around verandas that were now decked with tables and chairs.

Tall trees in front of the house ensured a lovely cool area where more tables and chairs were. The whole setting was like a massive garden party, which in fact it was. Waiters moved around with laden trays of eats and drinks. The hum of people talking completely blocked out the music coming from speakers in the trees. It was impossible not be engulfed into the festive spirit.

Buddy had been waiting for his mother to arrive, and opened the car door for her as they stopped. 'Mommy, you look wonderful.' He hugged her briefly and kissed her on her cheek, thinking how soft her skin was. 'God be with you and your children today my son. May they be happy together for many years and have lots of babies.' He smiled at her and led her into the house where he had a comfortable chair ready for her.

They came to her where she sat, one by one, all her children and their wives and her grandchildren that were there, and her daughter-in-laws', family, and their family, and everyone else. Each one respectably asked about her health, and that of her family, after they kissed her cheek or held her hand. Plates piled with eats, were everywhere and drinks were carried about on big trays. This was a feast like no other before it.

Today her grandson was getting married. A young boy, only seventeen, and his bride even younger, were to be united.

On the brides' finger her engagement ring glittered as she moved her hand. The light bouncing off the massive diamond sent off shafts of sparks that dazzled ones' eyes. Oh! She was beautiful there was no doubt about that. Long blond hair fell down her back and her green eyes glistened like emeralds. If it looked as if the groom was a bit nervous, one could easily miss it, with all the glamour around.

Waiters dressed in black trousers, white shirts, black bow ties and white gloves, flitted in and out of the marquee set out in the garden. It was huge by any standard and two smaller ones were set up on the sides where a bar was erected in each. No costs were spared on this day and the festivities had not even begun.

More cars were arriving all the time and were shown to the parking lot at the back of the property. The guests arriving could have been mistaken for attending an Oscar presentation, as glitz and glamour was the order of the day.

Manouch felt her eye throbbing where a glass eye now covered the cavity that once held her own eye. She put her head back to rest it on the chair and closed her eyes. Yvette sitting nearby, saw the tiredness in her mothers' face and went to her. 'Mommy, would you like to lie down for a while? It is still going to be a while before they start.' Manouch opened her eyes and nodded gratefully. 'Wait here mommy I am going to find out where you can rest.' Manouch closed her eyes and rested her head on the back of the chair.

Most of the bedrooms were all full of people getting dressed or just sitting around, and Yvette looked everywhere for her sister-in-law, so she could ask her where Manouch could rest. When she found her, she was shown to a room towards the back of the house where a bed was, and she fetched her mom. Once Manouch was settled, Yvette closed he door and went back to the lounge where more people had gathered, and took a glass of cold drink filled with ice, from a waiter. She knew her husband would be in the yard where all the men were, so she settled herself next to a cousin on the couch, and relaxed.

* * *

The 'ululating' of women announced the bride was ready and everyone went outside to watch her approach. The retinue of twelve bridesmaids, groomsmen, best man, matron of honour, flower girls and ring bearer waited at the foot of the stairs leading up to the house.

The groom stood in the centre of the group, waiting for his bride to emerge.

Manouch, now rested, stood just outside the door where she had a good view of everything with Finnie holding her arm. Yvette had joined her husband and they waited to follow the wedding party.

The bride was beautiful there was no doubt about that. Her face glowed in the afternoon light and her designer dress flowed like a soft mist around her.

The lace bodice of the dress was encrusted with beads and diamantes and the train stretching out for twenty yards behind her was held up by six flower girls.

The men in the bridal party were each more handsome than the other, their black hair neatly oiled back. Their outfit of black suits, white shirts, black bow ties, and black patent leather shoes was finished off with white gloves.

The bridesmaids looked stunning in their layered, beaded dresses with their hair in curls tied up high with flowers. Each young woman looked more exotic than the other.

It took a while for the retinue to get into their right places and then the procession slowly started.

It was exactly four blocks to the city hall and the streets were lined from end to end with onlookers who had waited for hours for the bridal party to emerge. When they finally made their appearance, the people shouted and waved and whistled as their expectations were not disappointed.

Arm in arm groom and bride walked side by side. The bride carried a huge bouquet of white lilies and roses. The six flower girls holding up the train of the dress came next and then the maid of honour and the best man. Behind them, couple by couple of bridesmaid and groomsman followed. After the wedding party the grooms' parents came followed by the brides' parents and then uncles and aunts, and cousins and friends. When the bridal party reached their destination not even all the followers had started from the house.

Manouch did not join in the procession and went back to her chair in the lounge. After a while it became quieter, and she closed her eyes thinking back to when Buddy was just a small boy helping his father loading the cart. 'If only you can see your son now, Salem, you will be so proud.' Manouch now often found herself re-playing scenes of the time when Salem was still with them. Sometimes it became so real that she felt as if he was there with her.

And then, just like in a theatre, another screen opened for Manouch as the huge curtains on the stage parted. Instead of a happy scene with celebrations going on, it showed a figure all hunched up, as if in the most incredible pain, sitting on the floor of a bedroom. The woman had her arms wrapped about her body and she was rocking back and forth. It looked as if she was screaming, but the scene was silent as Manouch saw it. Then a door opened and a man appeared. He walked to the woman and tried to lift her up, but she grabbed his arms and pulled him down to the floor, where they held each other.

Manouch, her eyes still closed, experienced the pain that flowed from the two figures on the floor, as an even more painful scene enfolded on the screen.

A car stood on the concrete apron in the back yard of a big house, with the back passenger door open.

A man emerged from the door of the house with boxes in his arms, leaving the door of he house open behind him, and walked towards the car. Manouch saw him bend down placing the boxes on the back seat, and then he closed the door of the car. He did not see the toddler crawling out of the door of the house, as his back was towards the open door.

Then he walked back to the house, and shouted a greeting, although everything was in silent mode, and closed the door of the house.

The scene changed to the rear of the car, where the toddler was crawling on the ground, in between the back wheels of the car. The chubby little boy had a nappy on and his shirt was riding high leaving his little stomach open and a dummy was firmly clenched in his mouth.

Then the man opened the car door at the driver side, and climbed in. He started the car, released the hand brake, and looked in the rear view mirror to make sure everything was clear, before shifting the gear into reverse.

The bump was slight, but he quickly disengaged the gear and pulled the hand brake up and opened the car door leaving the engine running to see what he rode over, thinking it could be a toy.

It looked like a crumpled up doll lying in front of the back wheel of the car, but he knew instantly that it was not and he threw his hands into the air and howled like a wolf, all in silent mode. When he turned his head Manouch saw her son Buddy, looking down at his little boy on the ground, and she wished at that moment that she could rather bear his pain, as she saw him fall to the ground to pick up his son.

Manouch woke up with a start, and felt her cheeks were wet, where tears had run down. It took her a little while to focus, and to remember where she was. Her heart felt like a heavy stone, and she felt her breath was laboured, so she closed her eyes and hoped everything would change when she opened them again.

* * *

The likes of the celebration that took place that day, were never equalled in that town again, and those who watched went home with stories, that sounded more like fairytales.

Inside, the vast hall, was lavishly decorated. The bridal table was very long, and turned in on the sides, to accommodate the bridal party and the parents. The tables closest to the bridal party, were filled with dignitaries covering a spectrum of judges, mayors, magistrates and police commissioners, advocates, racehorse owners and trainers and the odd lawyer. This was no ordinary reception but one of recognition of each ones' importance. Manouch was also seated on the main table with the bridal party and parents and grandparents. She would stay until the dancing began and then leave. This was such a wonderful day for her son and his family and her heart filled with pride.

Later when everyone was relaxed from the good food and wine, the dancing started. Belly dancers dressed in sheer voluminous outfits with gold medallions around their hips entranced the people with their movements. There were also fire eaters, comedians and a magician who entertained the guests.

Afterwards the bridal couple took their first dance followed by their bridal party taking up the whole floor. Manouch was happy to see David approaching to take her home. She had enjoyed the day and was ready for bed.

The celebrations did not end there. In fact it went on for days afterwards, as well wishers, still went to the house, where they were lavishly entertained.

* * *

Chapter Twenty-eight

There were more shadows now than light for Manouch, as her other eye grew dimmer and dimmer. No, the doctor said, there was nothing they could do as the sugar diabetes took its toll. Total blindness was imminent, and it was only a matter of time before she would be engulfed by total darkness. Her children cried for her, and she did also when she was alone at night, and prayed instead for the end of her life to be sooner rather than later. She did not know how she could accept the fact that not only would she not be able to see her children and grandchildren, but would in fact be dependent on them for even the most simple of tasks.

When they came to visit, she looked at them intently, locking away their faces into her inner being. She stroked their faces to feel the contours of their bone structure, and traced their lips with her finger so she could feel the lines. She had no problem with their voices, knowing them from childhood, and she reminded herself how fortunate she was to have been able to see them for such a long time of their life.

Yes, it was going to be difficult, and yes, she was going to long to see their faces, and yes, she would have liked to see those grandchildren who she had not yet seen, and yes, she would survive even this. After all, her name is Manouch and with the help of God, The Almighty, she can overcome all obstacles placed before her.

When the morning came that she heard the clatter from the kitchen and the voices of the children, while all around her was total darkness, she did not cry out or panic, instead she lay quietly, and waited for one of her daughters to come to her.

* * *

Sundays were special days, and this one was no different from those before it, although in fact, it was marked as the first Sunday that they gathered and were not seen by their mother. She knew of course that they were there, and did not see the tears in their eyes. Instead, she laughed with them until they forgot that she could not see them. The one thing that did not change was the fact that Johnny came in the early afternoon with his family to visit his mother, and David came soon after they left, with his family. When and why this feud had its roots, nobody but themselves knew, and one wondered if they even remembered why it was like that. Manouch had on many previous occasions tried to get to the bottom of the situation, but was unable to, so she, like the others, just accepted the fact that, that was how it was, and left it at that.

Now, when her sons came to visit, they hugged her and held her hand for a short while or sometimes kissed her cheek. She in turn lifted her hand and gently touched their face. The wives did the same and for a while it was awkward but as time went by everyone accepted the situation. Manouch made her own way from room to room and down the step in the kitchen to the bathroom with Alfred always around to watch out for her.

He would quickly pick a child up if he thought she could trip, or check to see if the bathroom was unoccupied or not. When he put her tea in front of her, he gently took her hand with his gnarled fingers, to touch the cup. Instead of just putting a small plate of eats down for her, he explained to her what was on the plate making sure it was not near the edge of the table where it could be bumped off.

Mostly she sat and listened to the daily chatter and only spoke when spoken to. She felt isolated and apart from everyone. It was difficult at the beginning even though the children tried their utmost to keep her close to them. Darkness was her daily shroud and she depended on others to help her dress, to check if her hair was combed right or if her slippers matched, or anything at all, that was out of place.

And so, isolated in a cocoon of darkness, she played her own movies.

There were many to choose from and she usually chose at random.

Sometimes it was when the children were babies, and other times when they were more grown up, but whichever movie she chose she saw Salem in the background, either busy in his garden or loading the cart. A soft giggle sometimes escaped her lips, and if anyone was near, they always asked 'Why are you laughing Mommy?' 'Just something that happened long ago.' She would answer, and then they shook their head, and carried on with what they were doing.

* * *

Today it was Jimmy, their second youngest son, who came on the screen.

Stocky and muscular he had his arm around the waist of a pretty girl.

She was smartly dressed and the two of them looked happy. 'Mommy this is my wife.' She remembered how shocked she was, why did he not tell her before? She could have prepared a feast for the family. 'When did you get married?'

'Yesterday.' He answered.

'Why did you not tell us so we could have made a nice dinner?'

'Naw, we wanted to keep it small, but Dawood and Badeo knew about it.'

Manouch shook her head. She never really understood this son of hers. Completely different from the others, he shied away from family ties preferring to be on his own. 'Come here my girl, let me have a good look at you.' She was even prettier when she came nearer and Manouch saw the shine of happiness in her eyes.

'Jimmy, you look after your wife. Remember you will be watched.'

He grinned from ear to ear as he translated what his mother said to his new wife. 'You see, I told you it would not be so bad.'

Yvette and Finnie joined them when they heard his voice, and congratulated them when they heard what it was all about. Phillip came a bit later and then Norman, and later David, and before long, the table was filled with family and food, as laughter and joking among the brothers filled the room.

Alfred was introduced as well and it was obvious that Jimmy had prepared his wife to meet him, as she extended her hand to him in greeting.

Later when Jimmy and his wife left, the family digested the event. They were not surprised at anything he did, and were happy for him. They knew he did things in his own way, and it was better to get married than to be alone. Besides, she was very pleasant to look at. Would she fit in with their family was another matter, but they knew that they would slowly teach her their ways if she was willing to learn.

What kind of a family did she come from they did not know, and whether they would ever meet her family was not certain. The only wish they had was for Jimmy to be happy. Manouch smiled when she thought of that day.

True Jimmy often felt unnoticed in his big family, being far down in the pecking line, and Phillip and Joe so close to Manouch that he and Yvette, and even Finnie, felt as if they belonged to another family. They were the ones who looked after the youngest and their older siblings, were as if from another time altogether.

* * *

Yvette was crying where she was busy in the kitchen. She tried to do so softly not to upset her mother who was in the bedroom, and she succeeded until Manouch came into the kitchen. Her soft slippers made no noise on the wooden floorboards and Yvette was caught unawares.

'What is wrong Yvette, why are you crying?'

'Oh! Mommy, I did not hear you come in. There is something wrong with Raymond's one leg, I have to take him to the doctor.'

'What is wrong with him?'

'He is limping and cries with pain.' Yvette sobbed.

'When are you taking him?'

'I am waiting for Badwa and he is late as always. He makes me so mad when he does this.'

'Well, take it easy, don't upset yourself, I heard a car outside, it must be him.'

Yvette went to look and sighed with relief. Finally, he knows they have an appointment. 'Mommy, you will be all right, Phillip will be here later. If you need any help just call Alfred.'

'Go Yvette, don't worry about me.'

Manouch found her way to the chair at the table where she always sat, and called for Alfred to bring her some tea. She knew it was always a worry for the children to leave her, but they had problems of their own and sometimes they had no other choice. Well, Alfred was always there and Finnie and Lizzie will soon be back from the shops so there was nothing to worry about, or was there?

She drank the tea slowly as her thoughts drifted away. Finnie left early taking Lizzie with her to get some nice fresh fish. Manouch always worried about Finnie when she went on her own, knowing she could take a bad turn at any time, so Lizzie went with her just in case. Yvette and the children were usually at home and it was seldom that she was left on her own. She knew Phillip would come a little later and she saw his smiling face in front of her. He often smiled in his own special way where the ends of his mouth curled up like a frill of a collar, and her heart softened just thinking about him. He had the most beautiful little girl with black curls, that he absolutely doted on, and a new baby son. She knew he must be happy and she smiled.

'Mommy, why are you sitting so alone? Where is Yvette?'

Manouch was startled when she heard his voice and laughed. 'You gave me a fright Phillip. Yvette and Badwa took Raymond to the doctor. His leg is sore. How is the family?'

Phillip pulled out a chair to sit at the table and called Alfred for a cup of tea. 'How are you Old Man? Are you looking after mom?'

'Ag, you know I always look after her.' Phillip laughed and took Alfred's hand when he put the cup down, and kissed it. Alfred pulled his hand away but not before he felt the warm glow of love pass through him. This was one of his sons and he loved him.

Then Finnie and Lizzie arrived and the room was filled with noise and laughter and Manouch was happy.

* * *

It was a very worried couple that returned from the doctor with their child. Tests had showed that the one leg was in fact shorter than the other and callipers had to be made to support the leg which was, not only shorter, but was also thinner than the other.

'Mommy' Yvette cried, 'why did it have to be like this.'

'Shush, don't ever be ungrateful, it is God's way. Be happy they can do something for the boy.'

'I know Mommy, but how will he cope?'

'He will, don't worry, you will see.'

And her words were true as the boy, after being fitted with callipers, was soon running around. It was remarkable how the young adapted and this was just another obstacle that was not impossible to overcome.

True, the boy was spoiled, but who could blame them, when he was such a likeable child. He was always smiling and with his black curly hair and warm brown eyes, was loved by all.

Chapter Twenty-nine

Always ready with a smile and a good word, Manouch did not know what to say to help her son. How do you tell him that everything will be fine when you know that it won't be? How do you tell him not to worry if you know there is nothing anyone can do to help? Nobody can help him or his wife or their child, and as much as you believe in miracles, you know that it will probably not happen in this case. They knew their son was slow from the beginning and accepted that they had to be patient, and they were. Love was never in short supply and the boy was showered with this. There was always the hope that somehow the child would emerge from the cocoon that he was in like a butterfly, and be perfect.

Although she could not see him, she knew if she touched his face, his cheeks would be wet with tears. She put out her hand and he took it in his own. He sat like that holding his mothers' hand and he cried. She cried with him and this upset him even more. 'Mommy, don't cry. Don't upset yourself. I don't want you to get ill.'

'My tears are for you and your wife, not for myself. I know it is hard but you must listen to the doctor.'

'How can we just give our child away mommy?'

'You will not be giving him away, but putting him in a place where he can be cared for in a way that you or your wife can not.'

Alfred put two cups of tea on the table. He took her hand from Phillip and brought it to the cup so she knew where it was. 'This is enough now the two of you. Drink your tea before it gets cold.'

After he finished his tea Phillip left and Manouch waited untill she heard the car door close, before taking the rosary from her apron pocket and silently went through the decades. She did not know how much pain she was meant to endure, and each time the weight became heavier. She sighed and for a moment forgot where she was with her prayers. Please God let the child in the mother's womb, soon to be born, be normal. She said this prayer many times through the day as she sat silently at the kitchen table, and even at night when she was in her bed. She never expressed her fears to her children knowing it may upset them, and smiled when they were near, but in her heart, the fear lurked like a monster ready to pounce.

* * *

Looking at the pinched little face, wrapped tightly in a blanket in his mothers' arms, hope rose like a phoenix and filled the fathers' heart. He was going be just fine, and he knew nothing would persuade him to believe otherwise.

This was going to be the son that he always longed for.

* * *

When they put the baby in her arms, Manouch lifted the little bundle up to her face. The smell of a newborn baby always made her happy. She hugged him to her breast and blessed him while laughter filled the room as her family chatted to each other. There was a festive feeling all around as dishes laden with food were placed on the table. Oh! What a joy she thought, to have your family around you.

Holding the baby in her arms she thought again of the day Phillip came home dressed in his army uniform. She had to control the laughter that welled up in her.

'Mommy, why are you laughing?'

'I am just happy to have you all with me' she answered Phillip. He gently took the baby from her.

Manouch raised her hand and blessed the child now in his fathers' arms.

When they left and the kitchen became quiet, Manouch again took the rosary from her pocket, and prayed as her fingers counted the beads.

*   *   *

'He is so gorgeous Mommy. I think he looks just like his father.'

'Yvette, bring me some water, I am very thirsty.' They were used to talking in this way. Manouch said one thing, and Yvette another, each one understanding exactly what the other said. Much later a remark would be made regarding the earlier statement and they would then either respond or even leave it for the next day. With Finnie it was different. She expected a response immediately and even badgered the person she was speaking to for an answer. This was how they were. Alfred again, usually made a statement and never expected an answer, knowing that his words were not taken lightly.

Sometimes he walked so softly on his bare feet that no one even knew he was there.

Silently he listened to their conversations not to pry, but to think about their problems so he could, when the opportunity presented itself, give them sound advice if they asked him. Sometimes he sat on the raised step in the kitchen for hours not saying a word, and at times even fell asleep sitting upright. Nobody took notice or objected, accepting him always, as a part of the family. If he was needed, he was there instantly. When he was not around, they worried and looked for him.

Now Alfred waited until he saw Manouch return the rosary to her pocket, before he spoke. 'What did the doctor say about the baby?'

'Later on he will do some tests.'

'Why? Are they worried about him?'

Manouch relied on others to be her eyes and so she always asked if there was anything they should tell her. 'How does he look to you Alfred?'

He gave no answer and got up and went outside.

Manouch thought about his words, knowing he did not say anything without reason, and made a mental note to speak to Yvette when she got back.

*   *   *

Of all the days in the week Manouch loved Sundays the most. From early in the morning the kitchen was like a beehive. If Badwa was home he usually took charge, otherwise Yvette and Finnie did the cooking. Lizzie was also there, rinsing the vegetables and preparing the basins, to mix the salads in and to clear up afterwards. By late morning, lunch was ready and the table set.

Whoever was visiting was automatically included in the meal. Before the grownups ate the children were fed so everyone ate and sat around chatting. Later in the afternoon, Johnny complete with wife and children, would visit. This was the only time they ever sat in the lounge, and bowls of olives and feta cheese with Lebanese bread was laid out and small cups of sweet Turkish coffee for the men and strong tea with hot milk for the women was served.

Much later, after Johnny and his family left, David and his family came.

David's first marriage did not last long and this was his second family. Manouch was happy for him, he had a good wife who understood his ways and made a comfortable home for him. They had four children and expected another soon. Jimmy and his wife usually came early, and at times, had their two small children with them. They did not always bring the children, preferring to leave them at home with her parents, whom they were sharing a home with. Yvette and her children were there and Finnie, and Phillip of course, and sometimes Norman. Oh yes! Sundays were by far the best days leaving Manouch relaxed and tired when evening came. Dawood rarely came on Sundays preferring to be at his own home where there were friends and family who could join him and his wife with food and drink. He enjoyed a more rowdy crowd who sat with him under the shady tree in his garden while his wife brought platters of food. These parties often erupted in arguments that Manouch only heard of afterwards and she usually paid little attention to this preferring his visits during the week when no drinking took place.

Sleep came quickly on Sundays after a busy day, leaving her content having her family around her. She knew they were blessed and thanked God at every chance she got.

* * *

They watched the new baby as he grew bigger and waited for him to reach the normal progress of sitting and crawling, and they waited and waited, and waited. And so with a heavy heart they took their second son to the doctor. When the final tests were complete, the result was the same as with their older son. Even though they had expected the outcome, their pain was almost unendurable. They cooed to the baby, and now and again, saw a flicker in his eyes and then their hearts would fill with hope. Doctors can be wrong everyone knew that, besides it would only mean that he would be slower than other children. They had to believe that a miracle would happen this time, and so candles were lit, and novenas were prayed.

A mothers' heart mourns for the pain of her children, willing if she could, to bear it for them. Even though Manouch did not see their faces she felt their pain, and tried to comfort her son and his wife. 'God is Almighty, my children. He knows why it is like it is, we have to trust him.' 'Mommy it is so hard to accept it.'

'I know, but you have to.'

'How can we let them go?'

'For their own good.' She replied.

'How do we know they will look after them?'

'Because they are trained to look after Gods' angels.' They cried and she cried with them.

Depression is an unseen steel box that entombs your very soul. How does one smile and talk to people when you are in a black hole? How does one even manage to live each day?

I am his mother and he is my son and we all, his brothers and sisters and in-laws and of course most of all Alfred, give our total support and unconditional love.

We went with them, David Yvette and myself, to take their eldest son to a place where children like him would be taken care of. Their agony was too sad to even describe. We held them close to us as they cried uncontrollably and knew that in a few short weeks we were going to have to do the same as the younger son was going to be given over for special care at another place. We tried to keep the brothers together but that was not possible.

If the first handing over of a child was traumatic, the second was unbearable. The parents of the boys, sunk into an abyss of pain and agony, until the family took them to the sea for a change of environment where they could breathe the crisp air and learn to smile again.

When they returned home, Phillip packed his bag, and left to stay on his own.

His wife, although hurt and fragile, understood why he had to go, and knew that he would one day return to her, and she would wait for that day.

Phillip now seldom went to visit his mother, and it was only when she kept telephoning him that he did go. He never stayed for long, not wanting to talk to any of his brothers or sisters, as he grieved for the sons he would never see growing up. When he saw the children of his siblings, it was more than he could bear. His daughter, thank God, was growing up nicely, and when he saw her on his infrequent visits, he was touched by her love for him. And his wife, always understanding his feelings, never made him feel as if he had abandoned them, believing her love was strong enough for both of them.

* * *

A long time passed before Phillip did eventually go back home and his family members were all happy for him. A man needed his wife and family. Before long, they expected another baby and everyone was happy for them.

When she was born, a mop of black hair encircled her little face, all pink and pinched up, and the parents, as everyone else, were relieved that it was a girl, and they smiled wherever they went. They dressed her in beautiful little dresses like a princess. She gave them much pleasure, and one could actually feel the love radiating from them. So cute, one just wanted to eat her up, and when they took her to Manouch she held the baby and nuzzled the little body smelling the baby smell she loved so much. They laughed and chatted and were content.

It was at a general visit to the doctor when he picked up that something was not quite as it should be. He said he wanted to do some tests to make sure everything was in order and they were not unduly concerned but even so was nervous waiting for the outcome.

When the results came, they were devastated. Not as severe as the boys, but definitely retarded. They looked at their little girl and they cooed and smiled and she smiled back. Doctors can make mistakes and they believed that such a mistake had been made. She was a beautiful little girl, and reminded them of their firstborn daughter, who was perfectly fine. When she gurgled and laughed, their hearts nearly burst with love. One thing, they were certain about, was the fact that they would keep her with them, no matter what, and care for her as if she was perfect. In many ways, for them, she was perfect, and even though it took a lot of energy and constant supervision, they marvelled in her progress no matter how slow.

While the mother gave her two daughters all the attention she could, Phillip became more distant, and then when he could stand it no longer, he left again. Nobody knew exactly where he went to, and he always made a plan to visit or telephone his mother, but he was not easy to find.

For Manouch his visits, now rare, were precious, and she stored his presence in her inner being, to tap on when the longing grew too much.

Sometimes, out of the blue he would visit his wife and children making it clear that he was not there to stay. There were no accusations or confrontations and tears welled in their eyes when he left. His own tears only fell when he was alone.

Part Three

Chapter Thirty

Hot sun baked on the sand where I lay on the beach working on my tan.

I know it was getting there because my skin was tingling from the sun burning on it, and the looks from the young men around me, confirmed it. The orange and brown full piece bathing costume fitted like a glove and sun streaks in my light brown hair pulled back in a ponytail, shone brightly. My parents left me at the beach earlier so I could enjoy the sun, while they took the younger children to another beach further along the coastline. I preferred this beach where all the action was. Talent was everywhere and everyone who knew anyone, met at the restaurant on the beach, where I was also going to later on.

The boys usually arrived later in the day after sleeping off their late nights, so I waited until I knew they would be there. Durban was the only place to be in December, and plans to meet were made by all those who could find a way to get there for the holidays. Anyway, I had made plans to meet someone there whom I had met a while ago.

Not that we were a couple or anything, really only friends who went out together in a group at times, but we enjoyed each others' company in a non serious way. When I first met him at a jive session, I was oblivious of the fact that he was the key to my whole future. He himself also did not know this of course, as fate played its hand. The fact that he was Lebanese was the key to the door. Not that his origin meant anything to me. I did not even know that such a country existed till then.

It was a happy group who met later that afternoon, first spending time in the waves, with the guys swimming too far out, and the girls staying in the shallow water.

It was good fun, and later we all sat at the restaurant and sipped our cool drinks soaking up the sun, and making plans for the evening.

Arrangements were made to meet again later that evening when we would all go to a party that someone had heard of. When my parents picked me up later in the afternoon, I told them about the evening arrangements. They were not keen to let me go, but nevertheless, dropped me off again later that evening, and waited till they saw my friends arrive, before leaving.

We were a big crowd, and some of them I did not know till later. There were two girls that I had never seen before, and the one in particular stood out. To me she was the most beautiful girl I had ever seen. She was taller than I was, and slender with longish black hair and light olive skin, with dark brown eyes that shone out of long black eyelashes. Her eyes were enhanced with black khole, and she had a beauty spot above her one lip, which I thought made her look like a movie star. Little did I know, that she was the next link to my own future.

Antoinette and I became friends and we met on Saturday afternoons with the crowd of young people we both knew. A month later she invited me to her home for a weekend where she lived in the adjoining town to the east.

There I met her family, parents, brothers and sisters, and later cousins as well. We were going to a jive session organized by another Lebanese family who stayed on a large old estate in the heart of a mining community.

Her younger brother, whom I had gotten to know from stage appearances at the local roadhouse where all young hopefuls showed off their talents, in whatever they were good at like playing musical instruments or singing, performed. Tall and slim like his sister, he had the most charming manner about him, and we liked each other from the onset. Not much older than I was, it was purely a feeling of friendship, and we felt comfortable in each other's presence. We had a lot of fun as he took us with his car, the smallest I had ever seen, to the event. He was the drummer in the band performing that night, and his music equipment, was taken there earlier by someone else, seeing his car was so small.

He also had a beautiful voice and sang as well.

What I saw when we arived was a typical mining residence with a corrugated iron roof and a big veranda. On a concrete area, which could have been a tennis court years gone by, lights were strung on wires high above, and the band was set up in one corner. It looked brilliant, and I could not wait for the dancing to begin, but first I was introduced to the hosts. We met in their lounge and the first thing I saw was a life size, cut out board on a stand, of a boxer with a heavy gold belt around his waist. Trophies were displayed on shelves erected on the walls right around the room. Impressed, I asked about the display, and was told it was their son, when he was a boxing champion of the world. They were obviously very proud of him, and they smiled a lot when they spoke of him and if there was a little sadness in their smile I did not pick it up. It was many years later that I learned how a cracker fired on a 'Guy Fawkes' night had ended his career as a boxer when a cracker blew up in his face.

The evening, turned out wonderful, and later when the band was packed up, we went home. The day before when I had arrived, my friends' mom had prepared a special traditional dish of small mince filled round flour discs covered in a sour sauce which became another important token in the plan of the universe which I knew nothing about.

A small helping was dished up for me to taste, which I did not enjoy, and amid laughter from them, they gave me something else instead, which was more to my taste. My friend told me it was one of their favourite meals and they had let her uncle know that a helping would be kept for him.

It was late when we got up the next morning and had breakfast. A lazy day stretched before us and we just sat around. Later that afternoon, both her brothers, and the two of us, went next door to her cousin's house. I had met them previously at jive sessions, so we knew each other. A lot of laughing and joking went on and a while later they went to make a snack to eat. When they returned and put the dish on the centre table, I had one of the weirdest feelings that I had ever had, and knew I would always remember it. Little did I know it would be the first of many new experiences that I would have.

Shock registered on my face, and they burst out laughing, as I looked at the plate piled high with absolutely raw pieces of meat cut into squares. Next to it they placed a small side plate with salt and pepper in little heaps and another small plate with cut up chillies as well as a few of the round flat breads that I had eaten with my meal the night before. I never said a word and holding up my breath, watched as they took a piece of bread and filled it with the raw meat and actually ate it. When one of them spoke, I felt a shiver run down my spine.

His face was serious, as were the others.

'After this, it's your turn.'

I did not know if I should laugh, or try to leave, so said nothing, even when they burst out laughing. I was worried as I saw them take piece after piece of the raw meat, with a torn piece of the flat bread, with salt and pepper and chillies. What was I to believe? Did they specially invite me to kill me? Flashes of a story I had read years ago, from a Readers Digest magazine about a woman, who advertised for a husband and then, when they were asleep, killed them, and made sausage from their cut up bodies, made me wary. Did I even dare to sleep that night? I laughed, but it sounded hollow to me, and I knew that I would be very careful just in case. I was happy when we went back to her house but did not say so.

A while later another visitor arrived.

Her mother's brother was the youngest of that family, and many years were between her mother, and brother. To me he looked old with his black hair and olive skin that looked quite pale. It was almost as if he never went out in the sunlight. He ate his favourite dish, which had been kept for him, in the kitchen, and then joined us in the lounge. The three of us, Antoinette her sister and I, had planned to go to the lake where the carnival was stationed for their final weekend, and she asked her uncle if he could give us a lift in his car.

He was not keen and said so, but Antoinette persevered till he agreed. His car was brand new, which immediately set him above the guys that I went out with, who mostly had motorbikes or really old run down cars. Antoinette sat in the front with him, and her sister and I sat in the back. I had a good view of his profile and was not impressed at all. He seemed so old and staid, and I wondered again about the paleness of his skin. And then he said something really funny.

'If I tell you to duck down you must. I had to meet my girlfriend and I don't want her to see I have girls in the car.'

I giggled at the weirdness of his request and then he saw his girlfriend walking along the road on the pavement, and quickly told us to duck, we all ducked down. He cursed in his own language and we all laughed.

We were still laughing when he stopped the car at the fair and we got out. Well that was the last of him, or so I thought, not knowing that another link had just fallen into place.

Chapter Thirty-one

Antoinette and I met regularly in the crowd we hung out with, to go to movies, or jive sessions, or just to have something to eat. Sometimes we made arrangements for the evening when we knew there would be a party or a jive session. Afterwards we would go home our own way. We were young, and had fun and we got on well. I left school at the end of that year although I was only fifteen, having completed the required schooling standard as stipulated by government. I started work in a bank in town, even though they had to obtain permission from the government as I was below the legal age of employment at the time. I began working on the second of January, and turned sixteen on the eleventh of that month. Antoinette worked in her hometown, at an outfitting shop and she usually came into town by train, while I commuted by tram. Antoinette was five years older than I was but we were good friends.

On a warm Friday nigh in March, just before the beginning of Lent, there was once again a jive session at the mining estate, and I was to meet her there. We enjoyed the evening and I hardly sat down all evening dancing with everyone.

I never saw him as he stood on the outskirt of the dancing area in the shadow, and only when he called me over, did I recognise him.

'Hey, Frenchie.' I looked at him from the dance floor and he beckoned me over. I had somehow acquired an accent while still at senior school and was sometimes mistakenly, thought of as French. Not that I ever said I was, but at the same time was not displeased with the attention it brought me.

So I slowly walked over to where he was standing.

'What do you want?' I asked him.

'Do you remember me?' He asked.

'Yes, of course.'

'Can I take you out?' I hesitated. First of all, he really was much too old for me, and secondly, I was not really attracted to him.

'I don't think so.'

'Well, why not?' He asked surprised. I knew I was right to refuse and said.

'I live very far away.'

'It does not matter, I will find it.' I hesitated again.

'Where did you want to take me?'

'To movies.'

'What about your girlfriend? Won't she be upset?'

'Nah, we broke up.' He saw I was still hesitant, and then he said 'it's my birthday today.'

Now I felt sorry for the guy. He broke up with his girlfriend and it was his birthday and he was on his own.

'Ok, movies only, I can't be home late.'

He asked someone for a pen, and wrote down my address and telephone number. Another link was in place, although I was still unaware of that fact.

* * *

My dad never let me out with a guy unless he spoke to him first, and I knew I had to prepare them before he arrived, after all, it was not like he was anything like the other boyfriends I had. I also knew my parents would feel he is too old, and probably too experienced in life, for me.

They would be right about this, as I had the very same thoughts.

When he knocked my dad opened the door, and invited him in. Then the interrogation began. 'Where do you stay? What kind of work do you do?

Do you have brothers and sisters? Are your parents still alive?'

I must admit he answered all the questions without fail. If he was nervous, he did not show it, and I knew too little of him to have an opinion.

The message that I think he got loud and clear, was to look after me, and to bring me home at a decent hour.

The evening was pleasant. We both enjoyed movies, so that was a plus.

He took me straight home afterwards and asked if he could see me again the next night. This surprised me, and I asked where he wanted to go.

'To movies.' He said, so I agreed.

The second night movies, was repeated on the third and fourth and fifth night, and by now we had seen most of the movies on the circuit, so I told him that we did not have to go to the movies every night, and that he could visit for a while if he wanted to, and he agreed.

Then on the sixth night, he asked me to 'go steady' with him. I took a while before I answered, and he saw I was reluctant. Up to now he had behaved like a gentleman, and I thought that even though he was older, and seemed more settled, as well as having a nice new car, and going to the movies every night, I was not really ready for a serious relationship with someone so old. I also realised from talking to him, and his friends, that he had many girls, who he went out with.

On the other hand, I thought we could use a little more time to get to know each other. My answer surprised even myself, as I said. 'On one condition.'

He waited to hear what it was. 'That you come every night. The first night that you don't come to me, will mean that you must not come back again.'

He did not hesitate before he agreed to the terms, and it was settled. We were now going steady.

What he saw in me I never understood, but it was as if he had made up his mind, and that was that. Every night his car came down the street and made a U-turn at the corner of the road to pull up on to the wide pavement in front of our house. My dad now chatted freely and my mother discussed her passion of horse racing, with him. We went to visit his brothers or sister and often just stayed at home. I got to know him better, like his religion, which was catholic, and was unknown to me or to my family. A rosary was entwined on the interior mirror of his car attesting to his commitment, and he leant forward many times while driving, to kiss the cross at the end of the rosary. To me, brought up as a non-catholic, it made little sense, and he explained how the religion was. We spoke a lot and he told me about his mother who was blind. It was obvious that he adored her. He called her his little olive. I said very little as he already knew my family, and slowly we learnt more about each other's ways. It was exactly two weeks since we started going out, and we were on our way to movies once again. We found a nice parking space close to the theatre, and before I could open the car door, he asked me to wait before getting out.

He leant forward and touched the cross hanging from the mirror, and then he asked me to hold it. I took the cross in my hand and wondered what was going on. 'I am going to ask you a question.' He said. "I am only going to ask it once. If your answer is no, I will never ask it again.'

Whow! I thought this must be serious and still holding the cross in my hand, waited to hear the question.

I was completely dumbstruck when it came. "Will you marry me?'

I knew a lot depended on my answer, and thought about it carefully. If I said no, he most probably would not ask again. If I said yes on the other hand, I could always pull out later, so I answered in a strange voice. 'Yes, I will marry you.' He was elated and kissed me. Now it was a different couple that emerged from the car. We were betrothed, and I was excited and I knew he was happy. Later I began to panic just thinking about what my parents would say.

* * *

When he arrived the next evening, he asked to speak to my parents.

'I have asked your daughter to marry me and she agreed, and so, I am asking you for her hand in marriage.'

My father looked at me in a stern sort of way and then said. 'You hardly even know each other, and she is very young. Although we do not disagree, we feel you should wait a while.'

'Fair enough.' was his reply' but you must know that I will not change my mind.' My dad shook hands with him, and my mother kissed his cheek.

We agreed on an engagement date for September, five months away.

* * *

I had met his brother Dawood and his wife, and Antoinette's family of course, and his brother Jimmy and his wife, who we sometimes met for movies.

He also took me to Anthony, his eldest brothers' house where he lived with his family, and I liked them all, and enjoyed learning about them. I had still not met his mother, who I knew was blind, or not been to his home. I was nervous for that day, having been told how strict his mother was. I also felt he had been reluctant to take me there, until he was sure of himself. Late one afternoon, he stopped in front of his house. I had been there before, but I never got out of the car, and always waited for him while he quickly fetched something. So when he asked me to go in with him, I was surprised. 'You know my mother is blind, so you must be very quiet, so she won't know you are there.' Now I was really nervous.

'I will wait for you in the car.'

'No, it is alright just be very quiet.'

My steps as we went in were soft, as he led me down the passage to the kitchen where everyone was, and showed me a chair next to the table to sit on, putting his finger on his lips showing me to be quiet. I sat like a mouse, and tried not to breath.

Phillip was there, and Dawood and Finnie his sister, whom I had not met before. I saw the kitchen was built on two levels. The top where I was sitting next to the window overlooked a velt at the back, which I saw stretched further to a ridge, where railway tracks ran. A step on the side of the room, next to the wall, led down to the lower part of the kitchen, where the scullery was, and a coal stove where pots were cooking. At a small kitchen table in the lower section, an old woman sat with her back towards me, eating from a plate in front of her. Her hair was snow white like silk, and fell to just below her chin. The people, when they saw us, smiled and nodded not saying a word. I sat very still and worried what his mother would do if she knew I was there, and what her reaction would be. They spoke to each other in their language, which I understood nothing of, and someone must have told their mother that I was there. Panic rose within me when Dawood spoke. 'My mother knows you are here, and she welcomes you.' I thought I was going to cry with relief and kept still.

'Thank you' I said in a small voice 'please tell her I am happy to be here.'

She spoke in Lebanese as she turned to me, and Dawood translated. 'My mother asks if you would like some soup?' Once again I did not know what to say, not wanting to offend anyone, so I said that would be nice. This answer caused some disturbance as they spoke to each other in their language, and then addressed me again. 'We gave my mom the last plate of soup and she says she will gladly share it with you.' I was so embarrassed and did not know what to say.

'Please tell your mom, thank you very much, I did not really want any soup, but was afraid to be disrespectful.' And so the ice was broken.

Later I learned that one never accepted on the first offering, or even the second, but once the offer is made the third time, it is time to accept, failing which, will place you in a position of disrespect.

There was a flurry of excitement as his sister Yvette, and her husband Badwa, arrived. She carried an infant wrapped tightly in a blanket, in her arms and wore a nightgown. Her long black hair was pulled back into a ponytail, and to me she looked beautiful. Her cheeks were flushed with happiness as she held her baby daughter.

Now the kitchen was filled with laughter and happiness, as she showed the baby around. Each had a turn to inspect the lovely little girl with black hair in her mothers' arms, and then they opened a path for Alfred to look at the baby. Norman had told me about Alfred, but I had not met him before this, and only saw him when he came in from outside.

He was small in stature. His shirt was tucked into his trousers, which were rolled up a few notches, showing his bare leathery feet. His hair consisted of tight little curls and was mostly white, and when he smiled, there were many teeth missing. The mother held her baby low so he could see her, and when he said she was lovely, happiness shone from the mothers' eyes. It was obvious to me that there was a special kind of love between all of them.

Then the mother carefully walked down the step and placed the little bundle in her mothers' arms, where she sat at the table. I saw the grandmother hold the baby carefully, and then she brought it up to her face smelling the baby, and then she nuzzled the little girl. A smile full of happiness lit up her face. I watched the family as they spoke to each other and wished that I could understand what was being said.

*   *   *

Josephine is my given name but everyone calls me 'Finnie'. I am happy that our youngest sibling chose someone so young. We are different in culture and religion and some changes don't always sit well if one is too set in ones' ways. She is attractive and has a nice figure and she is shorter than he is which is great. He measured five feet and seven inches, only just equalling his brother Jimmy, in height. Besides this, she is friendly and seems intelligent, and best of all, she laughs at our jokes and accepts who and what we are, although we are quite different from her own family. What she dislikes is all the swearing that takes place in our general conversations, and this she made quite clear. We joke about this among ourselves, but try to curb the cussing when she is around which is hard seeing as we are so used to it. Other than that, it looks as if she could fit in quite easily, and most importantly, was that Alfred took a liking to her and we trusted his judgement.

I never married for the simple reason that my mother and my older brothers did not think it would be wise because of the epileptic seizures that plagued me. In general I was fine, but every now and again it would rear its nasty head.

Not that I remember anything much when this took place, except for the fact that I would find myself in bed with a terrible headache, and weak for days, unable to get up. Perhaps they are right, although I had proposals from two suitors who knew about my condition and who were willing to live with it but my family did not want to take the risk of me having children, which was probably just as well.

I was commissioned to take the girl under my wing. I had to prepare her for her new and very different life.

Their engagement was set for September, and I showed her the diamond ring she would be getting. The ring was from a previous engagement to Jimmy's wife's cousin a few years earlier, which did not work out, but it was a beauty. Solitaire, brilliant white and weighed, 0.75 carats set in a plain gold band. But first there was work to be done. Religion was important and she had to attend classes before converting to the catholic faith. She understood this, and accepted it. She became a regular visitor and we got used to each other. Her parents also came to meet us, and there was an instant liking between my mom and them. It was obvious that they respected my mom, and although she could not see them, knew what they looked like, from details supplied by the children. My mother, was happy that her youngest child, whom she loved so dearly, would be among people who were decent and loving. My brothers also liked her parents and they joked together. After all, my elder brothers were like my father would have been, and were in fact, of the same age as her parents. They looked out for their young brother, and he respected them as father figures, all of them, and valued their guidance when given.

Respect was something my mother taught us well. We each, in our way, respected and depended on each other, even though many fights broke out among us we always apologised if we were in the wrong, or younger than the other, restoring the peace for our mother, if not for our own. Anyway, I think this girl will fit in when they do get married, which will be early in the new year, after her birthday. They will stay with us once they are married, so she can learn to cook the food that my brother enjoys, and learn more about our ways.

She is eager to learn, and asks many questions about everyone. When it came to the portrait paintings in the lounge of my two brothers Johnny and Joe, I knew it was time for me to tell her that all her questions were upsetting my mom. She took my words seriously, and chose her questions carefully, when my mom was around. I knew we had to be patient and bear with her until she knew us better.

*   *   *

Chapter Thirty-two

The wedding was a grand affair. I designed my own dress, and it was made by a bridal shop in town. It had a full white organza skirt with many starched petticoats underneath, and was drawn up in the front with three organza roses, with an embroidered organza train just touching the floor. The lace top was cut out in the pattern of the lace on the neckline with hand beading in the flowers, and fitted low on my shoulders. A halo of orange blossoms held the short embroidered veil in place. Long embroidered white organza gloves finished off the outfit very nicely with white high heeled shoes that peeped out from under the dress. My older sisters' pearl choker, which sufficed for the borrowed requirement, encircled my neck. Underneath the layers of organza a blue garter fitted snugly around the top of my leg, to comply with the something blue. The bouquet consisted of a single orchid fastened onto a church missal. My hair and nails were done at a salon in town that morning and everything was in place when the driver arrived. David had a beautiful Chevrolet, with long fish tails at the back and was our appointed wedding car driver. His wife helped me with my dress and they first took me on a roundabout route to the convent near their home so I could show the nuns who they were friendly with how I looked. The nuns were thrilled, and I received my first blessing for the day from them. On the day before the wedding we had gone to the market to buy flowers for the church and it was going to be arranged by the lady who took care of the church flowers. The flowers looked lovely on our day as I entered the church on the arm of my dad to the wedding march. Dolores the eldest daughter of Johnny, my new brother in law, was my bridesmaid and was the same age as I was. She looked beautiful in a green organza dress that fell to just above her ankles. As my dad gave me over to my husband to be I saw the pride in my fathers' eyes. Norman stood with Phillip his best man, at his side, and the two brothers looked like film stars in their dark suits.

In the front pew Manouch sat with Finnie and Yvette together with my mom and dad.

Manouch wore a lovely green silk dress, with a small bouquet of fresh flowers, pinned to her shoulder. Her white hair shone like silk, and on her feet, she had on a new pair of felt slippers, their shiny pom-poms reflecting little flashes of light as she walked on the arm of her daughter. Her face was lit up, by a smile that went on forever. My parents looked very smart indeed. My dad wore a suit, which he very rarely did, and my mom was dressed in a light bottle green suit with a soft cross over neckline and a pencil skirt in a shantung fabric. Her hat matched her outfit and her shoulder long black hair curled in at the edges. We certainly made a lovely group as the photographer took photos on the church steps after the ceremony.

Laughter and music from the band filled the air at the hall, where the reception was in full swing and everyone was having a good time. Manouch had left earlier, and my family I knew, would be clearing up after everyone went home. It was official, I was part of my new family and a new life lay before me like an uncharted map. We were, like so many millions before and after us, on the threshold of a new life together. The links of the chain were firmly brought together in an unbreakable clasp.

Chapter Thirty-three

Four days of bliss at the sea followed and then we moved in with Normans' mom and sister Finnie. Our bedroom was freshly painted and adjoined the lower kitchen next to the bathroom. Our brand new bedroom furniture filled the room. It was the latest design and had won the gold award at the annual show. The solid oak wood was sandblasted to highlight the grain, and then washed in pink and white.

I knew I had to learn the ways and culture of my new family and although young and eager to learn, was at times totally astonished, at the different way things were done.

My life with my own family was, although disciplined, very free and comfortable. I now found myself confined and isolated from my own family. I also went nowhere without someone with me, and found myself staying home with my in-laws, while my husband went out. I felt unhappy as it seemed to me to get worse each day.

I longed for my previous life, and saw no future ahead for us in the present state.

Evenings were usually filled with visits from brothers and wives, and weekends were the same. My life to me had become a prison. Seventeen was an age for enjoying ones' life and I was not part of a carefree life any longer. The very things that I thought were rich and vibrant were in fact ropes that tied a wife down, and I rebelled. I was pregnant and my in-laws attributed my difficult behaviour to this.

The person that I married, or thought I married, was not the same person I now knew. When he was with his family he felt compelled to show his power and dominance. Arriving from work in the evenings he was waylaid at the front door to hear how his wife had miss behaved that day. I knew I would not survive this life for long. My spirit was breaking and after a terrible scene one evening my husband telephoned my father and asked him to come and take me back as I was not obedient.

My dad arrived with my eldest sister and they sat with me in our room on the bed, and my dad my hero, looked at my tear-streaked face, and knew he had no choice.

'He is, your husband, I cannot take you away from here. You must understand that. It is not that I don't want to but I can't. You have to listen to him.'

I knew he was right and I knew I had no choice.

They left me in the room and went to talk to my in-laws. I did not hear what he said, but I know that he would have been firm. He would have questioned my safety and would have assured them that his wrath would be severe. He would also have told them that he would not allow his daughter to be a prisoner. They would have complained to him, how I behaved in a disobedient manner, and he would have reminded them of my young age. Peace was restored and respect for my dad was tangible. He was a fair man and expected fair play from others.

My position was clear. I was not going to win anything by behaving in the way that I was, and I needed to find a balance in my own way.

I truly tried, I really did but when an argument erupted late one morning after my husband left for work, I walked out.

* * *

I walked the streets for a while, trying to calm myself and eventually came to a decision. I went back and went straight to our room and packed a small suitcase with clothes. My options were basically none but I had to get out before it was too late. My mother-in-law tried to reason with me but I pushed past her and left with the suitcase in my hand.

* * *

There was only one place I could go to, so I walked the distance. It was far, but it was the only way I could get there. I had no money, heavily pregnant, and not much of a future ahead of me, but I had a perfectly good mind, and was going to use it.

It was already afternoon when I reached my destination and I was tired.

I knocked on the door and waited. When she saw me with my suitcase, she put her arm around me and led me in. On the day we got married my mom had whispered in my ear that if I ever needed help she had spoken to Normans' friend and his wife, and that I could depend on their assistance.

When the telephone rang we knew it would be Norman.

'Oh! Hello Norman, how are you?' 'No she is not here is everything ok?

Yes, if she comes I will let you know.'

We knew it would not be the end and saw his car riding up and down in the street in front of the house till late that night. When he telephoned again he got the same answer that he probably got from my father as well. No, I was not there either.

After a restless night, I was dropped off at my parents' home the next morning. We had no alternative but to face the fact that the marriage was indeed over. I slept with my sisters sharing their room and cried myself to sleep at night.

My husband now knew that I was with my parents and we spoke on the telephone. There was no way I was going back to the same circumstances and told him so.

Oh! I missed him very much and I knew he must also feel the same, but neither one of us was backing down. The first week passed and my mom bought me a packet of wool, to knit myself a jersey. Thick green wool and thick needles with a pattern of intricate cables was my consolation. I never spoke much and my parents did not force any issues. The needles flew feverishly in my hands and the jersey was nearly complete within days.

I felt hopeless for any kind of future and knew my parents were at a loss as they, also did not know, how to handle the situation. They realised that some sort of action had to be taken and decided that a lawyer was the next step. The enormity of such a step was not lost to me knowing that I would be dependent on them until my baby was born and then I would have to make other arrangements. I knew I could not stay with my parents permanently. Not only would it be a drain on their finances, but I was no longer that child that left my parents' home to get married. Three siblings, a sister, brother and sister in that order, were still in school, and they needed their space. My future as well as that of my unborn child looked bleak and uncertain.

Norman himself was probably also thinking along those lines and his mother, no doubt, had called in her advisers to discuss the problem.

Johnny was the one who was sent to discuss the matter. He and his wife came on the Sunday, and the visit was not unpleasant, as they chatted to my parents along general lines, before broaching the problem at hand. I did not say much, but stated my case when asked to. They did not stay very long in order to go and report to his mother who was waiting for them.

Although, I longed for him, he never came. The message from him was that I was welcome to go home but he was not fetching me. Like I went, I had to return. I knew that I would never do that, and said so. He now telephoned each evening and we spoke for a while, but no promises were made from either side.

My parents realised that it was time to take action and made an appointment with a lawyer for the following week.

When my eldest sister and her husband came to visit, my mom asked my brother-in-law, if he could collect my trousseau chest. The beautiful mahogany chest was the only piece of furniture that had accompanied me when I got married. It stood in the room where Manouch slept, as there was no space in our bedroom. This step would be an indication of the ending of a relationship, and the significance was clear. My brother-in-law came to me where I was sitting on my own on the narrow veranda.

"Mom asked me to fetch your trousseau chest. I said I would but I want you to think about it. If I fetch it the relationship will be over. Is this really what you want? You know I am behind you whatever you decide. My feeling is that you love each other and don't want to end it. It is up to you. I can make the arrangements if that is what you want.'

I knew he was right and asked him to wait before fetching the piece of furniture that had now become a symbol of finality.

Chapter Thirty-four

When the telephone rang that evening I knew I had to make a decision.

'We will collect the chest during the next few days if this is what you want.'

My statement was met by a short silence and I held my breath.

'You know I want you to come back.'

'Then fetch me.' I said

Again a silence. I was aware of the fact that his brothers had told him not to do so, as it would make him look weak. I also knew my parents would not take me, so I waited anxiously for his next words.

'You know I can't do that. You have to come back in the same way you left. We never chased you. You left on your own free will.'

Stalemate! He would not come and I would not go.

'I tell you what.' Were my next few words.

'I will call a taxi to take me back but you have to pay the taxi.'

'Hang-on.' He said, and I waited with my heart pounding knowing he had gone to his mother. Then I heard him breathing in the telephone.

'OK, let a taxi bring you and we will pay him.'

Tears ran down my cheeks as I put the telephone down.

My parents sat in the lounge and had heard the whole conversation and waited for me to tell them the outcome.

"Where do I find a number for a taxi?'

Their feelings must have been mixed when I told them what had been said. Were they doing the right thing to let me go back or not? They knew I had to give our relationship another chance however difficult it would be. I knew as I looked at them, that they would not welcome me back if things did not work out this time, and I realised it was up to me to adjust to whatever was needed. I was seventeen years old and felt very old.

* * *

It was late when the taxi stopped in front of the house. The front door opened and Finnie came out to find out how much the fare was and then went back inside, to get the money. I picked up my small suitcase that the driver took out of the car boot and went inside. I knew that my first step was to apologise to my mother-in-law.

She was in her bedroom sitting on her bed, and although she could not see me, knew I was there.

'I am very sorry Imme.'

She turned her face to me, her eyelids down but I knew she understood me.

He waited in our room for me and took me in his arms and held me close.

I knew I was where I had to be and would do whatever it took, or whatever was demanded from me, to make it work. I was seventeen pregnant and wiser than many people twice my age were.

* * *

An understanding developed between Manouch and me. She did not speak in a language that I understood but her words were translated to me. She realised as well that I had a lot of learning to do, and although married and with a child on the way, was actually only a teenager and she would have to be patient. Alfred was always nearby to help me, as I settled in, step by step.

Chapter Thirty-five

Still it was not easy living there. I was not used to the constant disagreements, and the profanity jarred on my very being. As a wife I did not have a voice, and had to obey any instruction. Slowly my confidence was eroding day by day, and I promised myself that we would move to our own place as soon as possible. Alfred and I got on very well and to be totally honest, the strangeness was interesting to me, so I asked many questions in order to understand the culture better. They in turn, saw I was willing to learn, and slowly warmed to me as well. It probably was as difficult for them to accept me as it was for me, to accept their ways. My parents now came regularly to visit, no doubt to make sure I was coping, and they were always welcomed. Finnie, my sister-in-law, had gone with me to the local clinic at the beginning stages, and my visits became more regular as the pregnancy progressed. I went with her on her weekly visits to the shops, and I was amazed each time, how the whole town knew her. We walked on the one side of the road on our way into town stopping off at each and every shop where the owner, not only greeted her with a smile, but also made us sit down for a chat, and refreshments. There was the chemist, the clothing store, the fish shop the jeweller and every other shop on the block and we had not even gone through the subway yet. This outing usually took all day, and returning home we walked on the opposite side of the road, popping in to all the shops on that side. Her popularity was beyond doubt, and I was impressed as I was introduced to everyone. My new family, was not only well known, but really well liked and respected.

I had heard about the convulsions that plagued Finnie but I was not prepared when it did occur. It came suddenly while we were in the kitchen as a cry from Yvette made Phillip run to grab her. I sat stunned as she was held down. Her eyes rolled wildly and foam formed on her lips.

I was quickly taken out of the kitchen, to another room.

I sat there until everything went quiet and then went to her room where she lay on her bed covered with a blanket. I wanted to sit with her but I was gently taken away again.

'You must leave her for a while. My mother is afraid for the baby.

Rather stay in your room.'

In truth I had never witnessed anything of that nature before and knew they were protecting me, so I heeded their reasoning and stayed in my room knitting baby garments.

There was no laughter in the house that evening, even when the brothers came to visit. Instead everyone spoke in softer tones. I helped with making tea and then retired to my room.

Finnie was a big woman. Her hair was always neatly done and I knew she had been a beautiful young woman from a photo on the dresser in her room. In the photo a slim beautiful girl with long black hair pinned back in bangs, looked at the camera and smiled. Now she looked washed out as she lay in bed with an unhealthy pallor to her face.

I was allowed to sit with her the next day and by the third day she was up and about as if nothing had happened.

Many doctors and specialists had seen and tested her and the answer was in most cases the same. Regular medication was necessary and a close watch was all that could be done and stress was to be avoided. I knew, because they told me, that they had tried every possible cure but to no avail. They were still prepared to try anything, and when I saw the man there the following day, I understood their desperation.

He came in from the back yard and had people around him. His body was painted with white clay, and pieces of animal fur covered his body. On his head he had a band with more fur hanging down his back. On his legs were bands of seeds that made noises as he walked and in his hand he had a stick covered in strips of beads with more animal fur hanging from the end. I tried to get into her room where she lay on the bed, but was blocked, and so I went out into the yard, and looked through the bedroom window. I knew he must be a sangoma or witchdoctor. I saw him chanting over her body and waving his stick in small circles over her, and then I felt someone take my arm and lead me away.

* * *

My life had become one learning curve after another and it felt to me more like a movie set than actual life. Soon my baby would be born and I did not have a clue how I would know when it was that time. And worse even, was that I was too shy to ask anyone, not wanting to show my ignorance, and I was scared. How would I handle being a mother when I could not even be a good wife or daughter-in-law? Eventually I plucked up the courage to ask Jimmy's wife as we sat in my room one evening. She was amused at my ignorance, but nevertheless, explained what the signs were to look out for, and I was relieved to know what to expect.

* * *

There he was, perfect in every way and I knew immediately that I would not only be a good mother but a great one. Fortunately I had people around me who could show me how to take care of my baby. Not that I agreed with everything they said or did, but it was comforting to have them around. Take for instance the medals. How we as children ever survived without the various medals to ward off evil spirits puzzled me. A blue bead for warding off evil eyes, a medal of Our Lady to look after him, one of St Anthony for protection, and so it went on as the medals were pinned to the small baby. But what really amused me, was that no compliment was ever allowed for the baby to avoid something dreadful happening to him. The sign of the cross was constantly made above him and if anyone, not knowing about the dreadful consequences, did pass a compliment, the baby was immediately blessed and taken away. Well I thought again however did we actually survive and grow up?

I had seen the visitors before and knew they were gypsies. Not play, play gypsies, but the real thing. Long time friends of the family, they always came to visit when they arrived in town with their caravans.

'Quick, take the baby to your room. Don't bring him out till they go.'

Of course I did what I was told and asked about it later after they left.

'Why did I have to take him away?'

'We have to be careful they have powers that can harm a small baby.'

And I listened to my family thinking that maybe there were things, that we did not know about.

I was to still learn many things about superstitions that I never even knew existed and I was amazed that people could actually believe that others had the power to control their destiny. My own family had always been a God fearing family and superstition, other than light mockery, never had a place in our home.

After living with my mother-in-law for nearly a year and learning new ways of living and actually learning to cook, it was time to move on.

I found a flat not too far away and so we began our own life. This was a place where I was not under scrutiny all the time and also a place where I could be shown love and care without making my husband look weak.

I missed the bustle and noise and the company but it was a place where we could grow together on our own. Mistakes would be made and fights would be many but we had to learn to cope in our own way.

Chapter Thirty-six

My days now consisted of taking my little boy for a walk to buy what was needed for supper. The flat was not far away from the cemetery and many days after bumping the pram down the flight of stairs, I walked through the rows of silent graves. On the far side, in the best spot was the grave of my father-in-law whom I never met.

I knew his son Joe was also buried there although his name was not engraved on the grey granite with Arabic writing. I wondered about that and only later learnt why the name was not there. I knew a daughter was also buried in the same cemetery and walked up and down the rows yet never found her grave. Now I sometimes bought a bunch of flowers and put it on my father-in-laws' grave as I chatted to him showing him his grandson.

One day, I went into the little office at the entrance and asked if there was a register so I could find the grave of Amiro. We found nothing in the register and I mentioned it to my husband.

'She is buried under our previous name.'

I knew my father-in-law and his brother had changed their surname at some stage, but did not know exactly why. I was told that there were too many families with the same surname, and I left it at hat. If there were other reasons, I did not know about them.

So I went back to the little office at the cemetery and there it was. I went to the grave that was registered and found it bare with no headstone. It looked forlorn and lonely, and I found an old glass bottle and filled it with water from the nearby tap, and put some flowers on the grave.

I regularly took our little boy for a walk in his stroller, among the graves of the dead, reading the messages inscribed by their loved ones.

Some were sad, while others said nothing at all but the dates of birth and death.

One day we went for a much further walk than usual, and towards the opposite direction. It was a long way to the centre of the suburb, where all the bigger shops were and we took our time. I saw a place where they cut tombstones and I went in to enquire about a small headstone to mark the forlorn grave of my long gone sister-in-law Amiro. I thought it would be more expensive than it was, and promised to go back again. I wanted to discuss my thoughts with my husband that evening.

"Why do you want to do that?" He asked

"Why not" was my reply "I would not want to be in an unmarked grave and I am sure you also would not like it."

"I don't know, it must be very expensive, you know we don't really have the money."

"It is just a small marker with her name on and really is not expensive at all.'

When he heard what the cost would be he agreed and a few days later with the number of the grave and the money I went back to place the order.

It was just a plain granite stone with a steel vase in the centre. There was no date and no message, only her name. When I looked at it I was happy that recognition had been given to her. I felt she would be happy as well.

Once a week, usually a Friday I now bought two bunches of flowers to decorate the two graves. I knew that over the weekends many visitors went to the cemetery and now they could see that these two graves were not forgotten.

* * *

A recession loomed in the country and when Norman came home one evening with the news that he had been retrenched we were not too concerned. He was a tradesman and would surely get another job.

But conditions became grimmer by the day as men were laid off daily.

The building trade that my father was in, was also affected and it was only with the help of Manouch, that we survived. She had Finnie make up portions of the vegetables and fruit, of what she was paid in, for the children who were in need. From our portion we helped my parents as well.

There was now only one possibility of earning enough money to eat and pay for our needs, and we had to take it.

The supply of alcohol to the illegal trade brought a small income, while searching for work.

Although we were thrilled with the news that I was pregnant again it was cause for concern and finding permanent work became critical. My mom saw the ad as she scanned the columns in the newspapers each day for some relief, and Norman went immediately to enquire. The pay was poor and it was the night shift, but at least a wage at the end of the week, meant we could pay our way again.

A girl this time, and we were thrilled. Fair skin and eyes blue like violets, with a pair of lungs, that she exercised to its fullest. A surprise was however sprung on me when I went for my check-up after a few weeks, at the local clinic.

'Congratulations, you are pregnant' The clinic sister said after the examination.

'No, that is not possible.' Was my reply. 'I have only just had a baby.'

'Well, there is another on its way.'

When I gave the news to my husband that evening, we were not quite as excited as the time before. Now we had to look seriously at planning for our future as well as that of our children.

On a visit to us, my mom took a walk with our eldest son, and saw a house just around the corner from where we were that was to let, and with great excitement we moved to our first house.

Yvette asked if we would need a maid, as she knew of someone who was very good, that could help us. At first I declined as we were already on a lean budget, but she persuaded us and it was settled.

Ten months after our daughter was born our second son was born.

Looking at him in my arms, I knew this was the baby that I had always thought of having. A mop of black hair, olive skin and brown eyes made him a replica of his father. Where the first two children were fair like me this baby was the opposite. Where the other two had blue eyes, his would be warm brown. I held him close to me and marvelled at his beauty. Our family was now complete and I was nineteen years old.

* * *

As happy as we were, we knew we had to earn more money to provide for our family and I began searching for a job.

Although our baby was only a few weeks old we had a good maid who could look after him as well as our other two children during the day. I was reluctant and sad to leave him so young and fragile but knew I had to work if we were to survive.

Nobody, except another mother, will understand how difficult it is to leave a newborn baby or even any small child with someone else. All day your thoughts are with them hoping that everything is fine. And when they are ill? Well, apart from having to be up all night with your child or children, you have to dress and report for work with a smile on your face. The pay cheque, at the end of the month, is a reminder of the reason why one has to make such sacrifices.

I was now accepted, as a full-fledged, member of the family and was a daughter-in-law and a sister-in-law, in its fullest sense.

Chapter Thirty-seven

Manouch sat in her chair next to the table in the kitchen. Where before she would have been looking out of the window at the tall grass flowing in the breeze, she now sat with her eyes closed and listened to the noises in the kitchen. She felt tension around her and it made her body tired. It had been many years since she actually saw her family but their faces were ingrained in her memory. She remembered Yvette as a beautiful young woman with long black hair and a flush on her cheeks. She knew Finnie was also a lovely girl, and pretty when young, although carried much weight now in her thirties.

Sometimes the fighting and bickering just got too much for her, and then she retreated into her world of darkness, blotting out everything around her.

Memories of happy days were like magic illusions that appeared and disappeared in a mist. In fact, some days it felt so real that she was sure she heard Salem calling her name. 'Manouch, Manouch! Why are you taking so long?' Her answer was always the same 'be patient, I'm coming.'

When she felt the touch on her arm she got a fright. Was it that time?

'Mommy, mommy, what are you thinking about? I spoke to you and you did not hear.'

Manouch turned her head to Finnie. 'I heard you say something but then the noise was too much. What did you say again?'

'What would you like for dinner tonight? Badwa brought a fresh sheep but he went out gambling so I am cooking.'

'I feel like rice and meat, but not too much my stomach is a bit sore.'

'Where is it sore Mommy? Must I get the doctor?'

'No, no it sometimes comes but then the pain goes away again. It will be better soon.'

'OK, but you must tell me if it gets worse.'

'Yes, yes, I will.'

Then Finnie left her side and she relaxed again. Actually the pain had grown worse lately but she was sure it was something she ate. Better to keep her diet simple for a few days.

* * *

The telephone rang in the bedroom but nobody heard it with all the noise coming from the kitchen. The yard was full of men drinking beer and laughing with Lizzie serving while Alfred kept an eye on them from his place on the little bench next to the back door. Finnie was busy at the stove and it was only when Manouch called her, that she heard the ringing.

Slowly she pulled the pot to the side of the stove and wiped her hands before walking to the bedroom to answer the telephone.

Manouch turned her head to hear who the caller was, and when she heard Finnie scream it was as if a cold bucket of water had been poured over her. She gripped the table to get up and Alfred was at her side almost immediately. He had also heard the scream above the noise and even though his body was frail, he rose instantly to go to Manouch.

'Slowly, get your balance first.' Manouch gripped his wiry arm and he waited for her, before leading her to the bedroom. He knew it was bad when he saw the look on Finnie's face and he prepared himself to go to her if she took a bad turn, so he helped Manouch to her bed where he sat her down, and then he went to the telephone and took it from her hand.

'Who is this? We will phone you back.' He put the telephone down and spoke to Finnie. 'What is wrong?' Through her tears she told him that the call was from David's wife.

'Its David, he's dead.'

Alfred was next to Manouch even before Finnie finished her sentence.

She wanted to get up from the bed but he held her down.

'Wait, we will call Phillip. Finnie, stay here, with your mother, don't let her get up, she may fall down and then she will hurt herself. I am going to fetch Yvette.'

Finnie sat on the other bed her body heaving with sobs. For a moment she forgot about her mother then realised what she was doing so she got up and went to her mother. 'Mommy, lie down for a while.'

Manouch said nothing, instead she put her head down on the pillow, and Finnie lifted her legs on to the bed. She pulled the chair around to face the bed and spoke gently to her mother. 'Don't upset yourself mommy,

Yvette is coming and she will phone to see what happened.' Finnie looked at her mother and fear gripped her heart. This was bad, really bad and she wished Yvette would come quickly.

They heard her, before they saw her, storming into the room. 'Mommy,

Mommy, are you all right?'

'Yvette, you must phone Katy, Alfred put the phone down before she could tell us what happened.'

'Where is the number Finnie why is the book not here?'

Finnie knew all the numbers off by heart and called the number to Yvette.

Silence was tangible as they waited for the phone to be answered.

The voice that came on the phone could hardly be heard between the crying. 'Hello, who is it?'

'Katy, its me Yvette, what is wrong, what happened?'

A few seconds of silence followed, and was broken by more crying. 'He said he was not feeling well and was going to lie down. When I got to the room he was already dead. What must I do?' The crying intensified and Yvette waited a short while.

'Katy, I want you to go and sit down. Do nothing, we are leaving right now, where are the children?'

'They are at school, they will be here in an hour.'

'Listen to me Katy, don't answer the phone. Go and sit and wait for us and Katy, drink a glass of water and put some sugar in.'

Yvette slowly put the telephone down and turned to her mother who was now sitting up. 'Are you sure you want to go with us mommy?'

'I must. Finnie will wait here and phone the others.'

'I am going to see why Badwa is taking so long. Finnie get mommy's slippers on and make sure she has her medicine with her. I don't know how long we will be away.'

Finnie wanted to go with but she knew Yvette was right. She had a lot of work to do, so she pulled herself together, and made sure her mom had everything she needed. She would wait with contacting her sister and brothers till her mother, was gone, knowing that the words she would be saying to them, would upset her mother.

She waited with her mother on the veranda till Badwa brought the car to the front of the house. After helping her mother in she went back inside, to fulfil her heavy task.

* * *

Katy opened the door even before they knocked and fell into Yvette's arms sobbing. 'What am I going to do without him?'

Yvette loosened her arms and led her to a chair. 'Sit for a while, tell us what happened.' Badwa settled Manouch on a comfortable chair, and went to the kitchen. He opened the fridge and found a big bottle of coca-cola. He took glasses from the cupboard and poured some for all of them.

He knew the sugar would be bad for his mother-in-law, so did not fill her glass. She needed this as much as they did and he took it inside.

She was sitting with her eyes closed and he saw her pallor was pale.

'Mommy, here is a little coca-cola, drink it slowly.' Manouch put her hand out and he placed the glass in her hand and waited till her fingers gripped it.

'Thank you.' The liquid was cool as she sipped and tears rolled from her unseeing eyes.

The task that lay before them was harder than anyone could imagine and they tried not to think about it until they heard the voices of the children as they started to arrive from school. They did not all arrive at the same time as the girls were in different classes at the convent nearby and the boys were at the local high school. When the girls came in it started.

When the boys came they were met with everyone crying. Stunned they went to their rooms and closed the doors. Manouch, although she could not see anything, felt their pain mingled with her own pain, and a heavy sigh escaped her lips. It was a pain that she knew too well, and she tried and her heart had constricted to a heavy metal ball that pounded against her ribcage. At moments when the pressure became unbearable, a sigh once more left her lips, but nobody even heard it, engrossed in their own pain.

And so the dominos began to fall.

Chapter Thirty-eight

I got the call while I was at work. We were not allowed to receive calls unless it was important and Norman knew that, so when I heard his voice, I held my breath, not knowing why he needed to speak with me.

'My brother David died. See if you can get away a bit early.' Well, that was not possible of course, and even so the buses only ran on their scheduled time, and linked up with the next bus to get me home. All in all the journey took at least an hour and a half so I waited for my usual time to leave knowing there would be no connecting bus at the other end if I left earlier.

When I finally got home, I sorted the children out, and asked the maid to keep an eye on them, while we went to the house of the dead. First I had to change to something darker. This was a term that was new to me 'house of the dead,' and I was going to have to get used to it. We were married now for four years, and during those years, I had matured and grown up in many ways.

There were already a lot of people in the house when we walked in, and I saw my sister-in-law sitting with an expression that clearly showed that she had blanked out, whatever transpired earlier. My mother-in-law looked pale to me, as I went to kiss them on their cheeks, and then I went to the kitchen to see what I could do to help. I saw a pot of food that had been cooked earlier. The pot of corn with meat and chopped onions, was still luke warm on the stove, and I went to look for the children where they were in their rooms. 'Have you eaten yet?' I asked. They shook their heads, so I told them to come to the kitchen so I could dish up for them.

The little group was very quiet and did not say much, even though I tried to make some sort of conversation with them. After I dished up I went to the lounge and asked my sister-in-law Yvette to ask Katy and my mother-in-law to come and have something to eat. They both ate very little and I cleared everything away, with the girls helping me. Then I helped the children to get ready with their schoolwork, for the next day, and bath and get ready for bed. We sat and spoke about many things that evening but not about their father, that I knew, their mother would do. I knew she was probably desperately wanting to be with her children, to hold them and comfort them, but she, as his wife had to remain with the people who had come to sympathise. Much later, when the people leave, I knew she would seek their comfort as well as giving her own to them.

It was my first experience of a close death, where I was required to carry out a duty, of some kind. The next day more senior sisters-in-law took over, and I helped with serving endless trays of tea and Turkish coffee.

It was a blessing to know that we had a reliable maid who lived in to take care of our own children.

The funeral was scheduled for three days later and I would learn many things before that.

We were now all dressed in black, all the women that is, wife, mother, sisters and sisters-in-law, and we would be in mourning for longer than we thought. Food was prepared by Badwa and Yvette each day, to feed the family, and relatives who came to the house each evening. Manouch was there each morning and stayed till late at night. She was in her own mourning that went deeper than anyone could know. She spoke when answered to, and said very little to anyone. Her children saw her sorrow and tried to comfort her as best they could, but they somehow knew their efforts were not enough.

When I arrived the next day, it was to see the coffin in the centre of the lounge resting on two chairs. The lid of the casket was open, and as he lay there, it looked almost as if he was sleeping. I walked around the coffin to go to the kitchen but was called back. 'Come, speak to

David.' Oh no! I thought how could I do that? I went anyway, and sat on the chair next to the coffin. 'Touch him, tell him you are here.' Reluctantly I put out my hand, to touch his cold hand, and quickly drew it back again. They saw my reaction and prompted me again. 'Tell him you are here.' 'David' I said in a small voice. 'Thank you, that I could know you.' Then I got up and went to the kitchen where I tried to control my feelings. What if he were my husband? What would I do? My body shook as I sobbed for him and his family, his wife and their six young children.

The next day his body was brought to the house again for the same ritual.

Katy was now only a shadow of her former self, and Manouch hardly said a word. The children walked in and out as if they were lost, and were not sure what they should do.

The day of the funeral finally came with some relief for everyone concerned. Some kind of closure would mean that future plans, could be put into place, and no doubt, would have a major effect on the family.

But what it would really mean, was that some kind of order, would be restored.

The grave was situated in a newer part of the cemetery nearer to where Amiro rested. The family grave was three rows from the road and big pine trees threw shade for the cars. It was a pleasant spot and everyone agreed on that.

Long tables were set in the garden of their house, and after the funeral, the people attending, were to be fed with traditional dishes of all kinds. I stayed at the house to see that everything was ready and waiting, and watched for the first cars to arrive, before filling the glasses with a cool drink. As they came in, trays of refreshments were offered around.

Filling large bowls with food and serving the men at the table, took a while, as places were filled again, and again, and again and the women waited their turn. The children only ate after all the grownups had their fill. It was a long day, and we were all tired when we eventually cleared away the crockery, and put the tables in the courtyard for collection the next day. Manouch left earlier with Yvette and Badwa so she could rest at her own home. She looked worn out, and was pale, yet never once complained.

Her world was torn apart as she grieved silently in the darkness.

Without fail she dressed each morning and waited for someone to take her to her daughter-in-law, so she could be there as comfort for her. For the next forty days, people came constantly, to show their support to the widow and the mother, while plans had to be put into place for the future of the children. Forty days later a mass would be said for the deceased, and the tables would once again be laid out, with a variety of traditional dishes, as with the funeral.

The women, including myself of course, wore only black, and every evening found us carrying trays of refreshments to the guests who came. All this, and more, I learned as the days passed. The family was drawn together and the brothers all helped in their own way, to smooth the way forward for their brother's family. It was trying times for the widow and her young children. She had been taken care of by her husband for all their married life, and now had to take charge, while she herself was fragile.

For the younger siblings, Phillip, Yvette, Jimmy, Finnie and Norman it was more like loosing a father than a brother. David was the one they went to when they had a problem. He listened and if he could, he took care of it. For him, David, the eldest of the children, responsibility for his family, was important. His father had relied on him and knew he could depend on his eldest son to do so. It was David, who was called when Manouch needed him, and he never, if it was in his power, disappointed her. It was he, David, who went to the local car dealer who refused to sell Norman a car on terms, and who pulled the salesman over his desk and throttled him, till he apologised profusely to Norman, and it was he, David who went with Norman to collect his new car. It was also David who signed as surety at the bank for Norman to buy his first home. All this he did not only do for his youngest brother, but for his family as a whole. He was the person who made decisions, and gave a helping hand, whenever needed.

Now I sometimes bought three bunches of flowers on a Saturday morning to put onto the graves. David was in a newer section where a family grave was bought, as his family was still young, and provision had to be made for future use. Space in the cemetery, was becoming in short supply, and they were lucky to still get a plot there.

Manouch, when she sat early mornings, in her chair at the table in the kitchen, grew quieter and rarely said anything. Alfred bustled around her bringing tea and olives and the feta cheese she loved, but she hardly touched any of it. He was worried about her, and always sat on the step in the kitchen, so he could see her. His eyes, now old and dim, watched her every move, and he was instantly at her side, if she made any movement.

Manouch knew he was there, and although never admitting it, felt safe in his presence. She knew that more than anyone he sensed her sorrow, and shared it with her.

Chapter Thirty-nine

December became February and the women were still in black. Six months would be over before one knew it, and they looked forward to the day when another colour could be worn. The six months however, would stretch to breaking point, although they did not know it at the time.

Evenings found the house filled with voices when the brothers came to visit. When they were there, Manouch was happy, and she smiled when she heard them argue. This was how she liked it, the noisier the better.

'Finnie, make some tea.'
'Mommy, we just had tea.'
'Never mind, make some more.'
Without protesting Finnie went to the kitchen and told her sisters-in-law, who were there, to make more tea. The same pattern emerged each evening, as the trays were filled again, and again.

Alfred sat on the step in the kitchen, through all the noise and the bustle, waiting for them to leave before preparing his bed in front of the warm stove, his food slowly baking in the warm oven.

Pain shot through her body and she clutched her stomach. It was not a new pain. In fact it has been there for a while although she cannot think when she felt it for the first time. Was it weeks, or months, it really did not matter though. It must be the olives, she thought. Maybe I had too many? Slowly the pain subsided and she relaxed again.

It came again and again and by morning she knew she had to say something. 'Finnie come and help me please.'

'What is wrong mommy?' Concern showed on her face although her mother was unable to see it.

'A terrible pain in my stomach.'

'You must have eaten something to upset your stomach. What did you eat last night?'

'I never ate anything, I was not hungry.'

'But mommy, you know you have to eat. Let me check your sugar.'

'No, first help me to dress. Call Yvette, and wake Badwa, they must take me to the doctor.'

Finnie felt her heart begin to race. Her mother never complained and never asked to see a doctor. She walked quickly to the house next door to call her sister and her brother-in-law.

'Yvette! Yvette! Wake Badwa.'

'What are you shouting for Finnie? We will come just now.'

'No, you must come now, mommy wants to go to the doctor.'

Yvette came rushing out of the house still in her nightgown and ran to her mother.

'Mommy, mommy, what is wrong?'

'Is Badwa here Yvette?'

'No, he is still sleeping.'

'Well, what are you waiting for, wake him.'

'OK, mommy we wont be long I'll tell Alfred to bring you some tea.'

Manouch sat still for a while then said slowly. 'Yes, let him bring me some tea but nothing to eat. Tell Lizzie to come and help me.'

Yvette felt her mothers' urgency and spoke the words she did not want to but knew she had to.

'Must I phone the others?'

Now it was Manouch who hesitated, but not for long.

'No, let us first go to the doctor.'

Yvette went to the kitchen to speak to Alfred and Lizzie, then washed herself in the bathroom, and went to call Badwa.

Lizzie came to the bedroom and helped Manouch to finish dressing then walked with her to the bathroom, and waited till Manouch was finished. Afterwards she helped her to the table, where her chair was. She saw Manouch was unsteady on her legs and gently guided her.

As she sat down Alfred brought her tea.

'Here is your tea.' He waited till he saw her hand touch the cup.

'Thank you Alfred.' He felt tears well up in his eyes knowing that her words were not for the cup of tea. In that moment, he saw her stand in the yard watching, while Salem loaded the cart. He watched as she brought the cup to her, lips and take, a sip.

His voice quivered when he spoke to her in her own language.

'It has always been my pleasure.'

She said nothing, and he turned away, to go and sit on the step, where he could see her, never taking his eyes off her, until Yvette came to fetch her, and even then, his eyes followed her as she left.

Chapter Forty

It was the second day that we were gathered at the hospital. Children, and their spouses, as well as some grand children, were there. The corridor, outside the ward, was crowded, as each waited their turn to see her.

She lay with her eyes unseeing, hearing the different voices of her loved ones as they spoke when they came in, but her words were few and they did not stay long.

Any movement caused her pain so Manouch moved as little as possible. She knew she should tell them to go home, although just knowing they were nearby gave her some sort of comfort. Earlier she heard the matron asking them to leave, but they stayed. Last night, Janey and Yvette, stayed with her, and she knew someone would stay with her again through the coming night. She made up her mind to tell them not to stay. They were better off at home tending to their family. Besides she knew the nurse would give her something to help her sleep if she asked. Her thoughts became clouded, and she drifted in and out of a light sleep.

'Your mom is resting now it is better if you leave.'

'Can some of us stay with her for the night?'

'If you feel you must, but it is better, if you let her rest. Tomorrow will be here soon enough. We will take good care of her, and the doctor will give her something to sleep.'

They spoke among themselves, and finally agreed that they would all leave. There were duties to carry out at home, and children to tend to, who had been neglected for the past two days, and it looked as if their mom was resting, comfortably. It went quiet in the corridor as the last of them left.

When the lights were put out in the wards for the night, the nurse on duty made a final check, and wrote on her sheet, 'all checked and resting.'

* * *

When he came for her, his presence was soft like a summer breeze and his touch was light, as the wings of a butterfly.

She saw him clearly, just inches away from her face, and she smiled as his lips touched hers.

* * *

The sky was still dark, when the nurses began their morning round, to check on their patients, and the clatter of pans and trolleys echoed in the corridors. The first thing the nurse saw was the smile on the old lady's lips. She smiled back forgetting for the moment that the woman was blind, then she bent down to touch her patients' hand. It was a feeling that she knew, very well and one she always dreaded. The cold skin had no elasticity and the smile on the face never wavered. There was no need to close the eyes of the woman lying there, as they had been permanently closed, for many years. Nevertheless, the nurse stood for a moment, saying a silent prayer for the woman. Then she took the dividing curtain, and pulled it around the bed, before making the entry on the patients' sheet clipped to the bottom of the bed.

* * *

We were already up and getting ready for work when the knock came on the door. When I saw Dawood standing there, I knew instinctively why he was there, and without a word showed him to go to the bedroom where his brother was. I stayed in the kitchen as a sob, so intense, as to nearly tear my chest apart, escaped my lips. I cried, not only for Manouch, but also for my husband, who I knew would be devastated.

It was early February and the women were still in black from December past. The mood at her home was sombre. No one spoke to anyone. They were too afraid lest they would start to cry. The brothers stood together but said very little. The sisters made no effort to hide their sorrow and in the kitchen, Alfred sat on his own, without speaking to anyone. He had not eaten or drank anything since early morning, and just shook his head when someone offered him something. Badwa was busy in the kitchen, and the daughters-in-law were helping him. He had gone into action in a military manner to move furniture out of the dining room, and getting chairs lined up, on the cool veranda. Big pots were bubbling on the stove and trays with teacups filled one whole table. Customers, who came to buy a drink, were told about the death and left. A sad feeling, hung over everything, and there were no words that could ease the pain, so it was no use saying anything anyway.

And just like that another domino had fallen.

Later that day I walked with Finnie to the up-market departmental store just the other side of the railroad. She knew what she had to buy and the saleswoman patiently brought out her selection of nightdresses. We agreed on a long white garment with long sleeves and tiny roses embroidered along the neckline. A new pair of slippers was also bought and with the parcels in our hands, we slowly walked back, calling in to all the shops on our way but today we did not stay to chatter, it was only to inform them of the news.

The last stop on our list was the undertaker, where we left the parcels that we bought, before returning home. When we got home I saw the lonely figure at the far end of the veranda, and my heart went out to him. I did not approach him because I felt he wanted to be alone. I realised that the hustle and bustle in the kitchen was too much for him and he had sought out a place where he could sit quietly. Since I met him for the first time, my affection for him, as a loving person, had grown steadily. He advocated fairness and respect for all and I knew he felt the same about me. Later, much later, I knew I would talk to him, but for now his pain was too great.

From early the next morning, gifts from the many shopkeepers started to arrive. Fresh fish from the fish store, vegetables and fruit from the vegetable store, and groceries and refreshments, from another, as well as meat from the butcher, and so it went on.

Each gift received, was solemnly acknowledged, as a sign of respect. People arrived from early in the day, and trays of refreshments went back and forth all day and evening. A place stood ready in the lounge for the casket that was coming later. Our own lives had changed over the past few months and I was grateful for the loving maid who looked after our children at home.

The grave was definitely in a prime spot. Right on the corner as you came into the cemetery, and as they say, business rights. The granite stone rose high into an arch chiselled out into an alcove, where a life size figure of St Joseph stood. Arabic writing squiggled on the sides, and along the bottom of the granite headstone. Many were the days, when I just sat there under the pine tree that shed its needles all over the base of the headstone, and looked at the writing, wishing I could read it. Little angels flanked the family grave on the corners, and three metal vases were embedded into the polished granite forming the border of the grave. Within the grave lay the remains of Salem on one side, and his son Joe, on the other side, leaving the centre space for Manouch, where she was now to be buried. Many years spanned the burials, and the many stories that went with it.

After the church service, the hearse first made a turn in front of the house as a last tribute, before it rode at its slow pace to the cemetery, which was not far away. On the veranda Alfred and Lizzie stood and watched in silence as the cortege passed. Their tears were also silent as it dropped down their cheeks and neither wiped them away to hide their sorrow.

Chapter Forty-one

Eventually I had no other choice. I had to call the doctor. He had been our house doctor since we were married, and before that even, with the family. He knew the trials and tribulations that the family faced over the years and his judgement was always respected. It was three days since the funeral and Norman has been in bed since then claiming illness, and not eating anything. I tried with special dishes that he liked, but nothing I brought or said, changed anything. I saw him fade away and was powerless to do anything, so I called the doctor for help.

I left them alone in the room and only went back when the doctor called me.

'I have examined him and everything seems in order, so I am prescribing a mild sedative. If he still does not eat by tomorrow, we will have to put him in hospital so a drip can be put into his vein to nourish him.'

The doctor did not look at Norman, as he spoke. Instead he looked into my eyes conveying a message, which I understood clearly.

'Thank you doctor for coming, I will let you know how he progresses.'

'Like I said, tomorrow is the latest we can leave it, before taking him to hospital.'

I walked out with the doctor then returned to the bedroom.

'You are going to have to try to eat something. I know you don't want to go to hospital.'

He nodded his head. 'Make me a soft boiled egg and a slice of toast.'

I sat with him as he slowly ate, and then the tears started to flow. I said nothing, my own feelings building up inside me and waited till he spoke again.

'She was my sun.'

'I know.' I said

'I don't know how I can live without her.' He said.

'We will help you.' I replied.

Later he got out of bed and sat in the lounge watching the children as they played. I knew it was not only the passing of his mother that affected him so badly, but also the passing of his brother, who had taken on the roll of his father. I felt for him and would help him as best I could, and I knew his brothers and sisters, were most probably feeling the same as he did. I knew Yvette would be busy with her young children and husband, but Finnie was now alone in the house, except for Alfred and Lizzie.

For the next forty days visitors would be calling and trays of refreshments, would be served constantly. After that period was over, things were bound to change. The gathering of brothers and their wives calling in the evenings, to visit their mother, would no longer take place. Visits once regularly, would be scarce. In fact, the feeling of loss was not only for their mother, but also for the closeness that they enjoyed as a family.

We still popped in for a visit, although not as regularly as before, and on those occasions when another brother also came, it felt comfortable but not the same. The front bedroom where Manouch and Salem slept was now unoccupied. The Sunday visits from David no longer took place since his demise and Johnny and his family, now paid a visit to Katy or to Badeo. The stream of clients over the weekend still kept the pot boiling, with Finnie and Yvette looking after them. The children, who used to be checked when misbehaving, now did whatever they wanted to. Broken chairs or cupboard doors were not repaired, and an air of neglect was slowly seeping in.

Finnie still worked at the vegetable shop over the weekends, and that was good. Here she met all her old friends and chatted to her hearts content.

Ulcers on her legs became inflamed at times, and then got better before getting worse again. She went to the doctor and asked how she could get rid of the problem. He prescribed treatment and encouraged her to loose weight as a matter of priority, and she went on one diet after another. It was difficult to loose weight, and when a doctor was recommended who gave injections to help, she made an appointment to see him.

He in turn recommended that she see a doctor he knew who could help her with her leg problems so she also made an appointment with that doctor.

She was excited when she got home and told Yvette that both doctors could help her.

'Why did you go to them Finnie when our doctor told you to first loose weight.'

'I know what he said but this doctor says I should be fine.'

'You must do what you think is best but I think you should wait.'

'You see' Finnie said 'you are just like mommy was. You want nothing good for me.'

'You know that is not true Finnie. We are only looking after you.'

'Well, I am going to do the operation on my legs.'

Yvette said nothing further. Maybe Finnie was right, after all what right did they have to forbid her anything?

Chapter Forty-two

'Why does Finnie want to do this now?' Norman asked Yvette where they were sitting in the kitchen. After work he stopped to visit her and Alfred. 'I told her not to do it but you know she is stubborn.' Yvette replied.

'Maybe we should phone our doctor and ask him.' He said.

'Leave her. She will only be upset.'

He felt uneasy but said nothing further, and when he heard his brothers' voice he forgot all about Finnie and her operation.

Jimmy was also happy to see his brother there, and soon the kitchen had a familiar buzz to it.

When Finnie came back from the shops with Lizzie she first went to her bedroom to put her parcels down. Although she had nice nightgowns in the chest in her room, she wanted to get something new for going to the hospital. Lizzie usually went with her to the shops for company, although everyone knew it was to keep an eye on Finnie, just in case she took a bad turn.

When Finnie joined her family in the kitchen, nobody spoke a word of the impending operation, and she was happy about that. She had enough flak from Yvette, and her mind was made up. It was time she did something for herself. Once her legs were fixed she would go on a strict diet and before long she was sure to loose some excess weight. She looked forward to the challenge and was determined to carry her plans out successfully. She knew she looked older than her thirty something years, but felt this would also change. She always felt she could not leave her mother alone to see to her own needs, and now it was time that she put herself first.

She was due to go into hospital on the Wednesday so they could prepare her for the operation on Thursday and she was not expected to stay longer than a few days at most. The doctor said she would have to rest her legs at home, but she was looking forward to the rest with her family around her.

* * *

Wednesday evening we went to visit Finnie in the hospital. She was looking forward to the next day when the operation to fix her legs, would take place. All the necessary tests were done during the day and she was as ready as she could be. We were not the only visitors and chatted to each other over her bed. We knew we would see each other the next day after the operation and left in high spirits.

On arrival the next evening we found other family members with her and the nurse asked us to wait, as they only allowed four visitors per patient at a time.

She looked drained and tired, but happy that the operation was over and thanked us for coming. We did not stay long knowing that there were other members of the family waiting to see her.

Friday evening found us waiting our turn to see her. She really did not look good.

'How are you feeling Finnie?' we asked

'Very tired but the doctor is coming later to see me again.'

'Oh, was he here earlier?'

'Yes, he says everything looks fine.'

'Do you have any pain?"

'Not too much, later they will give me something to ease it.' Her voice was very soft.

We were worried when we left and we were not the only ones.

Arriving at home we heard the ringing of the telephone and I rushed to answer it.

'The hospital phoned. They said Finnie is not good, and we must come.'

'Yvette' I said 'we just come from the hospital. She looked tired but she was alright.'

'It happened after you left. She had a bad turn.'
'Ok, we will pick you up.'

Yvette was waiting outside for us and we rushed back to the hospital where we found other members of the family waiting.

We all sat with her until the ward sister said she was more settled, and would soon be asleep so we left.

Early Saturday morning I went to get some fresh flowers to take to Finnie thinking it may cheer her up. The gladiolas and carnations in bright pink made a lovely show.

'We have to go. The hospital phoned.' Norman said as I got home

With the flowers still in my arms we left and drove in silence. Badeo and Yvette were with Finnie, and the men sat in the visitors lounge.

I went to the ward having left the flowers in the car on the backseat.

Finnie smiled when she saw me. 'You should not have come.'

'We wanted to come.' I said.

Finnie turned her head to Yvette. 'Yvette, did you see mommy?'

'Where is mommy?' Yvette asked.

'She was standing by my bed. Didn't you see her?'

'How did she look Finnie?' Badeo asked her sister.

'She looked so beautiful but you must have seen her Badeo, she was right here.'

'Yes' Badeo said 'I did see her and she looked lovely.'

Finnie looked at me again and said. 'You must go now.'

I said I would go and come back later but I only moved out of her line of vision, and stood behind her sisters. I knew she wanted to protect me and love for her made my heart constrict as I knew at that moment she would leave us.

A convulsion shook through Finnie and Yvette frantically called the sister.

The sister came and quickly went out again, returning with the longest injection needle I had ever seen. She cleared away Finnie's nightgown covering her chest, and inserted this long needle into her heart.

We waited with abated breath, the four of us, Badeo, Yvette and I, and the sister holding the needle in her hand. Nothing happened as

Finnie lay still on the bed, and still we waited until the sister looked up and shook her head. I turned away and left the ward, as another domino fell.

Within six months the family had diminished dramatically.

Norman was waiting in the car for me and I opened the door and got in without saying a word. He could see on my face what he had dreaded and silently drove to my parents' home, which was not far away. I took out the flowers and gave it to my mom.

They sat with Norman where he cried in the lounge, not saying anything till he could speak.

'Why Dad, why? She was so young. Why is this all happening to us?'

I had gone straight to the kitchen when we arrived and now brought a tray of tea into the lounge.

'We don't know why God has done this but he knows best. He is the only one who knows the way ahead and we have to respect his judgement.'

We stayed a while longer and then went home. Our children were with the maid and had hardly seen us over the past few days, and there were many things to take care of.

* * *

The casket was put on the big round table in the dining room next to the kitchen. The wives, with Badwas' help, were busy in the kitchen preparing food in big pots and setting trays with teacups ready for the stream of people arriving to pay their respects to the family. The women were all in black and hardly any words were spoken. Everyone seemed stunned and was too afraid to say anything.

I saw the two men come in, and knew they were not family but friends of Finnie. They had their handkerchiefs in their hands as they wiped away their tears.

I was busy with the teacups but when I heard the singing, I stopped to listen. The rich, tenor voice of the heavy set man, was amazing as he sang the 'Ave Maria' to the woman lying in the casket. His emotion spilled over to everyone and I had to sit down to gather my own feelings so that I could carry on with my tasks. I had I knew, without a doubt, never heard anything so beautiful, and I was happy for Finnie who had to make so many sacrifices and who had indeed been loved.

I did not go to the cemetery having to help with the preparations for the people when they came back to the house, but knew she was going to be buried in the corner grave, with the Arabic squiggles, next to her mom, on top of her father.

And one more domino was down.

Chapter Forty-three

There was now only one occupant left in the house that once upon a time, was a safe haven for so many people. He sat on the veranda in the far corner, and it looked as if his eyes were glazed, as he stared at nothing much. A lonely figure, thinking of his life, as it had been. He gets up very slowly, and shuffles to the kitchen, where Yvette and the children are.

Business went on, as before filling the days, and at night when they left to go to their house next door, he would be on his own again. Not that it bothered him being alone, that is considering how noisy the children were during the day, but he missed Manouch. The family now seldom came to visit, except on weekends, and then it was usually just for a little while. But life went on while the children grew up, and he made tea ready in the mornings before they went to school, just as before. The callipers that Yvette's eldest son wore did not hamper him in any way, as he ran all over with his brother. Why Yvette and her family did not move into her mothers' house, he did not know, but he was sure they thought it was haunted.

* * *

Many changes took place as the family circles grew, yet everyone kept in contact somehow, and the bond between the families were always there even though each had created their own family, and with it, another life.

Dawood once again proved his strength, when he fell from a thirty feet construction platform while working, and crushed his chest. We thought he looked bad when we saw him in hospital, and frankly feared for the worse, but he surprised us all and recovered quite well. The accident did however mean that he could no longer do the manual work he was used to doing. It was time for him to sit in the sun in his yard and relax. Not that his strength was in any way diminished, but he was ready to make changes.

The suburb where Norman and his family lived was very pleasant.

Neighbours were friendly and waved as they passed and sometimes stopped for a chat. There were also many children around who became friends with his children.

His eldest child, a son, had only just started school, and the maid took the walk each morning, and each afternoon, together with the two younger children, to take and fetch him from school. It was an uphill walk and at the end of the road, steps chiselled from rock over the hill, led to the upper road, where the school was. It was a pleasant walk on most days, when the weather was fine, and an icy walk during winter. Jimmy was living with Norman and his family as his divorce had become final and he did not have anywhere to go. It was not an ideal situation, but more like a coming to terms, kind of a situation. His two children were with their mother and he needed a place to adjust. The arrangement was initially for a short time but stretched to a year, and then he brought his son Cyril, to stay as well. Being a teenager, his mother had become disenchanted with his behaviour, and thought he would be better off with his father. There was a very strong bond between father and son and he idolized his father. He was a lovely boy but as all teenagers, had no idea what he wanted to do. School was out and college was tried and discarded while he decided what to do.

They had named their son after Jimmy's father Salem, as the English translation was Cyril, and Jimmy's older brother Johnny, had also named his eldest son the same, so these two cousins boasted the same name.

Jimmy was trying to build a new future for him and his son and had started a business of his own, and Cyril after much soul searching, went to work with his father. It looked like their life was finally taking shape again and they moved out.

* * *

One afternoon when I stopped at Yvette for a short visit, I saw the gypsy woman, there again. We chatted and Yvette said I should let her read my palm. I first made excuses but Yvette encouraged me, so I held out my hand.

'You and your husband will have a long life together. Are you pregnant?'

'No' I said. 'Definitely not.' I knew this for certain as I was taking modern day precautions that practically guaranteed that such an event would not occur. After all, three children were plenty and we were happy with our family, as it was.

'Well, you are going to be. As soon as your youngest child starts school, you will have another baby.'

'I don't think so.' I said smilingly with confidence. 'It is impossible.'

'You will see I am never wrong.' Although her face was serious her prediction did not bother me at all, knowing I was taking proper precautions, and I soon left.

Our eldest child was finding it difficult at school and I realised we were too eager to send him at such a young age. He was not really happy and dreaded going to school each morning, and hated the evenings after the cooking was done, when we worked on his reading. Some evenings when I returned home from work it was already getting dark, and I realised my son was tired by that time, but there was nothing I could do about that, as we needed the second income. Our daughter was starting school the next year and I sent out letters to all the schools in the area with the hope of finding an administrative post which would allow me to spend more time with the children. My enquiries did not produce anything and I thought I would try again at a later stage, and I was very happy with the work I had.

I took our daughter to her first day at school, and when I went to register her in the office, the friendly woman behind the desk, asked if I was the person who applied for a position earlier. 'Yes' I said with surprise.

'Well we did not have anything then, but out typist is pregnant and will be leaving soon, if you are still interested.'

'Of course.' I said and she took me to the principal who agreed that I could start when the typist left. I was thrilled with the prospect and could not wait to tell my husband the good news. It meant of course that my salary would drop by half at least, but there would be no travelling expenses as I could walk with the children. Most of all was the benefit of being with them in the afternoons as well as school holidays. All in all, I thought I was in paradise.

I felt as if I was walking on air and could not wait for evening to come to tell my husband.

As planned I started working at the school, and loved every minute of it. The walk in the mornings over the hill was invigorating, and time with the children was magic, and the following year our third and youngest child would also begin his schooling.

This son of ours with his big soulful brown eyes with long eyelashes and olive skin was totally different from the other two, who were fair with blue eyes.

We were all happy in the afternoon when we walked home from school while chatting about the day, as each one got a chance to tell us how their class was during the day. I knew that I was where I wanted to be, but a shock was waiting for me. I did not think it could happen with all the precautions in place but to my astonishment, the gypsies' prediction, was coming true.

This time the pregnancy was different. I was older, although twenty-six was not actually old, but the height of summer was not an ideal time to be carrying around extra weight, and the walk to school became a challenge and short rests in the shade of the trees on our way, became more frequent.

As much as I promised myself that I would never cry out in pain as I heard other women do while giving birth, I had no control as the pain in my back was unbearable. The birth was not only painful but the loss of blood was excessive and it left me very weak and I was hardly able to lift an arm to cradle our son. The bush of black curly hair and fair skin, made him look more like a doll than a baby and the staff in the maternity ward loved him. He looked completely different to all the bareheaded babies, and his skin was like marble. He was beautiful and hungry all the time. Fortunately our trusty maid was still with us to take care of our baby, and I was now working a walking distance away from home, and was only away for the mornings.

Our life had taken on a completely new meaning with a new baby in the house after six years. I chuckled to myself as I thought of my mother-in-law who chided me for taking precautions and I remembered clearly what my answer was to her. 'If God wants me have another baby nothing will stop Him.' There was no doubt that God was indeed Almighty and nothing could ever stand in His way.

* * *

Phillip went to visit his family more often and bought them a house on top of a hill, overlooking his brother Norman's home, which was nestled at the foot of the hill.

It was a lovely place, resting on top of the rocks, and the view overlooking the suburb below was beautiful at night when all the lights were on. He would stay for a weekend at times, and then leave again. Nobody knew exactly where he went to and he kept his other life to himself.

His wife was always happy to see him and never pressed him for any commitment. Their daughter was now in a home for people with special needs and they would fetch her on weekends to be with them. Phillip played with his daughter when he was there and loved her just as she was. Their eldest daughter was married for the second time, and he was now a grandfather to four perfectly fine boys, who all lived in the house on the hill. He knew they were blessed and thanked God every day for these gifts.

When he left, his wife waved to him, as he rode away. The hope in her heart was always there that they would one day be together as a family again. When he brought a little girl home to his wife and said it was his daughter from another woman she first cried, but later accepted the child as her own, and took care of her as only a mother could.

* * *

It was a Saturday evening and I was home alone with the children as Norman had gone to a boxing match with his nephew, when the telephone rang.

When I answered it was a woman's voice, asking to speak to Norman.

I told her he was not there and asked if I could help her, but she said no, she would phone later, so I put the telephone down, wondering who it could be. A short while later the telephone rang again, and it was the same woman who asked again for my husband, and now I was getting worried. I tried to get more information from her but she put the telephone down again. Not even a half an hour later, she rang again, and I knew I had to find out why she kept calling.

'Please tell me what is wrong.' I said.

'I have to speak to Norman.'

'He will only be back much later. Maybe I can help you. I am his wife.'

She hesitated and when she spoke I felt a cold shiver run through my body.

'I am at the hospital, where I brought Phillip. He had a heart attack and he is dead, and I don't know what to do. He told me that if anything should happen to him I had to speak to |Norman.'

I was stunned and yet I knew I had to find out what happened and where they were.

'He was not feeling well and asked me to take him to hospital and he died in the car before we got there. I have been here with him for hours.'

'Tell me exactly where you are.' I said.

When she put the telephone down I stood still as my mind raced like an engine. I had promised her that I would go to her but what was I to do? I was the youngest of the family and knew that I could not take any decisions on my own and there was no way that I could contact my husband.

I was uncertain what I should do. Who should I contact? What if she was not telling the truth? I sat down for a moment to think about what I had to do. I thought of his wife and how upset she would be, but I knew that I had to get hold of someone who could help me, and telephoned Badeos' home. Her husband was also the brother of Phillip's wife.

'Dawood' I said when he answered 'can you please come to me urgently. Something has happened and you must come and help me because I don't know what to do.'

I waited for him and explained what happened and together we went to the hospital.

At casualty they told us that he had been admitted but was declared dead on arrival. Then they pointed out the woman who brought him in.

I explained to the doctor in charge who we were, and that we had to establish his identity without a doubt, before we could inform his family. He took Dawood down to the mortuary, while I waited with the woman, who had telephoned me.

When Dawood came back he signed the documents they presented, and we sat for a short while with the woman to find out what had happened.

We were quiet on our way home, and he said he would go to his sister. While I waited for Norman to come home I telephoned his brother who contacted the rest of the family. And another domino toppled over.

She was devastated and cried uncontrollably for the husband she loved most dearly, and for the pain they had endured together. She was hurt that he was not with them when his hour came, and that she could not be there for him.

After the funeral was over that day, the family sat with Phillip's wife till late in the lounge where it overlooked the houses below. The curtains were open, and the first lights began to appear giving one a feeling of being one with the universe high up on the hill.

Buddy was also there, and a familiar feeling of family togetherness, enveloped them. He had become a stranger to his family over the years, and now this loss of his brother, brought him back again. He had forgotten how it felt to be with his brothers, and now in his later years, he realised he should have made contact more often. He promised himself that he was going to change that. These people were his family, and he laughed and joked with them, to lighten the air. And they in turn were amazed to find he was not as aloof, as they had always thought he was, No he was after all, one of them.

Buddy became a regular visitor after that day, and his family, brothers and sisters were enthralled with his stories and he basked in their admiration.

So when the call came, hardly two months later, they felt cheated, that they had so little time together with him. Just like his brother, completely unexpected while in his shop, he just sank to the ground.

An article, in the local newspaper, showed his photo and called him 'The Godfather.' Those, that knew him, also knew that it was in fact the truth.

The funeral differed from the earlier one of his brother, in the fact that he had a very large family of his own, and he was also well known in many other circles. Six black mourning cars stood behind the hearse in front of the church to accommodate his family, and the church was full to capacity. There were many people who were not catholic such as judges, magistrates, advocates, lawyers and other high office bearers who could be seen amongst the mourners.

A remark was passed, by someone that it was, as if a minister had died.

And so it was that within a few short months, another domino had fallen.

* * *

The house on the hill that Phillip had bought for his family became expensive to maintain and his wife took in a woman boarder to help with the expenses. Jimmy soon became a regular visitor and before long, bought a house, of his own. The woman boarding there had two little girls of her own, and they all moved in with Jimmy. The house he bought was on the opposite side of town in a new suburb, which was nearer to the place he was working. His own business was finally coming together, and he felt whole again.

Before long they were pregnant with a boy. Jimmy's own two children were grown up by this time, and this new little boy was like a fresh breeze in their lives. The relationship between Jimmy, and his eldest son, was of complete devotion to each other and there was no doubt that the arrival of a new child in the family had some impact on the relationship. Cyril did feel abandoned for a while, even though he had married and had a little girl of his own. It was a natural reaction but it soon made place for affection for the little boy who was his new brother.

Jimmy was like the cat that got the cream as he took his little boy with him wherever he went. Anthony was a sweet child that crept into everyone's heart.

Business was also picking up with Cyril working with his dad and he bought a house near them. Of all the brothers, Jimmy was the one that made a point of visiting his family regularly. He popped in for a cup of tea and a chat whenever he could, and usually brought his little boy with him. To Norman, Jimmy was always a part of his own family as these two brothers had depended on each other, since childhood. Their bond was tangible, and they were happy when the other was happy.

The suburb where Jimmy stayed with the mother of his little boy and her two daughters, from her earlier relationship, was in a new area so there were many children about. These children, who went to school or pre-school during the day, usually gathered outside in the early evenings, in front of their houses, to play with each other.

On this particular day little Anthony, who was now nearly four years old, had his small bicycle with fairy wheels at the back, with him. He felt so grownup when he was with the group of children, where they played in the road where their mothers could watch them. At this time of day there was not usually much traffic around, as all the parents were already at home so it was quite safe. His mother watched him from the lounge window never taking her eyes off her little son, and smiled indulgently, to herself. After so many years since the birth of her youngest daughter, this little boy was like a gift from heaven and she knew Jimmy felt the same way. Being with Jimmy made her feel safe and happy again and she loved him very much. She knew he would never commit in marriage to her, as he still loved his wife even though they were divorced. This she felt was not important to her, as she knew he was happy with her and the children.

She saw the milk lorry, stop a little way further along the road. The lorry came every evening to deliver fresh milk to the homes around her and it was nothing out of the ordinary. Except for this day. This terrible day, when their world, came to an end.

Instead of moving forward, she saw the lorry reversing and she started to run, but she was too late. The sound of the bicycle under the wheels of the lorry was not loud and there was no cry from the child that could be heard over the inhuman scream of the mother.

The red pick-up van turned at the corner of the road that led to his home and his family and he smiled in anticipation of seeing them. The smile turned to a frown when he saw the commotion in front of his house, and his heart lurched as he felt his chest gripped by steel bands.

Night fell, and a dense darkness enveloped everything around it, and not even a star could penetrate the black sky.

The small white coffin was not heavy as Norman's two eldest sons carried it to the grave. The mother of the child was not there as she was unable to walk or even talk or feel anything. She was sedated and could only stare in front of her not seeing anything at all. Her mind had left the world and nothing mattered any more. He stood to one side, the father, and his family was with him, although he did not even realise it. He was empty and had no feeling of any kind. His eyes were glazed and fixed as he stared at the little coffin. The grave was in the new cemetery where his brother Phillip was, as the old cemetery where his parents were, was full, but nothing mattered to him anyway.

* * *

And the years passed while the house where Salem and Manouch lived with their family became more and more neglected as rumours of expropriation for a new road was heard. Chickens now ran through the house, and the floorboards were broken, in places. The only occupant of the house was sometimes seen where he sat on the veranda staring into nothing.

When the letter did come it changed everything. The municipality informed them, that the property was indeed expropriated to allow a road to be built where the houses stood although the process would still take some time to be completed. The property could not be sold privately and the price offered, was not negotiable. It was time for Yvette and her family to look at other properties. The end of an era was at hand.

I asked if I could have the picture of Salem and Manouch taken on their wedding day that hung in the lounge. I cleaned it up nicely, replacing the old brown backing with fresh paper, and hung it in the passage of our new home. We had built a new house closer to town on an old mining property, where a new suburb was being established. It was closer to the high schools that the children now attended and a stone's throw from the cemetery where I used to take my babies for walks.

Norman was so proud and he invited Alfred to lunch so he could show him his new home. We made a special dinner for him and we all sat around the new dining room table enjoying our meal together.

After lunch we sat in the garden until Alfred said he was tired and wanted to go home. His heart was full of love that day knowing he had done a good job in raising the child that was left without a father at such a tender age.

Our new home was also not too far away from the house Yvette and her family would move to. The house they bought was higher up on the crest and was first renovated, as and when the funds were available. It took a long time to complete but it meant that Alfred now had his own room with a bathroom and a proper bed, as a row of outbuildings in the yard allowed for this. What, their move also meant, was that they finally ended their illegal business, of selling liquor. This practise had in fact also become absolute after the laws were changed and mining in the area, came to a near standstill. Time was moving on for all and progress was inevitable.

* * *

Chapter Forty-four

Changing from school to college for our two eldest sons meant that although three years separated them in age, they started on the same course and ended it together. According to law our eldest son was of age to commence his military training while the younger one, was not yet of age for this duty. He was in a quandary whether to ask for early admission for military duty, or to study further. In the end he thought it would be better to get the army training over with, so they both began their military training at the same time. Our older son would be stationed in Pretoria while the younger was going to the Heidelberg Army Gymnasium. They looked so handsome in their respective uniforms and our lives now revolved around visiting the army bases on weekends. We were very proud of our sons who both lived clean and healthy lives, not smoking or drinking and focussed on building a future. They were both slim and tall with black hair while the one had sky blue eyes and the other warm brown.

The first year came and went, and we revelled in the way our sons matured into men. From early the second year they were already counting the days for their duties to be completed. Whenever they could, they secured passes to be at home and we cherished each moment they could be with us.

Our eldest son was courting a lovely girl who also happened to be the granddaughter of Dawood, Norman's brothers' second wife. Before long he proposed and she accepted. The engagement party was a grand affair that was held in our church hall, and many army friends also attended. He was twenty years of age and although young, had his life mapped out before him as he had obtained an offer of apprenticeship before even starting his army duty. When we named this son of ours we gave him Salem as a second name after his late grandfather. This second name of his caused much interest with his friends at school and particularly in the army, and although he often complained, he secretly loved it.

The younger son was still unsure whether he wanted to study further or open a business with a friend, whom he had met in the army. He was eighteen and was an achiever, and looked forward to finishing his duty so he could begin his life in earnest.

* * *

The accident happened on the way to base camp one morning. A car swerved in front of them and by trying to avoid the accident our younger son and his friend who was at the same camp in Heidelberg, landed on the pavement into a garden wall of a house. The car, when I went to see it was a total write off, and we arranged for it to be taken away. Fortunately the two of them sustained only cuts and bruises but unbeknown to us it was strike one.

Depression took hold of our younger son with the loss of his much loved car, now mangled and parked in our garage. The insurance did not cover the damage as it was more of a collector's car and quite old, and we did not have the money to have it fixed. We knew his heart was aching and tried to cheer him up, but it was difficult. I knew I had to do something about it and after speaking to our pharmacist, bought him a tonic, which he took as prescribed. Slowly an improvement took place and when Yvette's son who had a panel beating business offered to help with the repairing of his car, he became more cheerful.

Yvette's eldest son, who grew into a fine young man having shed his callipers, had qualified as a panel beater and now owned his own business as he was one of only two beneficiaries on the will when Manouch passed away. He came to look at the stranded car and said he could repair it if a front half of a body of the same car could be found from a scrap dealer. What they had to do, in the interim, was to dismantle the car completely, to save on costs. So all spare time of our two older sons, were now spent in the garage, where they stripped the car. This was in a way, the best way to work through the depression, of our younger son, and soon the car was ready for the next step. Luckily a body for the front of the car was found, and things looked as if it could come together again. The front magnum wheels were also damaged and we started looking in the classified for replacements.

When his same friend from camp, invited him out one Friday evening, he first did not want to go, but after some discussion, decided to go along as his friend was celebrating the new wheels on his own car. Later they picked him up in their car, his friend and a cousin of his. We were happy for him to spend some time with his friends to take his mind off the state of his own car and we knew he never stayed out very late.

I was in bed but I never slept until I heard the last child come in, and when twelve o'clock came and went, I began to pray to Our Lady.

Next to me my snored contentedly after a night out playing cards.

As the one prayer ended I repeated it again, and again, and again, and when the telephone rang, I knew instantly that something was wrong.

'This is the sister from the casualty department. We have your son here. He is going to be alright but has concussion so we are keeping him overnight.'

'Is he hurt badly?' I asked as my heart was hammering in my chest.

'He is hurt but it is nothing serious, however it is necessary for us to keep him here overnight,'

'Thank you for letting us know' I said' we will be there as soon as we can.'

My husband had woken up when the telephone rang and was already dressing before I put the receiver down.

It was the early hours of a new day and the roads were quiet. Without knowing it, we were on the same road that our son and his friends had travelled on hours before. I saw the car first and we stopped and got out to take a closer look. How anyone could have survived was a miracle as the car lay on its hood with the front up against the pole of the streetlight.

We continued our journey to the hospital in silence, each with our own thoughts.

Relief to see him overshadowed our shock of his appearance. His face was burnt where battery acid had splashed, just missing his eyes, and dried blood, covered his one arm.

We smiled at him with love and although he saw us, nothing registered. The concussion to his head had brought with it amnesia.

A bundle of the clothes that had been cut from his body, was handed to me as we left.

Two strokes down and only one more to go for a strike out.

Home the next day he just lay on his bed sleeping most of the time. My parents came to see him as did some of his friends but he never got up. Special leave, from their commander, had been granted to him, as well as to his friend, who had also sustained minor injuries.

The burn marks from the acid of the car battery that had exploded on contact was fortunately not serious. X-rays were taken at the hospital of his arm, and although nothing was broken, he could not bend it.

Whatever occurred that night was totally blocked out in his mind and one could only imagine the terror before the impact as the car turned over and connected the pole of the street light.

Depression was now like a heavy blanket covering our son, and I was at a loss to help him other than to get some more tonic from the chemist. I sat with him in his room for hours in the evenings, to give him an opportunity to share his feelings with me. He was listless and I was worried. His recovery was slow.

When he got back to base camp and managed to get a sleep-out pass he was happy. It meant that he was home in the evenings, which was nice.

And now their count down from national duty was marked each day on the calendar.

Still, no matter what we tried, he just could not lift himself out of the state he was in. Progress on his car was slow and there was nothing he could do until the panel beating was complete. We spent many hours together, as I tried to be with him as much as he would let me, and when his long time friend came to visit I was glad. They were planning to go to the car racing on the coming Saturday, and asked if he wanted to go with.

At first he declined, but I encouraged him to go with, so he telephoned his other friend, who was with him at base camp to invite him along who was not well and first said no but then changed his mind. Now it was going to be a nice crowd of friends, which also included our daughter and I was happy knowing that he loved cars with a passion and felt the outing would be good for him.

How could I have been so wrong?

On the Thursday before that fateful Saturday, I had gone to the supermarket to purchase our groceries for the month. As I put my hand on the shopping trolley, a feeling, of such dread came over me, that I turned around and went straight home. I could not explain it, but I was powerless to shake the feeling off.

Michael and his sister left early the Saturday morning to pick up their friend before meeting up with the others. Our portable braai was packed in the boot of the car and I had earlier prepared the meat they were taking with.

The container with the meat and the rolls and cooler bag was the last to be packed in.

After I had prepared everything I crawled back into bed. When everything was packed and ready Michael came to my room.

'Thanks for everything Mom.'

I looked at my son and was happy knowing he would have a day out with his friends.

'Just enjoy yourself and have a good day.'

Then he leaned down and kissed me. I was pleasantly surprised as the older children very rarely did this.

'Please make sure you drive Michael. I will feel better knowing that. I know your sister wants to drive but she does not have as much experience.'

'I know, don't worry. I will drive.'

'Ok, have fun.' I said as he left the room.

When I heard the front door close I tried to doze off again but after a while gave up and got dressed.

It was a quiet day at home as our youngest child was spending the weekend with his cousins who were of his age, and earlier we had dropped our eldest son and his fiancé at the movies before Norman and I went to get the groceries that I failed to get on the Thursday. We planned to fetch them later when the show was over so we took our time to pack everything away and put the television on to watch some sport.

* * *

There was a festive mood among the spectators parked on the grass facing the racetrack and they mingled excitedly. The roar of the sports cars as they rounded the corner and accelerated on the flat stretch was deafening. The whole atmosphere was alive and exhilarating and the group of friends had their picnic basket laid out in a haphazard fashion, as they ate and drank. The portable braai was already cooled down waiting to be packed away. They had to shout at each other above the noise to communicate to share their views.

There was such a big crowd that they decided to leave before the end in order to avoid the traffic. Everything was packed up and ready but Michael just could not pull himself away from a conversation he had struck up with one of the guys in a group near to them. His sister was getting edgy as their friends were already waiting for them in their car so she got into the drivers' seat with their friend in the back and drove up to where Michael was standing and told him to get in. They saw their friends up ahead, but other cars fell in behind them, also hoping to miss the onslaught of people leaving, and when they saw their friends again, they were far ahead. There was nothing they could do but crawl forward slowly. Once they were out of the gate their friends were nowhere to be seen.

'What is the turn-off we have to take guys?'

'I'm not sure myself can't you see the others?' Michael answered 'Do you know which one it is?' He asked his friend in the back.

Too late she recognised the name on the signboard on the side of the road.

'Oh! I think we missed it. Never mind we'll take the next turnoff.'

And just like that fate played the cards.

The traffic control car was parked on a side road, when they saw a bakkie, speeding towards them ignoring the stop sign at the intersection. They put on their siren and raced after the car and saw it swerve in and out of the traffic lanes and increased their speed.

The driver saw the light flashing in his mirror and heard the siren and knew that if they stopped him he would be arrested. Hot sun while watching the motor racing and a few too many beers could only mean trouble and he pushed his foot down harder on the pedal and swerved again to overtake the line of cars in his lane.

And then he saw the oncoming car and his hands froze on the steering wheel.

* * *

Terror filled his eyes as he saw the bakkie racing towards them and instinct made him cry out 'Chips' as he grabbed the steering wheel away from his sister, to try to manoeuvre the car between the gap in the oncoming traffic. When his friend heard the warning where he sat in the back of the car he instinctively ducked down as he had been trained.

* * *

As they saw the car change lanes again, an opening in the traffic gave them a view of the road ahead, and their eyes registered shock as they saw the oncoming car. The head to head impact lifted both vehicles into the air and they saw them turn around in the air, and turn and roll again, before crashing down to the ground settling up against the steel barrier on the side of the road. A cloud of dust rose into the sky.

The patrol car skidded to a stop and both men were out of the car in seconds.

One officer ran to stop the traffic and the other ran to the cars, their patrol radio in their hands already shouting for help

* * *

I had warmed the pies that we had bought earlier for supper, and

I dished ours up, leaving some in the oven for our children to have later. As I put the plate on the small table in the lounge for my husband, the telephone rang, and I walked to answer it where it was on a small glass table next to the couch.

Why did my hand shake as I lifted the receiver?

'Hello.'

When I heard his voice steel bands clamped around my heart, and my tongue became dry and thick in my mouth.

'We have been in an accident, I have seen your daughter but I cannot find Michael.'

My heart hammered in my chest as a silent scream for help from God filled my very being.

'What do you mean, you can't find him?'

'I have looked everywhere.'

No! No! He must be there. Please God, let him be there.

'Is there a nurse or a sister with you? I have to talk to someone.'

When she spoke her voice sounded concerned.

'Your son is badly hurt you must come as soon as you can.'

The steel clamps grew tighter around my chest and my husband was next to me now. I knew I had to say the most dreaded words but I had no choice as a sob rose from within me.

'Please tell me if he is alive.'

'Yes he is in theatre you must come as soon as possible.'

I put the telephone down and for a brief moment my husband put his arms around me as I put my head on his chest. I knew there was a call I had to make before we left. My tongue was so dry and thick that I could hardly get the words out when I told our future daughter-in-laws mother to make sure they fetch the couple from the theatre where we left them earlier.

The food was forgotten on the table as I grabbed my handbag and the car keys as we ran to the car.

My husband did not turn where he was supposed to, and I said he was going the wrong way, but he answered that he was first going to his sister Yvette's house to fetch Badwa who he knew could handle the car much faster than he could. He stopped in front of their house, which was not far from ours, and he ran in to see if Badwa was at home, and when he came running out with Norman, I quickly got into the back seat. I knew why Norman did this as Badwa put on the emergency lights and drove like a demon.

For once I did not feel afraid or nervous going so fast, as prayer after prayer, rolled from my lips.

We left Badwa to park the car as we ran into the emergency entrance of the hospital.

Their friend was waiting for us at the entrance in a wheelchair with his uncle with him and took us to the sister in charge.

'He is still in theatre,' the sister on duty said 'He was not breathing when they brought him in but the doctor managed to get his heart going again. He has severe head injuries and we have called a surgeon from another hospital, where they specialise in head injuries. We are waiting for the helicopter to bring him.'

All I could think of was that he was alive and that he had a chance.

'Can you please send for a priest right away?' Norman asked the sister and she was on the telephone immediately.

His friend took us to our daughter where she was in a cubicle in the emergency section. She looked bad and was crying but the doctor on duty told us she could go home later as they did x-rays on her body and although her leg, arm and nose, was hurt, nothing was broken. There were lacerations all over her body and I asked if she should rather stay overnight, but the doctor assured us it would be better for her to go home.

Then our eldest son and his fiancé were there, and he held me to his chest. Then he told me that the man responsible for the accident was there as well and was badly hurt.

Anger and pain flowed through me and I said I wanted to see him but my son steered me away.

We left the two of them with our daughter and went back to the sister to find that the priest had arrived as well as the surgeon. We saw our son wheeled out from the theatre with a white sheet covering his body. He was unconscious and looked unharmed but we knew the injury was internal. We walked with him to the theatre. The orderlies were pushing him very fast with the priest almost running next to him, blessing and praying as he went. The passages seemed endless and then we came to the double doors leading into the theatre where the surgeon was waiting. Silently we watched as the doors closed behind him.

The priest stayed with us for a while, promising that he would 'storm heaven' for help and assistance, and I believed him.

Dawood, Norman's brother was there when we got back to casualty, and silently gave us of his strength.

The operation was expected to take at least seven hours and I told him later to go home and rest. After all, it was not in our hands and all we could do was pray.

Seven hours later in the early hours of the morning, they came out of the theatre, and we walked with him to the ICU ward where we left him. Badwa went back with us to the emergency section where we collected our daughter. It was cold and raining when we helped her into the backseat of the car and I was concerned that there was no blanket to cover her. No words were spoken by anyone on the way home for fear of breaking down emotionally.

Sunday morning found us early at the local police station to apply for a petrol permit as there were national restrictions in force. After much explaining the necessary document was obtained, and we could fill the car with petrol in order to make trips to the hospital possible.

The professor was in a private room with two students with him when he spoke to us. 'The operation went as well as can be expected and we are cautiously optimistic.

It will take a long time before he is well, and much work will have to be done. You have to understand this.'

'Anything you say we will do for him.' We replied.

He looked at us then spoke again.

'I don't just mean that it will take him a long time to get well, we will have to teach him to walk and talk again. His brain was severely injured.'

Silently we nodded, as words failed us and we clung to his words 'cautiously optimistic,' which meant hope to us.

He looked serene as he lay there silently, with his eyes taped closed.

Apart from the bandage around his head it was only his one arm that had some abrasions. His body was covered with a white sheet from the waist down and wires were connected to monitor screens on the wall. We stayed with him in silence for a while and then returned to the waiting area where the commodore found us.

He was not a young man, and had a kindly face. He looked resplendent in his white official uniform with gold braiding.

'I am the most senior officer in this area and it is my duty to offer you my assistance in caring for your son. Firstly I want to inform you that everything regarding any charges will be taken care of by the army so you don't have to be concerned about that. He will get the best care that he can have.' He waited a short while before he continued.

'As you know he is in our care and will be airlifted to the army hospital shortly.' Then he handed me his card and said we could call on him if we needed to. I put the card in my bag for safekeeping.

Our position was clear having been told by the sister who admitted our son, as well as the commodore, that we had no jurisdiction over our son as he was the responsibility of the army. This was not a bad thing, I said to myself, although it made me feel a bit afraid, I knew at the same time that they would do whatever was called for.

For as many hours as was possible I was at the hospital near our son. I was hopeful and positive. The sister in the ICU ward where he was, told me the next day, that the helicopter had arrived to airlift him to the army hospital but the specialist said his condition was too critical to move him, and that he would stay where he was. We did not know whether this was good or bad but we knew we had to accept whatever they decided.

At home the atmosphere was emotional. Our daughter had sick leave from her work and looked bad. Her nose was in fact broken, and her leg although not broken, was cut and swollen badly. I took her to our house doctor and he prescribed medication and treatment. She needed me but I left as soon as I could in the mornings to be at the hospital, and went again in the evenings with my husband. Daily duties had to be taken care of and I knew I was needed at home and at work but my whole being wanted to be with my son. Even if he could not see me I was certain he knew when I was there with him.

The accident happened on a Saturday and on the first Thursday after that they performed a Tracheotomy to enable them to clear his chest to lessen the danger of pneumonia. He lay there unmoving linked to monitors and drips in his hands that now showed swelling. We spoke to him and held his hand and hoped for a sign from him, which did not come. The fluid draining from his body was clear in the glass container underneath his bed and this gave us hope for his recovery. On the cabinet in his private ICU ward was a large register where every single movement was recorded in, and which I covertly, checked each day. On some days when I arrived, I found my mom and dad standing silently next to our son with love and concern in their eyes, and I could not look into their faces for fear of breaking down.

Two weeks had passed and I had already made mental arrangements of how I could help our son when he finally came home. I knew I would do anything and everything to help him and knew my husband would do the same.

Then his brain began to swell and fans were erected above him to try to get the fever down. Our prayers intensified and the priest was called again who anointed our son once more with the most holy oil. The priest assured us that prayers were being said in all the parishes and we felt comforted and hopeful. Surely all the prayers would help.

* * *

Twenty-one is an age announcing maturity, and thus must always be celebrated, so we did that on the day when our eldest son became of age. I cooked a lunch and invited his fiancé and her parents and if our smiles were laced with sadness, we knew that it would be understood. We were truly blessed with our children who never failed to make us proud.

The slim gold watch on our son's arm was selected very carefully and he was happy with his choice. This time with our eldest child was important although we were anxious to be at the hospital and we left as soon as we could. How precious time had become to be with our children.

There were times that I sat in the private corridor of the intensive care unit with other people who also had a close loved one in the ICU ward and we exchanged our concerns and prayers for each other. I saw the commodore when he came to check on his charge and he always stopped to say a few words.

When I arrived that fateful Wednesday morning and saw the medical register open on the cabinet my breathing became laboured, as I read the word written across the page in red, 'decerbrate'. I was not sure what the word meant but I knew it was not good and would look it up in the dictionary when I was home.

I rubbed his arms and held his hand and spoke of things at home and he lay unmoving with only the sound of the bleeping machines and the whirr of the fan to cool him down from the temperature raging within him.

The liquid draining from his body into the glass container under his bed had become cloudy and was now more green than clear. I knew it was not a good sign but hope and belief kept me going.

The sister told me that our son would be moved to another ward the next day. I begged her to keep him there for a while longer, and a doctor came to speak to me. I took the card that the commodore had given me, from my handbag, and asked to use their telephone. When he came on the line I asked if he could intervene on our behalf, as we had no jurisdiction over our son. Just a few more days I pleaded. The commodore asked to speak to the doctor in charge, and then spoke to me again, explaining that they were making the right choice, and instructed me to come to his office to sign some documents.

It took all my courage to sign the papers put before me knowing it was to close a file.

I left in a daze with tears blurring my vision. I knew his end was near and prayed incessantly, not for his life this time, but for his release of life.

Too late I realised that I had taken the wrong turnoff and found myself driving towards the wrong side of town.

We sat next to our son who now only had an oxygen supply point above his bed. Gone were all the monitors. The ward had six beds and it was clear that those who were there were not likely to recover.

Lights shone like gold coins through the darkness outside the window of the ward where we sat on either side of the bed. Norman held our son's one hand while I held the other. In the bed opposite a man was screaming in agony from a knife wound to his stomach and in another bed an old man was moaning constantly.

I kissed our son's hand and began to tell him how proud he had made us. How we loved him and always would, and that he was not to be worried about us, and that we would surely meet again one day.

The men in the other beds were silent now as they heard me speak to our dying son, and only a sniffle could be heard coming from them.

I saw a tear drop from the corner of his eye and wiped away with a kiss.

When I was finished I got up and walked out of the ward to be by my own for a while and saw the parents of our son's best friend arrive with the priest.

Once again our son was anointed with the holy oil and I persuaded Norman to leave with them. I stayed the night next to the bed of our son and on that Friday morning at 09h00 a shudder passed through his body and I held him tight as he breathed his last breath.

Chapter Forty-five

The church was packed to capacity. It was the same church we attended each Sunday as a family, and where our children were baptised, and where our son, would be buried from today. Family and friends could have filled the church besides the boys in uniform who sat close together filling row upon row. Our parish priest as well as our Lebanese priest, served at the altar where the candles flickered. His coffin was draped with the flag of the country with his beret fixed at the top end, while our wreath of red roses filled the remainder. He lay inside in full military step-out uniform, except for his beret. All the brass on his uniform, as well as his shoes, had been polished the night before until it shone. His older brother had made sure that everything was in place as it should be.

When we were given the option of a military or private burial we opted for the military knowing that our son wanted grand things in life that would now never happen.

The catholic service was solemn as each one tried to control their feelings and when it came for communion, our family went first and then our eldest son, being in uniform, and followed by a close friend, also in uniform, made all the soldiers rise as one and follow them to the altar. The priest, realising that the soldiers who were not catholic, were told to follow the example of our son, never wavered. When his chalice containing the host emptied, he went to replenish it, as soldier after soldier received the host that day.

The coffin was mounted on the gun carriage with the flag draped over it and the beret on top, and the cars followed the trucks with the funeral escorts as they made their way to the cemetery.

We rode with Jimmy and when the silence grew too heavy he said.

'Anthony is there and he will show Michael around.'

We smiled through our tears and knew he felt our pain. It was only a parent who had lost a child that really understood and we loved him for the support he gave us.

The cortege moved slowly with soldiers on motorbikes controlling the traffic. A group of men working in the streets stopped what they were doing and took off their hats in respect, as the coffin on the gun carriage passed them by.

Outside the gates of the cemetery, the cortege stopped as the entry was registered in the office. The military band played a slow march as the gun carriage was followed by the platoon of soldiers on foot.

The pallbearers were not all in the same uniform as they took their places.

At the head was his brother dressed in the uniform of a another regiment, with his long time school friend, wearing his air force uniform on the other side, while the four other soldiers wore the same uniform, as the body dressed in his step out uniform, that lay in the coffin.

As the bugler played the last post, rifles were fired into the air and the flag covering the coffin was folded up. With a salute from the officer in charge the beret that had been fixed on the coffin, was presented to us. Slowly the coffin was lowered into the earth, as we watched unable to tear our gaze away. It was a cold winters' day but we hardly noticed, as we shook hands, with soldiers, family and friends, thanking them for their condolences.

* * *

The photo of Manouch and Salem on their wedding day, hanging in our passage, was taken down, and carefully packed away. It was because I knew that I was not as strong as she was, and my husband understood my fears. There are no words or emotions that can even remotely be conveyed or understood when such a tragedy befalls a parent, and it is something that no parent, should ever endure.

Tomorrow is not considered and next week does not exist and even today is a blur and the body is only a robot in motion.

Chapter Forty-six

Original wedding arrangements were cancelled and although the couple were prepared to wait a while, we decided against it. They had waited nearly two years to be together, and a small family affair was arranged.

Their happiness overshadowed our sadness, as tears rolled freely at the mass in the church where our son was buried from a few short weeks before. His presence was tangible among us, and my gaze scanned those present hoping to get a glimpse of his smiling face.

And life is a joy, for although, tragedy may befall a family, there are many blessings along the way, to ease the pain.

Alfred, who now more resembled a fossil than a human, spent his days basking in the sun. Tight white curls on his head were sparse and left the top of his head shining like a marble where there was no hair.

His hands and feet were knarled like the branches of a very old tree.

He ate very little these days and had hurt his foot when he bumped it on a rock when he went walkabout. His mind sometimes, although not all the time, strayed a bit, and he had left the yard without anyone noticing him. When his absence was noticed a frantic search of the neighbourhood ensued and he was fortunately found a few blocks away.

His foot was cleaned and dressed but the healing was slow as the skin on his slight frame resembled dry wood instead of flesh. By our reckoning his age was around one hundred and sixteen years, but we could be out a year or so either way.

*   *   *

After a few weeks had passed with the foot not healing as it should the doctor advised amputation of part of the foot.

We lovingly dressed the wound but a fever filled his ancient body and he stayed in bed where the doctor came to see him regularly.

And then, just like that an era came to an end. A knight had fallen, so to speak, but one could also argue, that he had completed his life's work, and was probably needed elsewhere.

His funeral took place, in our catholic church, and was attended by all who knew him, as rows and rows of his family whom he had helped to raise, filled the aisles.

Later when his ashes came, we scattered them on the grave of Salem and his family in the old cemetery under the majestic pine.

An article in the newspapers gave him the recognition of a true and loyal father, grandfather and friend, and also one of the oldest people who ever lived.

*   *   *

Badeo had passed away on the very day that her granddaughter was born a few years earlier and her husband was now gravely ill with emphysema. We had been to see him and knew the end was near, but first, another domino had to fall.

After the death of their son, Jimmy had built a house in a new part of town, and his business was running well. Cyril his eldest was still working with him and he was satisfied that he had lifted himself and his family from the darkness that had enveloped them, into a place of light. He knew what his brother Norman felt after losing his son, because he had been in that terrible place as well, and Sundays when he saw his brother and his family at the cemetery where they came to put flowers on their respective graves, they chatted and laughed. These two brothers had always been good friends, and understood each other as none of the others did, and they drew strength from each other.

Cyril finally seemed to take on some responsibility and although he had been married twice, only had one little girl who was most adorable. Jimmy was always worried about his son's lack of direction, and he wished his son, whom he knew he had spoilt too much, could find lasting happiness with a good wife. The values of the younger generation just seemed so shallow and somehow had no substance. The fact that his son was covertly seeing the wife of one of his workers, had not escaped him, and he did in fact warn Cyril that the consequences could be bad, but Cyril just laughed and told him everything was under control, and Jimmy really hoped so.

Dressed early that morning as he always did, he put the kettle on to make his usual cup of tea before leaving for work. On seeing that it was the last teabag in the container, a feeling of panic rose within him. It was such an insignificant incident, and yet it left him unsettled, and he suddenly felt weak.

Coming up behind him and still in her nightgown, his partner saw how upset he was and she took his arm to lead him to a chair where she sat him down.

'It's the last teabag.' He said

'Don't worry Jimmy there is another box in the cupboard.'

He smiled at her and shook his head for being so silly. What was he thinking? Of course there was more tea, but the beat in his heart did not slow down.

'Are you alright Jimmy?'

'Yes, I just feel a little faint.'

'Let me call Cyril, I don't want you to drive.'

She was surprised when he agreed and went to telephone his son.

'Cyril, can you please come? Your dad does not feel so good and I don't think he should drive to work.'

'I'll be there soon but please call an ambulance.'

'Don't you think he'll be cross?'

'Just do it, I am on my way.'

Cyril arrived soon after she called him and the ambulance right behind him. Jimmy refused to be put on to the stretcher and insisted on walking to the ambulance. He knew he was only doing it to please Cyril and hated all this fuss.

In the ambulance he sat on the side bench refusing to lie down on the stretcher, while the medical attendant wrapped the sac around his forearm to take his blood pressure. The attendant pumped the small hand pump till it was tight then read the meter, saying nothing as he worked. He took down a clipboard from the shelf behind him, and wrote the results on a form, and then he looked into Jimmy's eyes and throat, and wrote some more. He could see that Jimmy was pale and firmly pushed him over to lie on the stretcher. This time Jimmy did not resist and he felt a warm blanket being put over his body. He would just close his eyes for a second, just until he got his balance back.

When the ambulance stopped at the hospital he insisted that he could get up but the attendant pushed him back on the stretcher.

'Lie still, it's better this way.'

So he relaxed and felt the bump as they took the stretcher down. He saw Cyril was already there and smiled when he saw him walking towards him.

'Are you OK Dad?'

'Why did you bring me here? You know I hate hospitals.'

'We just want to make sure Dad. It won't take long.'

Jimmy smelled the disinfectant from the open door as they wheeled him into the theatre

Cyril waited in the corridor not wanting to leave his father and wanted to speak to the doctor once they were done. He was worried about his father who smoked a lot and never stopped working. He knew his father as a workaholic and accepted that, but he had seen his father moving slower over the past few weeks, and knew he was in pain, although he never once complained.

He moved out of the way a few times as trolleys, with people on them, were pushed passed, but he refused to leave, even when a nurse asked him to do so.

It felt as if they were taking a long time with his father, and he felt himself becoming agitated. He left his watch at home when he rushed to his fathers' house, but he was sure it was almost an hour since he saw his dad go in to the theatre, so he stopped the next nurse that passed.

'Can you please find out for me why they are taking so long with my dad? It is almost an hour and I am worried.'

'I will see what I can find out.' She said and walked to the sister in the nearby cubicle.

He saw her talking to the sister who looked at him and put the file she was busy with on the desk and followed the nurse to where he was standing.

'Are you related to the patient?'

'Yes, I am his son. Can you please find out why they are taking so long?'

'I'll check. Wait for me in my office.'

'No, I will wait here.'

She nodded and walked to the theatre where she pushed the door open.

As the theatre door opened Cyril tried to look inside, and a feeling of dread that was unbearably intense, left him breathless as he saw the door close behind her.

Then the theatre door opened again, and a doctor in his white coat, came out and took Cyril by his arm, and led him through a doorway where chairs lined the walls.

Before the doctor spoke a word, Cyril burst out crying, and the doctor took his head and rested it on his chest. Not a word had been spoken and yet everything had been said. A sister came in and the doctor asked her to telephone someone to fetch Cyril, as he could not drive himself.

And just like that, another domino fell.

* * *

The oxygen tank hissed softly where Dawood lay on the bed. His eyes seemed to take up his whole face and his words were short while sucking the oxygen in between each word.

'Did you tell Jimmy that I am sick? Why has he not been here to see me?' And his daughter turns her face away so he cannot see the tears

'He will come Dad you must rest now.' And he closed his eyes and slept.

* * *

Jimmy was buried with his small son. The family grave was nearly at the beginning of the row while Norman's son, was halfway down the same row. Phillip was in the first row from the road in a prime position.

Cyril was not a pallbearer as brothers and nephews, carried the casket to his final resting place. The family who awaited the death of their brother-in-law and buried their brother instead were still in shock. Always full of jokes and finding time to visit all, it seemed unreal to say good-bye, while he was still so young. For Norman the loss of this brother whom he loved so much was enormous. For Cyril, Jimmy's son, the whole world, had collapsed.

And so, days later, we stood under the shady trees of the old cemetery, to bury Dawood, whose family grave, where his wife Badeo rested, was a few rows behind the grave of Salem, where Joe, Manouch and Finnie were, and pine needles crunched under our shoes as we lined up to accept sympathy from those attending.

Chapter Forty-seven

The family circle was shrinking rapidly with only four remaining siblings. Sunday mornings after church seemed endless. Jimmy usually paid us a visit and we missed him, although in some way we felt comfort that our son would now have someone with him who knew and loved him. When Cyril came to visit, I knew it was because he had to connect with his fathers' brother, to ease his pain. Although he had fathered a daughter a few years previously, he now had a little boy from his third wife. He was a beautiful boy, with big brown eyes, and black curly hair, who he named Jimmy, after his father. A bit slow the doctors said, and he would need constant care, and progress would also be minimal. We looked into Cyril's soulful eyes and smiled with love as we knew how lost he felt.

'Did the doctors say why he was slow Cyril?' I asked.

'They are not sure but it could be that I was on medication at the time.'

'Well I am sure he will progress just fine. You have to be patient.'

I saw how he loved the little boy wriggling in his arms and knew the task before him was not an easy one, but kept my thoughts to myself.

'He also gets fits but he is on medication for that.'

'You know, Cyril,' I said 'he may surprise you and outgrow all these problems. You know that prayer can move mountains.'

His voice was hoarse when he spoke again, but I did not show him that I noticed.

'The doctors said I should put him in a home where he could be better cared for, but I don't want to do that.'

'What about his mom?' I asked, having already heard that she had left them.

'She left us. She says she can't take the pressure of watching him all night and day.'

I had seen this anguish before, but smiled at him.

'You will know if it will help him or not, but wait a while, and see how he progresses.'

'Yes, I thought so as well.' He said relieved.

When he left my heart felt sad as I waved to him.

His mother did not live near to him but spoke to him a few times each day. Fortunately, Cyril did have his sister nearby, and although she saw him almost daily and babysat little Jimmy on occasion, I knew it was his father that he longed for more than anything.

Dawood, was not feeling well and had difficulty in eating. It was not that he did not want to eat, and even though his wife made all the delicacies he used to love, he was unable to eat any of it. We knew that it was the same as it was with Badeo his sister, and although we joked with him, who was in fact the eternal joker, we were concerned.

I brought my special trifle that he loved, and he somehow managed to eat a little from a small bowl as we sat with him. He promised to have more later and we smiled indulgently.

'I don't know what food to make anymore.' His wife said in desperation.

'What did the doctors say when you took him to the hospital?' Norman asked with a worried frown on his face.

'They say it is bronchitis and have given him medicine but he won't take it.'

'It makes me nauseas and you know how I hate to throw up.'

Norman laughed when he spoke. 'I know I also hate it.'

We stayed a while and left.

Although we knew he was not well, the call I received the next morning, was not expected.

After a bad turn his wife had taken him back to the hospital later that night but he was sent home again. With difficulty he had gotten out of the car and he had only walked a few steps into the house when he collapsed.

His strength could no longer save him, as one of the last remaining dominoes fell.

There were only two brothers that lined up to carry the casket as sons and nephews helped. Two funerals would take place that day for this man who was as strong as an ox. His first wife and their children, together with her family put out a spread of eats at her home, while his second wife did the same at her home. We attended both.

* * *

When Johnny passed away it was more a blessing for him than anything else as he had battled with emphysema for some time. His family, now grown up, were fine adults just like their parents, and two were married with children, who were nearly grown up as well.

With his passing it left only two members of the family of Salem and Manouch, Yvette and Norman.

Yvette was widowed when her husband died in a freak motor accident as a motorist on the opposite side of a highway suffered a heart attack, and veered across the middle, into the car that Badwa and his friend were travelling in.

So here they were, the second youngest, and the youngest who fortunately lived close to each other, so their children were not only cousins, but good friends as well.

* * *

For Cyril it was an uphill battle. Once the business that his father left him was sold, it was not long before the racing cars in his garage went, and then the house, until there was nothing else left but himself and his son.

His daughter lived with her mother and he did not see her very often.

His own mother did the best she could and supported him financially as much as possible. His sister watched over him like a mother hen and with her help he was able to sometimes get in a good night's sleep while she kept little Jimmy with her. This however became more difficult as the boy became stronger and more demanding and his sister was happy when her brother found someone again who could help him through the jungle of his daily life.

All this they did for Cyril, but his burden became heavier by the day, as the constant vigil, watching over his young son, took its toll. He was torn apart by wanting to keep his child with him, or to put him in a place where he could get more specialised care. He loved his son with all his heart and soul and knew the choice was too difficult for him to make.

And so one evening, after checking that everything was in order with his sleeping son, he went into the small lounge in the shabby apartment where they now lived, and sat on the comfortable chair facing the television. He was so tired but had one last thing to do. Carefully he put the dull steel shaft of the gun into his mouth.

Yes! His son was placed in a home that was scrutinised by his mom who took care of everything. She was torn apart inside her very soul for the pain she knew her son felt in making such a drastic choice but she hoped that he would be at peace and that he would be with his father whom he had adored.

There is something in losing a loved one that is so close, in that the very thought of not remembering that person, was unbearable. The need to establish a place among others for this person, seems so important, and yet it has absolutely no significance to anyone but for ones self. And yet it is by having that person near that ones' own life is sustained.

What pain, what agony. How could they not have seen the signs?

How can a mother, or a sister, accept the fact that they could not have done more for the person they loved so dearly?

Chapter Forty-eight

The scene I was looking at was more beautiful than any words could describe. The sea had a colour of turquoise that looked totally unbelievable while the mountain in the background looked like a paper model that was pasted on a sheet of drawing paper. As I sat there looking at the beauty the thought of leaving it all behind when we leave for home in a few days time, made me sad. And with a feeling of surprise I realised that it did not have to be the case.

Why could we not stay? What were we going back to anyway? We had spoken of retiring to the Natal coast many times, and now that the children were all out of the house and Norman had retired from the firm where he had worked for many years, our life seemed empty although at the same time we felt free for the first time. Our marriage had lasted for thirty-eight years and our children had all made a life of their own.

When our eldest son took a work contract in Cape Town he knew he would never return to his hometown. There was no comparison between industries where mine dumps marred the horizon and the beauty of the Cape and in particular Table Mountain. When we were invited for a visit, we were awed by the beauty surrounding us and could not wait for the time when we could visit again.

I sat there trying to lock the beauty into my heart to take home with me and just like that, I made a decision. I knew it would not be easy but it was possible. When I got up to walk home where we were staying, plans were already taking shape in my head.

I waited for the right moment before laying my cards on the table to Norman. He found many excuses and most of them were valid but in the end I persuaded him and he indulged me. We were setting a new course and it was exciting.

The first step was to sell our home that we built so many years ago and where the children grew up. It was not an easy task but once a deal had been signed the packing started. This was even more difficult than we thought. So many things accumulated over the years and everything had a special meaning that we now had to ignore. We first thought of buying another house in Cape Town but after much deliberating we decided that we might as well scale down and take a flat.

* * *

How small we are in the universe, and yet it takes its time, to plan the path that each one of us must take. Sometimes we need to be nudged a little to keep on track and other times the reins have to be pulled tight to steer us straight again. Whatever we think we plan, is only the culmination of what fate, has determined for us. We are given some latitude, but the bigger plan, is set during our early years.

We took one last look around at the house we had built for our young family so many years ago, and then a quick walk in the still dark garden, and then the big black gates were closed for the last time. Our memories were many and our hearts were heavy and nobody spoke for fear of breaking down as the two cars slowly rode away. Our youngest son had arranged with his friend to drive us to our new destination knowing it would be long and arduous.

There was some consolation in the fact that the new owners had three young sons and we knew that they would be happy growing up in our home.

On the backseat of each car, a sedated dog, rested on a blanket. The journey would take fifteen hours and we hoped the sedation would last.

We had planned to put the dogs down before our move, but somehow could not find the courage to do that. After a telephone call to the managers of our new home, which was in a large newly built estate, near the beach, we were given the assurance that we could bring them with us. Restrictions were of course in place, but were not unreasonable, so there was no question about it and they were on their way with us to our new home by the sea.

It was late that night when we arrived and everyone was tired but excited for the new life that lay before us.

And it was good. The air was crisp and clear and the sea and the mountain looked just like we remembered. Although the flat was much smaller and space was limited, we soon adjusted, and the dogs thought they were in heaven.

The estate we were in consisted of blocks of flats as well as houses, and sports facilities including tennis courts and a swimming pool and a clubhouse, but the best of all, were the open spaces all around the buildings, making it look like a big park.

Once we were settled we invited Yvette to come and visit. We truly felt blessed and enjoyed our new adventure. My dad being the sceptic that he was felt sure we would go back within six months, but once he came to visit, he knew that it would not be the case. He loved it as much as we did. I knew my mom would have done the same had she still been alive.

Yes! We went back to visit a few times, and once to attend the funeral of Yvette's eldest child. The boy who wore callipers when he was young and the one who built a thriving business, and who was now busy having a mansion built for his family, died suddenly just like his uncles and grandfather, before him.

Very young still, he left his wife and two daughters, to face life without him. He also left his mother devastated, and though we tried to console her, we knew her pain would not easily be quelled.

A whole new generation was facing the uncertainty of what tomorrow held for them. What was this element that caused this to happen? David or rather Anthony, the eldest child of Salem and Manouch, who died as suddenly as his father did, was no doubt watching from his perch high in the sky, when his youngest child, a daughter, died from a heart attack in her early thirties. And Buddy probably did the same, as his eldest son veered off the road and into a fence, when the same thing happened to him.

Thank goodness Norman who had his first heart attack at the young age of thirty-three was on medication and the air from the sea had somehow been of benefit to him. We were blessed that we could enjoy being together, and he fact that he could retire after many years of work and raising our family, into independent and successful people. Our four grandsons were our pride and joy, and we were happy for each new day as we basked in their achievements.

* * *

When we later moved into a cottage on the estate, we were even happier than before, as we now had our own garden. The clubhouse had become a vibrant pub for the inhabitants of the estate, and the couple running it became good friends of ours. A pool table and dartboard was also an attraction and offered relaxation and a means of stress relief. Sunday evenings found us all playing cards, with jokes and laughter filling the air.

Meals were also on offer, and Sundays usually offered roast with veggies, at a reasonable cost. The tennis courts were next to our cottage ensuring complete privacy and sport entertainment on our doorstep. Yes! Life was wonderful.

My dad came to visit again and I hired a wheelchair. Now we had the freedom that we lacked before, with him not being able to walk any distance. He loved being pushed in the shopping centres taking in the new fashions displayed in the windows. He enjoyed riding out into the farmlands and the little seaside villages and the fortnight passed too quickly. I was sorry we did not arrange for a longer visit, but then again, it would be a strain on Norman. Not that he, did not enjoy my dads' company, but he felt neglected after a while, and I understood this. We had become used to just being the two of us, and he relied on me more with each passing day, as his eyesight became weaker. I wondered if it was the medication that he took for his heart but we could not risk him not taking it.

When my son came to take my dad to the airport I looked into my dad's eyes that had somehow lost their lustre, and I wondered if I would see him again. Even in his advanced years he was my hero, and sadness, filled my very soul. The house seemed empty without him although Norman tried to make me smile. He somehow always had this knack of knowing how I felt, even when I was not sure about my own feelings.

Later when the telephone rang I knew it would be my dad to thank us for having him. I assured him it was our pleasure and that he could come at any time. His voice was a bit hoarse and I knew he was also emotional.

We both knew without saying anything, that it was unlikely that we would see each other again.

And after only a few weeks had passed since we saw him, the call came to tell us that my dad was ill. I called him up, and as he spoke to me, I heard the rustle of water in his lungs, and I knew without a doubt, that his time was limited.

'Dad I think it is better if you go to the hospital.'

He paused for a short while.

'How will I pay for the hospital, it can be a lot and I don't have much money.'

The closest hospital was in fact private, but I knew my dad would not stay in the state hospital, even though he went there every month for his check-up and medication.

'Don't worry about it Dad, we will pay the hospital if you don't have enough.'

A deep sigh followed.

'I will rather go to hospital then, if you are sure.' He said. 'But maybe it is not necessary.'

When I put the telephone down and told Norman what my dad had said, he took the telephone from me, and dialled the number again.

'Dad, we want you to go to the hospital. You must not worry about the cost, we will pay and if we don't have enough, I will speak to my children. Promise me you will go.'

'Thank you, Norman.' My dad paused again and then he said 'for everything.'

When Norman put the telephone down, tears filled his eyes and hugged him. Gratitude for his generosity filled my heart for I knew that our resources were very limited, and yet he had not hesitated for even a second to offer what we had. Although he never spoke about it I knew that my dad had also been to him, the dad he never knew.

I telephoned our daughter and son who went to the hospital as we could not go being so far away, and spoke to my dad for the last time while they were there. I could hear in his voice that the time was near as he thanked us again, and during the night when we slept fitfully he left us.

Two days later we flew back to our hometown to pay our last respects to my dad. Looking at my husband where he sat next to me on the plane I wondered how long he would be with me. I hoped it would be for a long time and I took his hand and squeezed it in mine. He turned to me and smiled.

Chapter Forty-nine

That summer passed and as autumn approached the flu virus left nobody untouched as we all battled to shed it from our bodies. For Norman it lingered and when we arrived back at our hometown once more to finalise the sale of our business our son had managed, he was lethargic and wished instead to be home near the sea. Even when our son fetched him to show him the new car that he was getting, he went reluctantly.

Later he apologised for not fully appreciating the significance of it, as he felt too ill, and asked me to tell our son that it was in fact a beautiful car, and that he was very proud of him. When we left he was relieved and anxious to be home. We had grown used to our surroundings near the sea with all its beauty and of the magnificent mountain we saw each day.

Where he had been eager to visit our hometown when we first left, he now knew that he was happy where we now lived. In fact, he went to great pains to tell not, only myself, but the whole family, as well as our friends, that he was indeed happy, and would never want to leave.

If only he could shake off the after effects of the flu, he knew he would be fine, and for now he rested as much as he could. Fortunately there was the anticipation of good rugby on television to keep him entertained and he took a little flutter on the horses on weekends, and added to that was the pool competition to be held in the pub on the coming Saturday.

Serious practice had taken place around the pool table by the entrants to get ready for this event, which was organised twice yearly.

All in all, he was quite content with his life.

And then it was Saturday, the day he had been looking forward to. Sitting in the lounge with the sun streaming through the window, he prepared his bet for the racing, which I would take to the local Tab a little later.

When the telephone rang, I answered to hear Yvette's voice, on the other side.

'Hello.' She said 'How are you?'

'Fine, thank you and how are you?'

It was always nice to hear her voice although the first impulse was always a bit guarded.

'Is Norman feeling better now?' She asked.

'Yes would you like to speak to him?'

'No I have to tell you something, and I don't want to upset him. I am sorry but I have to tell you that Alice passed away this morning.'

Alice was Dawood 's second wife and they were already married, when I got to know them. I know they loved each other and she had taken good care of him until he died.

'Oh! Yvette, I am sorry I did not know she was that ill.'

In fact Alice had been plagued for years with an ulcer in her stomach, and this had gotten worse. Alice was not only my sister-in-law, but also the grandmother, of my daughter-in-law.

Norman had heard this whole conversation and asked to speak to his sister, so I handed him the telephone.

'What happened Yvette, was she sick?'

'To tell you the truth Norman, nobody told me she was so sick. She was put into hospital yesterday, and this morning they phoned to tell me.'

'When you go to them Yvette, will you please tell her family that we are very sorry to hear that she died, but I am not too well myself, so we will not be able to fly up for the funeral.'

'No Norman.' She said. 'Please don't even think of coming. You must look after yourself. I will tell the family and they will understand.'

'Thank you Yvette' he said 'you must look after yourself as well, and give the children my love.'

Norman was subdued when he sat down again and stared out of the window without really seeing anything. His mood only lifted when he heard the voice of our eldest son as he opened the front door.

'Hi Dad! Did you hear about auntie Alice?'

Although Alice was the grandmother of our son's wife, she was to him always his aunt, as being married to Dawood, Normans' brother.

Norman was happy to see our son, and he got up to embrace him. 'Yes, auntie Yvette phoned but I told her we would not be able to go. I am still not feeling well enough.'

"I know Dad that is what I came to tell you. It's no good that you even consider it. Sandra will go because it is her grandmother but you are not well enough.'

Whenever this son of ours came to visit it was like a ray of sunlight warming us. He had inherited his father's voice where a timber sound caused it to break as he spoke. I could listen to them forever, just drinking in the richness of their voices.

He did not stay long as he had to go somewhere, and Norman walked with him to his car, where he stood until he saw the car disappear from sight, before going inside again.

When the telephone rang a short while later, it was our youngest son to speak to his dad about the rugby match later that day.

'Dad we have tickets for the match and my friend and I will be watching it live.'

'It is going to be a good match you must enjoy it, but there is something I have to tell you.'

Norman told him about his aunt that had passed away earlier that morning, and he promised to go and sympathise with the family. They chatted a while longer about the rugby, and then he rang off.

The pool competition in the pub at the clubhouse, was scheduled to begin around noon, and snacks as well as curry and rice was going to be served.

There would be a break in the competition, to allow the men to watch the rugby match, and I knew that Norman would come home to watch the game

He was always superstitious and preferred watching the game on his own at home, which was only a short distance from the pub. At home he could cheer, or curse, as much as he wanted to without upsetting anyone.

I usually left him on his own when he watched a match, so he could enjoy it, to his hearts' content.

Rugby, golf, cricket and boxing, and of course horseracing, were the sports that he enjoyed most, although he watched most sport, having been an avid sportsman in his younger days. Our two eldest sons preferred motor racing, but it was the one sport that Norman never took a liking to. It was our youngest son who took after his father by enjoying a game of golf or cricket and rugby of course was the highlight. Horseracing never interested any of our children.

Joining the boundary of our cottage, were the two tennis courts, and then the clubhouse area, which included the laundry facility.

This facility was convenient for me as I could do the whole weeks' washing all at once while being busy at home.

* * *

And when you looked into the mirror that particular morning, did you see anything different? Was the look in your eyes dimmer or brighter? Did your skin feel softer or harsher? No, everything looked the same as yesterday, and the day before that. Only it was different, it's just that you never noticed the sadness in your own eyes or the tremor in your smile. Did you hold your loved one just a little bit closer, and did you touch the objects around you, which reminded you of happy times?

No, the day begins just the same as it yesterday and a telephone call does not change anything. It is only a telephone call, but it does bring your son on this day to see you, and that is good because when he comes into a room the sun follows him.

Chapter Fifty

When he opened the front door I could hear how excited he was.

'Bring me my ticket I want to make sure the numbers are right.'

'Did you win?' I asked.

'I hate to ask anyone for the results but it looks like a winner.'

I handed him the racing ticket and he put his spectacles on to make sure.

He smiled and gave me a kiss before he sat down on the couch.

With his team winning the rugby and now winning a trifecta on the horses his spirits were much lighter than they were after he had the news of his sister-in-law.

'Are you finished now?' I asked. 'Can I make you a cup of tea?'

'No, I just came to check the numbers. I have to play in the final.'

'OK, I will come with you.'

He looked at me and shook his head. 'Rather wait here. The men have had a lot to drink and you know how they can swear.'

After he left to walk down to the pub I decided that I could just as well do the laundry while I was waiting. The laundry room was in the same building as the pub and I carried the two bags of washing to put into the machines. The washing cycle took thirty minutes so I went back to the cottage.

We had requested a mass for our son the next day in church. It was the twenty years' anniversary of his death and we wanted it to be the Sunday just before his birthday so I was happy that I could get all the chores done.

How is it possible that when one feels the most content disaster is just around the corner? It is almost as if one has to be on guard at all times just in case something should happen. But I was completely unaware of lurking shadows as I walked back to the laundry and transferred the now clean washing to the dryers. I enjoyed doing the laundry at this hour when it was quiet and there was nobody about. Mornings were usually busy and then one had to wait for a machine. I did not see Norman standing in the doorway of the pub watching me with affection as I went about my task. I wondered whether I should pop into the pub to see how things were going and then discarded the idea again. I might just distract him if he was playing and so I went home instead.

This next cycle of drying the laundry would take a whole hour so it was enough time to have a cup of tea. Norman should also be home by the time the washing was done so we could enjoy our Sunday without any commitments. I carried the cup of tea to the lounge where the television was on, and sat on the couch, so I could watch in comfort while I drank my tea.

The loud banging on the door startled me and I jumped up to open it. I saw our friend who runs the pub, in a state of panic.

'You must come quickly. It's Norman. Something is wrong.'

I was up and running with her behind me. My lungs felt as if they would burst and my mind was racing.

He sat at a high table in the pub. His elbows were propped up on the table with his chin resting on his hands. I touched him and called his name but knew it was too late for him to hear me. His eyes were open but glazed and a tiny bubble of spittle had formed on his lips. I ran back to the house to call an ambulance and our son.

The day had ended as it had started, in death but in between, the hours were filled unmistakably with happiness.

When I went back I was unable to look at the man whom I loved for so many years, and said three Hail Mary's as he had asked me to do, so many years before.

'You must promise me' he said early in our relationship' if anything should happen to me you will say three Hail Mary's for me.'

'How will I know what to say?' I had asked.

'In the car is a card with the prayer on.' And he showed me where it was. I was not a catholic then so knew little of the faith at the time.

Now, of course, I was a converted catholic and I prayed the words that I knew off by heart and that I have prayed so many times before.

Within minutes the emergency services were there, with our son and his wife, right behind them. Gently they laid him down and applied resuscitation before declaring him dead.

And another domino fell while the sun was setting in the most beautiful array of colours and laundry was spinning around in the dryers. It was just another day like so many others, and yet everything had changed.

I hardly slept that night and Sunday morning saw me up early. There was a lot that had to be done but first I had to get ready for church and I wanted to be early. The clothes I wore was black and I realised that I had hardly any black garments in my cupboard since retiring to the coast where bright colours or white was the order of the day. I made a mental note to buy some more black tops to wear.

I knocked on the door of the presbytery long before mass would be said.

When the door was opened I said 'We requested a mass for our son today but can you please make it for my son and my husband. He passed away last evening.'

* * *

Cars were stopping as they drove by and people craned their necks to get a better view of the whales so close to shore. I parked in the nearest parking I could find and joined the watching crowd. I took in the beauty and the majesty of the privilege to see them. I looked not only for myself but for my husband who I knew would be looking through my eyes. Although he was gone from this world and his body was with the undertakers, I believed that his spirit was still with us. I eyes drank in the scene before me, to take with on my journey back to bury my husband.

I was happy that he could share this beautiful place with me for a while.

We were fortunate in having the blessing of spending time together after his retirement. I knew there were many couples, who never got to do that, or to see their children grow to adulthood, and we were fortunate to experience this. We had lived under the shadow of death for so many years since he first had a heart attack while the children were very young and every year since then, had been a bonus. I looked at the mountain draped in a cloth of cloud and got into my car not looking back. In my bag was the money that I collected from his winning ticket on the races, which I was taking with me. It was his gift to me knowing that I would need it.

* * *

The photo of our son looked on as his fathers' body was laid to rest with him. The space in the centre was reserved for me to occupy one day.

Many of the people around the grave, including myself, and my children, had been there the previous day to bury my sister-in-law and grandmother and great-grandmother to my grandchildren. Our eldest two grandsons had in one day lost their great-grandmother as well as their grandfather.

My eyes, filled with tears, looked out over the gravestones. A few rows to the front, was the imposing gravestone with the photo of Phillip so handsome, looking at us. His wife was with him but her photo had never been added. To my left was the grave of Dawood with a modest stone. Next to him was a fresh mound with flowers where his wife had been buried the day before.

Further up in the same row where we were now gathered, was the grave of Jimmy and his son Anthony, and behind me was my mother and father and Badwa and Raymond, and for a fleeting moment, a smile played on my lips as I thought of the celebration they would be having as a brother, and an uncle and a father and son-in-law, joined them. And then I heard her as she laughed that hearty laugh and I saw the look that passed between Salem and Manouch transcend through space and time, as they waited with open arms for their son.

She stood with her son and her daughters to one side and as I looked up I saw her looking at me. I felt the affection and respect we always had for each other like a beam of light in a dark sky. It was only Yvette and I left now, and I knew I had to try and write about everything and everyone I knew of, so that our children and their children would know of the love that surrounded them.

* * *

Her name was Manouch and she was ten years old.